To: Rose

Tiger's Heart
Shakespeare's Lost Years

A novel

Leslie Rocker

New Generation Publishing

Prologue

Of the many uncertainties and even mysteries that surround Shakespeare's life and work, none has aroused more speculation and surmise than how he spent his time during what have become known as his "lost years", ie from leaving his home in Stratford-upon-Avon to his emergence in London as a major playwright. As John Masefield remarked: "At this point, he disappears, we know not what he did, where he went".

Well, he certainly was not lost. One theory suggests that he was a sailor, which is highly unlikely. If he did go to sea the possibility is that he would never have been heard of again, even if he survived. Another theory is that he was a schoolmaster, which also seems highly unlikely, although he may have consented to give the occasional lecture.

Countless theories have also been advanced suggesting that a poor, ignorant provincial lad could never have written masterpieces that have enthralled the world. They must have been produced by an aristocrat like the Earl of Oxford, or Southampton; a Cambridge graduate with an established reputation as a playwright such as Christopher Marlowe; even, one suggests, by a woman – perhaps Queen Elizabeth herself!

Then how did he acquire the knowledge implicit in his plays – the details of historical events and characters, things that happened in foreign countries, particularly Italy? How did he know the way things worked at sea, in commerce, among kings and princes, lords and ladies? Printed books of the right kind were scarce. There were no libraries for him to go to, no encyclopaedia to consult. He would not have been able to travel easily and certainly not abroad.

This book attempts to provide answers to these questions and, at the same time, introduces the reader to some of the extraordinary characters the budding playwright and actor would have encountered: fellow playwrights, particularly his friend Christopher Marlowe, so cruelly murdered in the Deptford tavern; the Cambridge *eminence noire* Gabriel Harvey; the Earl of Oxford, with whom he might have collaborated; the Earl of Southampton, who became his patron; the theatre managers, Burbage and Henslowe; and perhaps most important of all Thomas James, who developed a reputation as the "cleverest man in England" after his appointment as the first librarian to the Bodleian Library in Oxford.

The secret to Shakespeare's genius is quite simply that he was a wordsmith, perhaps the greatest of all, fortunate to be living when the English language was at its most formative and creative. It was a period too when the aristocracy and the literati communicated through the medium of poetry. And although the majority of the populace could not read, a medium had been devised called the Theatre (from the Greek "place"), in which the treasures of the vernacular could be conveyed to them, where all levels of society could gather not just to watch bears being bated, or to see a sword fight, but to hear wonderful words proclaimed by actors with stentorian voices and grandiose gestures.

This book tries to imagine the historical conditions in which Shakespeare would have worked, the people he might have encountered. He became involved in their lives, but he found himself standing outside them, observing their stories. In this book one of them has a happy ending; another ends in death. Shakespeare would have learned from both

ii

PART 1

Chapter 1

The thorns of the gorse bushes scratched the young man's arms, but he scarcely heeded them. Keeping low he moved into position on the lee of the low prominence and waited. He knew the herd was gathered in a small copse to his right and felt sure they would pass across the field ahead of him until they reached the denser woods on the left. He had judged this because he had seen their tracks on earlier excursions and knew they kept to a fairly regular routine.

He had not wished to approach them directly because that would only serve to panic them and off they would sprint, heels kicking, heads tossing, making an accurate shot difficult. Now he could just wait for them to emerge and select his target with care. They would move slowly, but once he had shot an arrow they would be off like the proverbial wind. So it was important to be accurate. If his first shot did not bring down one of them a second must do it, otherwise they would be in the trees again and all his care since early light would have been wasted.

The sky was tinged with pink, now fading like the blush on a maiden's cheek. He welcomed the sharpening light as it would throw his prey into silhouette. The air was cold and he shivered despite his homespun. The frost had come early that autumn, but it was worth waiting. If he was successful his family would feed well for weeks. Even his father might secretly approve, although he would perforce turn his official eye away from the illegal spoils of his son's endeavours.

As he lay there the young man, as he often did,

allowed his mind to wander on to a subject far removed from the business in hand and yet in some ways analogous to it. On the previous day he had attended a performance given by strolling players in the local inn yard. They were a professional troupe, containing a number of talented performers and led by an actor with a fine presence. They had been well received and would be staying on to give additional performances, but he thought the material they presented was very poor stuff.

Somewhere a bird sang an exultant note. It was a lark, he thought. A flock of rooks flew noisily up out of the trees to his left and he wondered what had disturbed them: stray sheep from the meadows beyond the wood, perhaps, or a hawk He had seen one gliding imperiously over the downs on the previous day. It was hunting its prey, as he was. He allowed his thoughts to dwell on the immutability of nature and lines of verse began to form in his mind, but then suddenly he was alert. There was movement to his right.

It was no more than a thin object breaking the line of the horizon, like the branch of a dead tree, but this was not dead. It moved from side to side as if directing the unseen herd. Then there was another, and another. Heads appeared in profile, sniffing the air, searching for danger. But he had chosen his position well. The wind was in his face, it would not carry his scent to the wary beasts.

They broke cover, at least a dozen of them, led by a magnificent animal with a head like a monarch's crown. With him were one or two males only slightly smaller, followed by the females and then the younger males. They moved across his field of vision grazing as they went. He gently raised himself on to his knees. He did not aim at the leaders. They were fine deer, but he was not looking for trophies. Their flesh would be tough. It was the younger ones at the rear that would provide the tenderest meat. Besides if he hit one of the leaders without bringing him down the whole herd would disperse in a panic.

He raised himself very slowly, drew back the string of his bow and released an arrow. The herd was immediately on its guard, but did not flee, until one of them was struck. Then they started hurrying towards the safety of the trees. The young man cursed under his breath. He had struck the animal in his rear haunch without killing him. It staggered and followed the rest of the herd limping. There were only seconds to spare. He fitted another arrow to his bow and shot. Then another. The two shafts struck home almost simultaneously, one in its fore-haunch, the other in its throat. The animal staggered, then fell. The rest of the herd fled. The bowman's task was done.

He did not immediately rush to examine the effects of his kill. He knew the animal was not going anywhere. He had to make sure no one had seen. He was fairly certain he was alone at that time in the morning, but it was well to be sure. Then, keeping low, he made his way to where the deer was in its last paroxysms. The bowman carried a knife to end the creature's torments, but found it was not necessary. The animal was still.

He retrieved the arrows, wiped them on the grass and put them into his quiver. Then, disregarding the blood that still oozed from the wounds, he hauled the animal on to his shoulders and began to walk across the field. He felt good as the sun rose and warmed him. There was something immensely satisfying about tracking, stalking and eventually defeating an animal the flesh of which would serve to feed his tiny community. His wife, his mother, his children, even his father would benefit from his efforts and for once he could feel his existence was justified. His wife, he knew, would be particularly appreciative and he allowed himself to dwell on the happiness he felt when enwrapped in her loving embrace.

His mood of joyous exhilaration was ended, however, by a rude encounter. Its immediate impact on him could be disastrous, but in years to come he would look back on it as the moment when his whole life was changed. He would come to see how apparently innocuous incidents and decisions could change the destinies of lives and men. To reach his home he had to pass through a wood. He left the bright sunlight and found himself in the opacity of the trees. There he was confronted by two men. It must have been they who disturbed the rooks. He stopped. They stopped. They confronted one another.

To the young man's further dismay he realised he knew the men. They were employees of a local landowner, with whom his father had been in dispute. He was not aware of the details, except that it was something to do with the illegal sale of wool. They were not likely to be sympathetic and let him off with a warning. At the very least they would confiscate the deer. The penalties for poaching could be severe. At one time it had been punishable by death, although that had been mitigated in recent years. Nevertheless it could mean imprisonment, confinement perhaps for years and an end to all the hopes and ambitions he had for the lives of himself and his family. What would his father say? He dreaded his wrath even more than the punishment of the Court

One of the two spoke: "Well, if it baint young master Shakespeare."

"I – er – I found this animal dead in the field and thought I had better move it before the foxes got at it."

"Dead were he? Fancy that now. And narry an arry sticking out of its poor hide. Perhaps there'll be blood on your'n. Shall us take a look in your quiver, young man?"

"There's no need. You can take the animal. I'm sure your master will know what to do with it."

"Oh Ah. He'll be knowing that aright. And he'll be knowing what to do with yoursen, too, young man. Poaching be agin the law as thou well knowst."

William Shakespeare felt his panic rising. They were going to arrest him. He would be charged. Imprisonment stared him in the face. There was a small round building at the end of the town with no window and the only view of the outside world through a barred doorway. The story was told of a prisoner who had died there and been forgotten until a later prisoner encountered his corpse.

There was nothing for it. He had to escape. They were large, cumbersome men and he could outrun them, although he would need a good start.

"I really think it would be much better if you acquired this handsome beast", he said.

"Yes, but thou canst carry he and then we'll take he offen when we arrive."

They laughed at this, nudging one another at the joke.

There was nothing else for it. He was a strong young man and with a thrust of his shoulders he threw it at them, knocking one off his feet and over-balancing the other. Then he was away, into the woods, following a track well worn by generations of those possibly engaged in a similar escapade. He ran aware only of the sound of their heavy footsteps. They had thrown down the deer and followed shortly behind, intent only on his capture. He must do something to delay them and as he ran an idea grew in his mind.

He turned off the main path onto a narrower one he knew well. At a certain point he judged it carefully and leapt high into the air, covering a good three feet before stumbling and continuing to flee. One of those behind him did not leap, however, and there was the dread sound of snapping iron, followed immediately by the agonised scream of his pursuer. A glimmer of humanity persuaded him to stop and turn to see the man writhing in agony and clutching at the leg caught in the mantrap. His companion was trying to free him and paused only to wave a fist in his direction. He gave a shrug of the shoulders and a wave of his hand hoping to communicate regret and sympathy, although he reflected ironically that it would have been they, or their fellows, who had set the trap.

So he ran, free of the burden of the deer, but still clutching his precious bow and arrows and reassured that the sounds of pursuit had died behind him. Fate had decided that from being the hunter he had now become the hunted. He was not exactly fleeing for his life, but certainly to avoid his future being proscribed by prison bars and that of his family by ignominy and disgrace.

He decided not to go to his home in Henley Street. They would be sure to seek him there. Instead he made his way to Newlands Farm, his wife's former home in Shottery, a mile outside Stratford. Her father, Richard, would not have welcomed him, but he had died five years earlier and the young man had always been on good terms with her brother Bartholomew. From there he would get a message to his father, who despite any disapproval he might have of his son's actions would at least do what he could to save him.

What would John Shakespeare say? Would he disown him, point out that his predictions had been proved accurate and his son's behaviour had brought the whole family into disrepute? Even if his father was able to rescue him from his current scrape what was there for him in the tiny rural town? He had resisted his father's attempts to involve him in his glove-making business, and he had neglected his studies at school and failed to attend university. He had divided his time idly between pursuing syntax and grammar by the light of a candle late at night and chasing animals at sunrise - not to mention a certain licentiousness when it came to the opposite sex. Instead of handling a leather-worker's knife at a bench he had chosen to wield a quill pen at a writing table, bow and arrows across the early morning fields and a weapon of a more promiscuous nature in the bedroom.

His future certainly looked bleak. The excitement of the chase, as hunter and hunted, left him and even the warmth of the sun and the beauty of his surroundings failed to lift his leaden spirits. So far the sum total of his scribblings had been verse of an amorous nature and attempts at plays reflecting his rural environment. As he made his way through the soft green fields of Warwickshire he was scarcely aware of the history that lay only a few miles distant where the castles of Warwick and Kenilworth lay. Such matters would only be revealed to him through books. The life he had led had been happy and carefree. In the not-to-distant future he would find himself taking on his shoulders the cares, the heart-aches, the tragedies of the world, and a little of its humour too.

The concerns of his father were ill-founded. The family's name was safe and would, in fact, be even venerated for centuries to come.

Chapter 2

It seemed as if winter had come early after a long hot summer. The air had turned very chill and the wind blew through the cracks in the woodwork and around the edges of the canvas blinds that offered only partial protection for the shivering men who huddled together in the rickety conveyance. They were dressed in a variety of costume, donned in an attempt to keep warm. One wore a king's cloak, but with a fur hat on his shaven head. One had even assumed a voluminous woman's dress and draped its skirts around his shivering limbs. Another sported half a suit of mock armour that protected his breast and back, but left his body below the waist vulnerable in the extreme unlikelihood of an attack.

One of the company stood out from the others. Unlike them he was dressed in more traditional wear, his warm leather doublet befitting the scion of a well-to-do family. Nevertheless, he still found it necessary to cross his arms over his chest and plunge his hands under each armpit in an effort to keep them warm. A young man with a mind full of poetic thoughts he compared the shafts of wind that assailed them to the showers of arrows that would pierce the ineffectual armour of fighting men, trying to endure the tedium and misery of the journey with thoughts of battles, deeds of derring-do.

Reflecting on the pain and death of those who fought and died, however, only served to increase his own misery and he turned his mind to thoughts of Elysian fields, of lovers dancing in daisy-strewn meadows, nights spent in the warm embrace of a loving partner. Even this led him to lovers who quarrelled, parted and sometimes sadly even died. He went over in his mind the lines of poetry he had been working on before he found it necessary to leave his home so peremptorily. They were inspired by the lament of a young woman he had encountered in the fields near his home. She was wandering apparently consumed with grief and for a while he watched her uncertain whether or not he should approach her. Eventually he did so, but she turned her tear-strewn face towards him and cried out in an agony of despair. Then she ran and although her suffering affected him deeply he felt unable to follow. Later in the calm of his own room he tried to recall the encounter in a few lines of verse, but failed to convey the depths of the woman's emotion on to the page, becoming embroiled in considerations of scansion and rhyme. He drew the image of an echo from a hill giving birth to her story, but had been unable to find a rhyme for echoed. Should he change it for reworded, which could then rhyme with accorded.

Some of the time he wondered why he was there in the cold and discomfort, leaving behind him a warm home, with a warm wife and children who might have contributed many inconveniences to one's life, but at least were warm. His mother exuded a degree of warmth. She would need to, having borne seven children apart from himself. Sadly, three of those had died, which eased the pressure on the family's economic situation, but left the survivors with an awareness of mortality. He himself had narrowly escaped being smitten with the dread pestilence that had ravaged the country in the year of his birth and as he had matured he had increasingly been aware of a responsibility to make some restitution to the providence that had spared him.

As for his father, he remembered no sensation of warmth emanating from that source; quite the reverse.

With an additional shiver he recalled the cold expressions of disapproval that had greeted many of the steps he had taken to fulfil what he had come to believe was his destiny. Why should his father, who always seemed to enjoy the company of actors and who, as sometime bailiff, would encourage their attendance in the town and license them, refuse even to acknowledge his son's ambitions to join them? And why should he regard with contempt his son's predilection to write the scripts he hoped they would perform?

His father had agreed to help him leave home, but that was presumably to try and mitigate what he saw as the shame that could be brought upon the family by his delinquent son. His position as bailiff carried little in the way of legal authority. That was the provenance of a Justice of the Peace and it was that eminent official who would be responsible for judging the severity or otherwise of his son's latest malfeasance. In earlier generations the killing of a deer on someone else's land could be punishable by death. In these more enlightened times it might bring upon the culprit little more than a fine, or a few days in the town's lock-up, but the reputation of both the offender and his family was something that could last a generation. If the miscreant was absent and not to be found, however, it was likely that Sir Richard Lucy (a nobleman known more for his exploits in London society than for his concern over the animals roaming his estate) might instruct his gamekeepers to drop the charge.

So, the young man thought, his father had cut him out of his life as if he had been a corn troubling him, had sent him off "without a penny", to follow the life towards which he had persisted in directing his wasted youth. The father abandoned the attempt to direct his son into the noble trade he had followed most of his life, or a similar occupation, or any occupation except the one he seemed determined to follow, one that directed his steps on to the precarious, temporary stages the acting companies erected on their visits to the town.

Oh! they might serve a social purpose, in the same way the cleaners cleared the ordure from the streets after market day. They provided a vent through which all the immoral tempers and cravings of the populace could be released into the cleansing air. But the father believed that the members of those companies comprised the dregs and cast-outs of humanity. They may have been inspired with the words to declaim and the ideas to act out their manifestations of the world's ills, but they carried those sins and vices around with them as they travelled from town to town, village to village.

So John Shakespeare would license them. He would give them the right to perform their tragic and comic scenes of human depravity and then he would see them go on their way and perhaps leave behind a community that had been in some way purged. What he did not expect to happen was that his son, one of the fruits of his loins, would involve himself with them and their sordid life of make-believe. The father had been born into a real world of industriousness and service and had become a respected member of a well-founded community. Let them act out their fantasies on their make-shift stages. He wanted no part of it for himself or the members of his family.

Now here was his son, set out on the long road to London. He had taken little with him but the clothes on his back, a few extras to keep him clean, the bow with which he had so skilfully shot the deer (and a few arrows in case of another fruitful encounter), and a pouch containing the precious pages on which he had so painstakingly scribed the early results of his inspiration. Unknown to the father it also contained a small leather bag containing twenty crowns given surreptitiously by his mother when she lavished her farewell kiss on him.

Will moved aside a corner of the canvas screen and peered out at the scene that limped so slowly past them. To his relief he saw that the sun had risen and was delivering a flame of burning gold across the fields and woods in their late autumn plumage. The sadness of his departure from home and family and the dreariness of the early morning had dampened the elation he had felt at the prospect of his journey and plunged him into a depression, but the spectacle of the new day blessing the world around him lifted his spirits and he began to view the prospect of his immediate future with more optimism.

What could be more exciting than to arrive at a village, or a town, help unload and set up the company's platform and perhaps even play some small part on it as an actor? Then there were his scripts to be considered. He had shown one to the leader of the troupe before they left Stratford and he had liked it, although he suggested they might need what he called editing to accommodate the needs of the stage and his particular company of actors. Nevertheless he would consider including it in the company's repertoire – a French word Will gathered meaning a list of all the works performed.

The young man had seen many of these plays as Stratford frequently received visits from the travelling groups and he made sure he attended all their performances, despite the disapprobation he received from his father. He had not, however, always been impressed by their quality – a manifestation of arrogance condemned by others in the audience, who thought what was shown on the stage was fine stuff, full of fights and grand speeches. He regarded the words given to the characters to speak as stilted and unrealistic. The representation of Robin Hood was, for instance, much too full of braggadocio. In his view the characters were too broadly drawn and lacking subtlety, particularly the villainous Sheriff of Nottingham. Robin Hood was, after all, a ruffian and a thief. It was said he stole only from the rich and gave the results of his activities to the poor. Of course he stole only from the rich. What would be the profit of robbing the poor? Where was the evidence that he passed on his ill-gotten gains to charity? No doubt he dropped the odd penny to beggars who gave advance warning of rich travellers passing through Sherwood Forest, but it was doubtful if he and his merry men habitually swelled the plate of the local church on a Sunday.

The comedies were quite funny, but full of leaps and falls. There was not much room for what he understood was called repartee – another French word. One play called *Ralph Roister Doister* seemed to have some merit, but the quality of *Gammer Gurton's Needle* was adequately exemplified in the play's title. Then there was a piece called *Gorboduc*, which seemed to him to be dull and stilted, with dumb show introduced for no good reason that he could see. He understood it was a convention borrowed from the Italians and for his part they could keep it. What was the point of having actors strutting about the stage saying nothing? He would make sure his characters always had plenty of words to utter.

This last performance had been followed by a play about the weather, which he had seen before and still found achingly unfunny. In it Jupiter was supposed to have summoned a series of characters before him to complain. Predictably they all wanted something different – the farmer rain, the laundress sun, a "gentleman" something calm and temperate, and so on.

At one point a quarrel breaks out between the participants resulting in a certain amount of knock-about comedy and it all ends with Jupiter deciding that the weather should be changeable, providing something for everyone, which in the young man's view was hardly earth-shattering.

Sometimes he found the performances of the actors very moving. There was something about their powerful voices and their declamatory gestures that stirred unaccustomed emotions in him. The antics of the clowns amused him, but he liked it best when they would suddenly throw off their comic personae and for a few moments tug at the heart-strings of the viewers. Even then the actual lines they spoke and the plots of the pieces they presented were very poor stuff. Often they were based on the works of Latin writers, particularly one called Seneca, translations of which he had read at school.

Why did the writers not give genuine characterisation to the people they portrayed instead of turning them into ciphers? The dialogue in the more serious scenes was mostly in verse, usually to a strict scansion of iambic pentameter and he thought that men and women in real life did not speak like that. In his plays he was determined to make his characters behave like real people, whether they spoke in verse or prose.

When he tried his hand at writing play scripts, however, it was more difficult than he had anticipated. He tried to envisage a kind of realism existing on the stage, but there were all sorts of technical difficulties involved in getting characters on and off, particularly when they died and thus tended to clutter up the acting area. There was one script in which he felt he had been reasonably successful. It was, he thought, very close to home, involving as it did not only the woods and lands in which he had spent his childhood, but folk lore and fairy tales with which his mother had fed his mind and those of his siblings from their earliest days.

He had woken up one morning from a deep sleep and remembered a dream involving fairies and magical transformations. He had transposed these on to stories he had been reading from ancient Greece, the Athenians, the Amazons and the people who lived in those happy far-off days. One of these coincided with an incident involving a girl he had been courting at the time. They had quarrelled because she thought he had been seen with someone else. He had protested his innocence and suggested it might all have resulted from the intervention of magic – upon which she had slapped him soundly on the face and told him that she never wanted to see him again, a penance that fortunately she was prepared to redeem not two days later.

Reading the script again he realised he had done something special, something the plays of other writers seemed to lack. He had put together a number of different motifs (a word relating to music he had also garnered from the French). They could be in opposition to one another creating a constantly changing interest, unlike the pedestrian themes that often marred the presentations he saw in Stratford.

The men around him were beginning to stir. They had slept heavily since setting out on the journey, for they had worked hard through the night dismantling the stage erected in the town's inn-yard. This had involved taking down the backing of the stage and folding it into a transportable size. The platform itself with its temporary supports was dismantled. Costumes and items they called properties were bundled or packed into large cases.

The two plays performed had been so well received they had gone on into late in the evening, resulting in the necessity to light torches and candles. Members of the company had then been rewarded with a satisfying meal, involving a whole boar's head, mutton pies, local cheeses, bread hot from the oven and much ale, as well as the new-fangled beer to which hops had been added. Some of the actors had partaken too well of the latter and had been scarcely fit to deal satisfactorily and safely with the arduous business of packing up. But they had gone to it with a will, sometimes dropping and even breaking things and receiving well-deserved curses from the company member who seemed to be in charge of the proceedings. The large items that made up the stage and backing were loaded on to a trailer. All else, including the cast, travelled in the coach, the sides of which were screened by canvas decorated with scenes of dramatic episodes, involving pictures of royalty, scenes of battle.

The man in charge of all this activity was not the leading actor. That glamorous person did not take part in the physical aspects of closing down, partly because he had been on stage for most of the duration of the two plays and was plainly exhausted. It was also his job to ensure that the financial and social aspects of their departure were satisfactorily fulfilled. A charge had been made for entry to the inn-yard for those who wished to view the spectacle. The inn had two levels of gallery, occupation of which involved an extra payment. The inn landlord retained a percentage of the takings, but made no charge to the players for their food or accommodation. He regarded the extra income earned from the audiences and for the food and drink consumed in his bar as sufficient recompense.

The members of the company were sprawled in various attitudes about the cart, resting on bundles and cases, folds of canvas, even costumes due for laundering at the next port of call. As they slowly

16

achieved varying degrees of wakefulness they coughed and sneezed and farted, making ribald comments when they did so, partly to hide their embarrassment. The young man knew none of them, except their leader with whom his father had negotiated for his passage.

His name was Charles Knight and he introduced the others to the young man. Their names were not, he said, their true or original titles, but had been assumed for various reasons, perhaps to hide their identities from legal authorities, or to escape from recalcitrant spouses, or in the case of the children because they had never known or had forgotten their parents' names.

Charles was a tall, distinguished figure of a man who managed to dominate the company he was in whether on the stage or at a social gathering. A great contrast was provided by Robin Goodfellow, a large ebullient character, who was so fat that his girth was almost as wide as his height, which was not much above five feet. His age could have been anything between 40 and 50, but this did not deter him from exuding the energy of a much younger man. His natural vivacity did not manifest itself, however, in any form of jollity. Rather he was taciturn, with a tendency to outbursts of almost uncontrollable temper, particularly when he had imbibed quantities of his favourite tipple, what he described as "good old English ale". He seemed to be regarded with great respect by other members of the group, as much for his quality as an actor as for his ability to withstand the effects of alcohol.

A total contrast was provided by the slim young man who was introduced as the company's juvenile lead, a phrase puzzling to William until it was explained that the word "juvenile" did not relate to a child, but to someone who still retained the qualities of youth. His name was John Pike, which, Robin Goodfellow suggested, had been adopted because the man was as thin as a pikestaff.

Before Charles could introduce the other members of the company, Robin interrupted and demanded to know how they should address the new arrival. The need to reveal his name had not occurred to Will and it was as if his father had reached out and touched him on the shoulder. Should he invent one and, if so, what? Then Charles came to his rescue, clapped him on the shoulder and said: "Like the rest of us, he shall assume a new name. We ought to give him a little time to consider and meanwhile perhaps he could be known as Will".

Then Will had an idea. He looked up and smiled: "And perhaps my family name could be Shivershaft".

A man he had not been introduced to leapt to his feet and cried: "That's good, for he stands there shivering and is certainly as lean as our friend Pikestaff".

The rest of the company laughed in a way that Will thought quite excessive for the very poor joke.

"You mustn't mind Corin Clout. He is our clown", said Charles

"Then as a clout he should be more target than targeted", suggested Will.

The clown laughed even louder. "A literary gent", he cried. "In which case you must know that my full Christian name is Corinthian, which means a very mettlesome fellow".

Will made him an elaborate bow, which the clown acknowledged and settled himself down again. Will pointed to two children who were still sleeping.

"And who are these?" he asked. "They seem too young to be travelling so far from their domestic hearth".

Charles seemed quite sad when he replied: "They have no domestic hearth, I fear. They are orphans. The

18

parents were snatched away by the plague when they were young. They were taken in by a monastery, where they were taught to sing quite beautifully. Then our noble king Henry dismantled the order, the monastery was closed and they fell into the hands of itinerant monks who made a living singing sacred music. The boys' treble voices were a tuneful contribution to the performances and they enjoyed their role, but did not realise that their masters had the intention to perpetuate their ability to sing such high notes".

"You mean – " Will hardly liked to put the idea into words. Robin had no such reticence: "They were to become castrati", he said Robin an expression of disgust pulling his face into an even more grotesque shape.

"But you do not need that to sing high, like a woman", said Will and burst into treble notes of melody from a church chant. There were a few moments silence, followed by expressions of astonishment.

"Is he a man or a woman, or a woman masquerading as a man. If she is a woman she cannot appear on our stages", said the clown.

"I am no woman", said Will, "and I can prove it", and with that he sang the bottom line in a deep bass voice.

"Why! he sings both high and low. He is a phenomenon", cried the Clown. "He'll certainly be able to sing for his supper".

Once again the company laughed and the Clown jigged about turning from one to the other as if trying to ensure that he was able to bathe in the reflected glory of the young man's performance.

"So we rescued these two unfortunate young people", Charles continued, "and they have served us well playing the younger female characters".

"What about the others, the matriarchic characters, the queens the mothers?"

"Robin Goodfellow there has been known to adopt the coiffure and gown of a fat female character as has our other character actor, Henry Stover, who is just waking there. Then we have two other young men, one of whom is still sleeping and one has been driving our horses since we set out. He is due for a break. They have not been with us long and are still learning their profession. They play many parts, including women, when speech is not important. They are becoming very proficient and if you are ambitious to act you will have to compete with them."

"I do want to act", Will said, "but as you know my principle interest is in providing you with scripts that your company can perform."

"Well, as for that, something of quality would be welcome", said Robin. "The rubbish we are expected to declaim brings shame on a noble profession. The comedies are not so bad as we can extemporise. But otherwise it is all kings and princes, lords and ladies. What we want are plays about real people, people with a little girth, people who enjoy a mug of ale, good trenchermen."

Charles laughed : "Like you master Goodfellow".

"Yes, if you say so. Like me."

"I must see what I can do", said Will. "I have here a script that does include such a man".

"Yes, but more of that later", interrupted Charles. "We need to think about what we are going to do at our next stop Also someone should relieve our driver. Henry Stover I think it is your turn"

"It always seems to be my turn", said Henry rubbing his eyes and getting grudgingly to his feet.

"Now it can't be that", said Charles, "Otherwise you would have been driving since we left Stratford. Go on and see if you can't keep those horses on a straight line."

"I might be able to if we had any sort of road", he grumbled, as he pushed past his companions and found his way through the canvas screen at the front of the coach. Will could hear much muttering as an exchange took place then, to his surprise, Henry seemed to return and make his way to the rear where he lay down with moans of relief.

In his astonishment, Will turned to Charles, who looked at him and laughed. He pointed to the young man and the rest of the company joined in. The man himself seemed not to welcome the attention. He pulled a coat over his head and tried to shut out the laughter.

"They're our twins", said Charles. "They make a great pair, don't they? You really cannot tell them apart. We have lots of fun with them on stage I can tell you."

Will did not join in the laughter. As it subsided he sat looking sad. The others also fell silent and looked at him questioningly.

"I have twins", he said. "They are not identical. A boy and a girl, in fact. Will I ever see them again, I wonder".

Before anyone could respond to him the conveyance stopped with a jolt, throwing some of those who were standing on to others.

"Now what can that be", said Charles. "I just hope we have not hit something. I'll do for that boy, see if I don't".

He made his way through to the front of the coach and for a moment there was silence.

Then Charles burst back through the canvas screen crying: "Thieves, robbers, murderers!"

He opened one of the large chests, took out a sword and rushed out again. One or two of the company followed. Others, more cautious, peered round the

21

screen. They saw a number of men standing in front of and on either side of the horses. One of them was holding a crossbow. Others had drawn swords or daggers. They were roughly dressed in hempen or home-spun and had made no attempt to hide their faces. The cart had been driving on what was little more than a cart-track on one side of which was a dense wood from which the robbers had obviously emerged. On the other a wide meadow dropped away steeply to the distant horizon. There was no prospect of aid. The men had chosen their spot well.

Charles raised his sword and was about to leap down and challenge them, but one advanced towards him raising his own sword in the air. Charles swung his towards the attacker, who parried and succeeded in cutting the defender's weapon in half. The robbers laughed and one of them shouted: "It was only wood"..

Charles was dismayed. "That was my best prop sword", he cried.

The gang's leader said: "Let that be a lesson to all of you and before anyone gets hurt, or even killed, hand over all your valuables and we will allow you to go on your way in peace".

"Fool", cried Charles. "We have no valuables".

"The sides of your wagon show pictures of crowned heads and handsome robes and precious jewels. What are you? The potentates of some foreign power?"

"No. We are but poor strolling players. We have nothing to offer you."

"Then you will have come from Stratford, where you will have put on your entertainment for the great and mighty of that town."

"That is correct. So please let us go on our way unmolested."

"You will have taken a goodly amount of the queen's coin. I am told that many hundreds attend your performances."

"But you would not rob us of the fruits of our labour. We shall starve or freeze to death for want of shelter."

"You lie. They will feed you well enough when you next put on your show and as for shelter, I think some of you are accommodated rather better than my men. Now hand over your takings or by heaven some of you will suffer grievously."

He went back to one of his men and said: "Hand me that sack. We will fill it up for sure".

Then a voice called loud and clear: "Hold there!"

The robber stopped surprised and turned, his sword aloft in one hand, the sack in the other. On the deck of the wagon another figure had appeared beside Charles. It was the young man now known as Will Shivershaft. He stood there holding a bow, a notched arrow pointing straight at the robbers' leader.

"Move one inch and you are a dead man", he cried. Then he swung the bow round so that the arrow was pointing at the crossbow man.

"Drop your weapon", he said, "in the time it takes you to bring it into play I can direct six arrows at your men."

The leader laughed nervously.

"That'll be a sight to behold", he said.

The young man lifted the bow. An arrow sped towards them. The crossbow man dropped his weapon on the ground and fell upon it. The others crouched down, their arms across their heads. They looked up with expressions first of relief and then derision when they saw the arrow was lodged in a tree. Their scorn turned to astonishment, however, when in a movement too quick for them to follow Will restrung his bow and an arrow was again pointed at their leader.

Charles was quick to take advantage of the young

man's intervention:

"He's right. I have seen him down three deer in a fleeing herd before the first has been able to seek protection in the trees". He raised his arm in a grand gesture and declaimed in a voice Will had heard him use on in a play. "My sword might have been a stage prop, but his bow is made of the finest English yew, the like of which led our great king Henry to victory at Agincourt. Let us go on our way. We mean you no harm. There will be much richer pickings to be had on this road before nightfall."

The robber was stunned by the power of his oratory and the spectacle the actor presented. More importantly he was aware of the arrow pointing directly at him. He lowered his sword. The bowman picked up his weapon, keeping a close eye on Will's bow. The man holding the horse's head relinquished it and joined the rest of the band in a group around their leader. A tense impasse followed. Then their leader laughed.

"So we have been defeated by a band of strolling players. Well, so be it. We'll let you go on your way. And good luck to you."

"I cannot offer you the same", said Charles, "but I hope God may help you find the means to mend your ways".

The band went to the woods, which seemed to absorb them so quickly it was as if they had disappeared into the ground. Charles put an arm around the young man's shoulder and led him back into the wagon's interior, where he was greeted with cheers and almost collapsed under the weight of patting on the back and shoulders. The company resumed their seats and the vehicle started with much urging of the reluctant horses. Will sat, putting his bow and arrows on the floor and his head in his hands. His shoulders began to shake.

"Well", said Charles. "That was very brave, but I can see nothing to laugh at."

Will lifted his head and they saw that his eyes were full of tears. His trembling grew and he sobbed almost uncontrollably.

"What is it?" one of them asked. Another cried: "What's the matter? You have saved the lives of all of us".

Robin Goodfellow lumbered to his feet and leant his great bulk against the young man. "You wouldn't have killed anyone, would you", he said.

Will shook his head and sobbed some more.

"I thought not."

Charles picked up the bow and admired it.

"It is a beautiful piece of yew", he said. "You must have worked hard on it".

"Actually made from elm, not yew", said Will, "But dried for two years and worked into shape for another four".

"The finest bow is useless if the bowman lacks skill and he was magnificent, magnificent", cried John Pike. "He was like – like Apollo. Standing there with his bow and arrow at the ready."

"Or Artemis aiming at the sun", suggested the Clown. "With his voice and that figure, he could be the goddess herself."

"A woman perhaps", said Robin with his arm affectionately around the young man's shoulder, "but with a tiger's heart".

Chapter 3

The cumbersome cart trundled its slow, tedious way along the ill-defined lanes of Western England, using the remains of drovers roads where they still existed, struggling down ways little more than paths trod by residents from one village to another, skirting woods, fording streams and at times even having to venture along the edges of fields. Will Shakespeare felt the excitement of the encounter slowly subside. With hands that still trembled he laid aside his bow and arrows and clutched to his chest a package that seemed at the time more precious than anything in the world. Even the care and love he felt for his wife and family faded into the background as he contemplated the possibility that the offspring of his intellectual copulation might have been wrested from him by the robbers. The pages of manuscript the bag contained might have been of no value to them, but the bag contained a purse of gold coins and was one of his father's finest, in expensive leather, with hand-wrought patterning. The robbers would have had no hesitation in snatching it from him with all its contents and it had been the thought of losing his precious scripts that had prompted him to act with such heroism, although guiltily he did not admit that to his companions.

The manuscripts represented days, weeks, even years of effort. The floor around his desk in the tiny room he used as a study was littered with broken quills and the surface of the desk itself was stained with the residue of ink he had ground with his own hands. His fingers would ache from the effort of guiding an unwieldy implement across stiff parchment. But this was nothing alongside the mental effort, the discipline, needed to produce quite a modest body of finished work. It would have been a bitter irony if he had been bereft of it now he was at last with those who could help fulfil its true purpose before an audience.

The actors were all now fully awake and talked in increasingly animated tones about the venues they had left and the destinations that lay ahead. There was also much comment on the plays they had presented and the experiences they had shared with their audiences. They huddled together for warmth and generated additional heat by their gesticulations and frequent jerky movements of their bodies. The exhalations from their mouths and other bodily apertures created a miasma of smells that seemed to bind them into one corporate body of humanity. He wanted desperately to be part of it, to join in their conversation and share their exciting activities, but despite his keen interest in their work and all it entailed he felt excluded.

Strangely, it was something he had already experienced, even in relationships with his family and those closest to him. He loved his wife and his children, always bonded with his mother and, although he felt little affinity with his father, he acknowledged a filial duty towards him. Yet he felt something of an outsider, an onlooker, concerned for their welfare, but unable to participate fully in the conjugal process. He had few friends and those who did exist were little more than acquaintances. Even hunting, his principal recreational activity, tended to be solitary.

He was only fully fulfilled when he sat at his work table, his mind crowded with characters who acted out their tales of fantasy and fable. He actually saw them coming to life before his eyes, speaking not only to each other, but to him as an audience. He was sometimes an arbiter controlling and directing them and even saw himself taking part with them, joining in their jollity,

27

suffering their heartache. Somehow all this was transmogrified on to the pages he had guarded so carefully. Their loss would have been like seeing those he loved stricken down before him.

It was something his father had never been able to understand. To his father there was more value in the leather satchel holding them than in all the pages of literary endeavour. John Shakespeare was a successful businessman, although perhaps "had been" is a more accurate description. Of late his fortunes had taken something of a downward turn. It is in such a situation that men hope they can turn to an offspring to help restore the family's position commercially and socially. Sadly for John this was something young Will failed to do.

There was a time when John Shakespeare's position both socially and in the business world had been unassailable. As a maker of leather wear, including gloves, belts and purses, his products were constantly in demand. He had been appointed ale taster for the town of Stratford, which meant he was responsible for ensuring correct observation of weights and measures not only by publicans, but also by butchers, bakers and the like. He had been an alderman and was in one year appointed High Bailiff.

Like so many of his generation, however, his religious affiliation had adversely affected his fortunes. He had been born and brought up in the Roman Catholic faith and had not seen any justification for changing his beliefs, for either spiritual or political reasons. He might have felt justified in this during the dreadful persecution of Protestants under the former Queen Mary, but it had been followed by oppression of Catholics – although less severe - by her successor, Queen Elizabeth. However much he tried to keep the spiritual predilections of himself and his family out of the public eye, the cold stare of prejudice had turned towards them. They were expected to attend the Protestant communion and there was a limit to the number of times excuses relating to illness could be proffered. The fines that were occasionally imposed for non-attendance only served to reduce the family's coffers even further. He was confident that his religious waywardness under the present hazardous conditions would be pardoned by his God, but he did not enjoy such forbearance from his neighbours and sometime friends.

Then he was confronted by an additional cross to bear in his own family. William was not his eldest child. There had been two daughters before him and a second son shortly after William's birth. But he was his heir and it was in him he had placed all his aspirations. He accepted that William was a clever child and showed intellectual brilliance as a man, but John never experienced the empathy of spirit that was supposed to exist between father and son. The hope that those developing powers of mind and imagination would be applied to the family business and help it to survive difficult times was never fulfilled.

Sometimes the father tried to talk to his son and reach through to the mysteries of the young man's mind, but he found it was full of stories, some of them relating to far-off kingdoms and even to fairy-land; others based on the legends and folk-lore passed down from generation to generation in the hamlet defining the family's horizons. The boy would sit for hours penning his verses, sometimes gazing into space as if hoping to find the words engraved on the wall above his head. If only, his father thought, he could see there the designs of shapely gloves and purses and turn these to profitable account.

At first John thought William's lack of interest in the

family business was because he lacked manipulative skills, but he demonstrated dexterity in the art of fletching and would spend hours trimming feathers to fit into his arrows. A similar sort of manipulation was required to produce writing materials, quill pens and ink compounds. To the father a quill pen was a quill pen, but for the son it was of the utmost importance to ensure smoothness in the way it passed across the page.

The boy did evince an interest, even a fascination, in the more abstract world of financial affairs and indeed this was something that was to last him all his life. Indeed, privately Will thought that if his father had paid more attention to this more arcane aspect of business he might have withstood the misfortunes afflicting him. In an attempt to justify the cost of maintaining himself, his wife and increasing numbers of offspring he tried to put this commercial aspect of his life to practical use, by persuading his mother to initiate a legal dispute relating to property at Asbies. She claimed it was her inheritance and there was some justice in the claim, but like so many disputes involving inherited property this dragged on for many years and profited the family little if at all. In fact it had an inverse effect as the action earned the family few friends. William's unsatisfactory relationship with his father was reflected in his approach to all forms of authority, particularly school. Before his father's financial position deteriorated he was able to send the boy to a grammar school of reasonable pretensions, and one which was said to be the equal, if not superior to, the nationally famed Eton. He was fed with the *trivium* of grammar, dialectic and rhetoric, as well as the *quadrivium*: arithmetic, geometry, music and astronomy. He was an assiduous scholar and had a desire - even anxiety - to absorb knowledge from the meagre supply of books available. In those days, however, schoolmasters attempted to beat knowledge into what they saw as the rebellious hides of their pupils. Any failures in the acquisition of learning attributed to indiscipline or intransigence The beatings an emerging poet suffered from one fearsome teacher when he resisted the attempt to be force-fed the terra incognita of Latin, while he was seeking to piece together aspects of the vernacular only made him more determined to follow his own path in life whatever the consequences.

His learning was augmented by the translations of Latin and Greek plays carried about by the travelling troupes of actors who frequently visited Stratford and neighbouring towns and villages. From them he learnt of a world of gods and goddesses, battles and strange journeys through fabled lands. He discovered that men and women could express themselves in words that rang loud and clear in the mouths of the lordlings who strutted about the miniscule stages set up in the inn-yards.

He struggled to put his own ideas into plays he hoped one day would be presented by these wonderful people. He had introduced himself to some of them, but they received his approaches with little enthusiasm. Now, at last, he was to be part of the company. Once he got to know them, worked with them, perhaps even shared their stage, they would be bound to view his writing with greater sympathy.

As he bounced and jolted along, ignored by his potential future comrades, Will turned to his favourite mental pastime, allowing thoughts and images to form themselves into words and phrases in his mind. There was little in his immediate surroundings to stir his poetic imagination, but there were many aspects of his earlier life he could call on. Words would come into his mind unbidden at the sight of wild flowers in a spring meadow, or the smile from a beautiful girl. They were often accompanied by what he could only describe as a tingle at the back of his neck, something no more material than an itch requiring to be scratched. But it would stay with him and urge him to write it down and when he did he would look at it and think: "that is good". Then he would put it on one side and forget it, until perhaps later the feeling would come again with more words and he would put them together, arrange them as a verse, then join those verses in a stanza. Echoes of his school work would remind him of such matters as rhyme and scansion, of a job-trot learnt from his classical studies and he would try to force his inspiration into the mould. But this often led him to feel he had only succeeded in marring it, so would tear the pages in frustration.

Hunting was always a source of inspiration although inevitably also a cause of contention between him and his father. It made a contribution to the family's well-being, adding to its store of food, but his father said it was illegal, although Will would point out that the deer roamed freely and were only occasionally culled by the landlords. He further justified his activities on moral grounds by pointing out that such game would feed the poor of the community for a whole winter season and all he was doing was to ensure that his family was able to enjoy a reasonable standard of living. Local gamekeepers had different ideas and were determined to interpret the law as strictly as their poor resources would allow.

To Will there was a correlation between the chase and wooing a beautiful woman. He recalled how once he had watched a herd of deer coursing across a meadow. They were not fleeing from him and their action seemed to be part of a mating ritual. One young deer had its tail up and its rear glowed red. The deer was a hart, he thought, and if I choose I could pierce it with an arrow as cupid might the heart of his love.

For much of his young life, love was nothing more than a pastime, like hunting, something to be enjoyed and about which to write poetry. The enjoyment of love however, like hunting, produced its consequences. One day Will came home and told his father he had fallen in love and proposed to marry. Indeed, it was somewhat imperative that he should as the young woman was pregnant. Her name was Anne Hathaway and she was several years older than Will, who was only 18. It was necessary to read the banns only once, instead of thrice, so that he could be bundled into a marriage with someone whom he did, fortunately, love dearly. A daughter was born and subsequently twins, one a girl and the other a boy Hamnet. The initial anger and despair of his father was mollified by the thought that his errant son might now be forced to give up his scribbling and musings, apply himself to more practical matters and settle down to a normal paternal life in his parents' home..

He was to be sadly disillusioned. If anything the need to provide for a growing family and to establish himself as someone of significance led the young man to distance himself even further from industrial activity and spend his time in what appeared to be nothing more substantial than recording the everyday trivia he heard from those around him. It certainly encouraged him to pursue his pastime of hunting, in which his skill with the bow and arrow helped him to become very proficient.

Then the day came when he was caught *in flagrante*, as it were. His captors seemed to take a special delight in hauling him before the magistrate and he was bailed to appear before the Court in a few days' time. If he appeared there his father could do nothing to save him from summary justice. There would be a prison sentence of indeterminate length. There was no alternative: William had to flee. Fortunately, his father's position enabled him to arrange for a licence to travel, without which he would be regarded as a vagrant. An actors' company was currently visiting the town and as the official responsible for granting them licence to perform John was able to persuade them to take his son into their company. The irony was not lost on him. At one time he had been an assessor of fines for crimes of malfeasance not covered by common law and now he was having to deal with a criminal in his own family

The theatre company's leader made much of the extra expense this would cause, not to mention the responsibility of providing for the young man. With arguments like this Charles Knight was able to extract a few shillings recompense from the worthy businessman, although in fact he was not averse to accepting a presentable and healthy young man in his company. Even if he was not proficient as an actor, there was much work he could undertake in the business of setting up and managing backstage as they went from village to village, town to town.

So it was that very early one autumn morning Shakespeare bade a sad and tearful farewell to his beloved wife and children, was embraced by his mother and received a few last- minute words of wisdom from his father:

"Come embrace me" John Shakespeare said. "We may not always have seen eye to eye, but you are my son for all that. Who knows when we shall meet again, but I hope your mother and I will receive news of you and that it will be meritorious. And I am sure it will be, if you act judiciously. Try not to be quarrelsome or judgemental. Make good friends and keep them, but discard those who might lead you astray. Fashions may be different where you are heading. So follow the custom of dress, remembering that you are a citizen."

William gently extricated himself and turned away, but his father restrained him.

"Oh! and one final thing – do not lend or borrow money. Remember I speak out of experience."

"I will take your words to heart, father. I know you have always advised me in what you thought was my best interest, but you must allow me to live my life in a way that is true to myself. I can be no other than I am. The thing I am shall make me. From now on I shall be my own man. It will be one consolation for the sadness I feel at leaving you and the rest of my family."

And he truly did feel sad, although it was combined with a sense of exhilaration. He thought of the wonderful prospect opening up before him among the colourful characters of the theatre company. It was as if he had spent his life as a peasant gazing at a castle to which he had no access, longing to mix with the fine knights and ladies who strolled through its gardens and its grounds. Since a boy he had attended the performances of the strolling players not only in Stratford, but in neighbouring towns and villages, watching as the stories from the books he read come to life on the tiny stages. Now he was to be a part of them, to share in their glory. And even more than that there was a chance that material from the plays he had been working on, which were so much a part of his world, would be spoken by those superior beings, that the characters he had imagined would come to life and reach out to audiences of which he had once been only a humble part.

Moreover, he was travelling! – an activity rarely experienced by those of his generation in a small west of England town. The opportunity to visit other villages and towns – perhaps even London - would bring something to his writing he had always felt was lacking.

He had been aware of its parochial, even bucolic, limitations. But he could only write what he knew or had read about. Now, he could gain experience of the wider world.

He could have no idea how wide that world would eventually become.

Chapter 4

They had hoped to reach Shipston-on-Stour by dinner time, but the hold-up had literally held them up and it was early afternoon before they drove into the tiny village and parked on the square. Robin complained that the inhabitants would have eaten all their pies and there would be nothing left for the players but the bones of mutton shoulders.

"We'll have to make do with quantities of cheese", he said, although he was mollified at the thought of the ale that would be forthcoming from local housewives.

The great stage coach house that would later grace the village had yet to be built, the efforts and resources of the locals having in recent generations been directed to completing a magnificent tower on their church. There was, therefore, no place to set up a stage, so the company rested the wagon on the village green and when they were ready to perform opened up one of its sides.

Their arrival in the village, which they announced with much banging of drum and clashing of cymbals, shouts and singing of popular choruses, was welcomed by an unrush of local inhabitants from the houses and surrounding farms. The housewives stopped cleaning the dishes they had used in their midday meal and lifted their skirts to come running to the side of the wagon in order to catch an early glimpse of its glamorous passengers. Shepherds left their sheep in the fields partly so that they could enjoy the show, but also to ensure that their wives did not shame themselves by gawping too long at the strangers and that they did not offer excessive quantities of their precious brew. Children leapt from the tiny schoolroom and could not be restrained from running to join the fun. They were followed by their schoolmistress, who came to chivvy them back to their desks, but stayed with them to enjoy the spectacle.

A space had been reserved on the grass at the side of the wagon so that the talents of the company could be displayed in advance, such as the athletic tumbling and jumping of their clown, to which the archery skills of their new companion were added. These entertained their audience while the principal actors were preparing themselves for their performances behind the wagon screen. But to those watching it was all part of the show. People whose sole form of entertainment woud be reading passages from the Bible by candle-light of a winter's evening, or a show put on by local mummers at Christmas time, could now laugh with joy and clap their hands at the silly antics of a clown, or gasp in wonder as a young man placed arrow after arrow in the centre of a targe.

More excitement was to come. The painted picture on the side of the wagon was lifted with the roll of a drum to show a magnificent figure clad in red and gold, with a tall crown on his head, holding aloft a sword that seemed to be strangely shortened. Kneeling before him was someone less richly clothed, but still obviously of high estate. He held a shield that bore a strange device, but had nothing on his head. Then a beautiful maid wearing a flowing gown and with long golden tresses joined the sovereign and linked hands with him. For a moment they stood unmoving, as a young man who could be identified as a page passed across the stage holding aloft a card bearing an inscription.

Most of those watching were unable to read it, so the schoolmistress called out :"It is our great King Henry receiving the surrender of the King of France at Agincourt". This raised a cheer from the gathered multitude and someone shouted: "And that is the fair Katharine, the French king's daughter, who became our queen". More cheers, combined with a few ribald comments, which in turn brought cries of "shame" and hissing of teeth.

The curtain was lowered on the scene and immediately a minstrel appeared around the side of the wagon to sing a song about the battle of Agincourt, telling how the king went forth to Normandy, with grace and might of chivalry, and how God wrought marvellously for him so that evermore the people of England might cry: "Deo Gratia". The singer accompanied himself on a stringed instrument and encouraged the audience to join in the refrain, which they did enthusiastically if somewhat unmusically.

When he was done the screen was raised again to show that miraculously what appeared to be the trees and undergrowth of a wood had grown. Into that scene a figure appeared in full armour and carrying on his head a half crown or coronet.

He identified himself as King John and claimed to be ruling the country in the absence of his brother Richard who had died in a crusade. This information was greeted with boos and expressions of dismay from the audience. These were repeated when another figure, also in armour, entered and said that as the Sheriff of Nottingham he would loyally serve the King by ridding the land of thieves and brigands, and all those who protested against the king's lawful rule. The reaction of the audience to this was so strong that certain members had to be restrained from advancing to the stage and attacking the character, who in turn inflamed the situation by turning on them and snarling in a most contemptible way.

This unpleasant character then told his monarch he had devised a plan to entrap the leader of the worst

39

robber band by kidnapping a woman who was known to be his paramour. Two thugs appeared holding between them a beautiful woman with long dark hair and wearing robes torn and stained from her captivity. This brought gasps from the audience and cries of shame, which increased when she said her name was Marian, that she was no woman, but a virtuous maiden, betrothed to Robin. The King commended the Sheriff on his initiative and left the stage providing the villain with an opportunity to press his advances on the helpless maid.

She repulsed him, but it seemed his superior strength would overwhelm her when, to the delight and cheers of the audience, the hero himself appeared arrayed in glowing green and carrying not only a long bow almost as tall as himself, but also the truncated sword of the earlier presentation. The evil sheriff told his henchmen to seize him, but Robin was joined by two of his fellows, one a portly monk, who seemed to be bristling with ungodly weapons and the other dressed in red doublet and hose. A fierce battle ensued, accompanied by shouts of encouragement from an audience becoming increasingly involved in the conflict. Children began striking adversaries about the head. Mothers attempted to separate them and fought with one another. This brought male adults into the fray and the whole event threatened to develop into a full-scale riot until suddenly a new figure appeared on the stage. He was royally dressed with a crown on his head, a sword in one hand and an orb in the other. He held these aloft and cried in a stentorian voice: "Hold all there!".

The audience looked at him stunned and immediately obeyed his injunction, producing a tableau of raised fists, supine bodies and aggressive stances.

"Do I return from bitter wars to rescue the holy places of Jerusalem from the infidel, only to find my own people engaged in violent conflict? Cease and bow in unified allegiance to your King. King Richard and England!"

The crowd did cease and as one they lifted themselves up, raised their hands and cried: "King Richard and England". Even King John returned to the stage and knelt in allegiance.

The actors then bowed and embraced one another, with the exception of Maid Marian who reacted to an attempt by the Sheriff to kiss her by slapping him firmly around the face and lifting her knee in a most unladylike manner into his groin.

The screen was lowered and the crowd started to move away, but their entertainers had not finished with them. A roll on a drum turned them back towards the stage. There they beheld a page bearing aloft a placard, which they were told bore the legend: "A morality play. Equity repulses Justice". Two characters then appeared in robes that seemed to have little significance. They engaged in a diatribe largely meaningless to the audience, who began to mutter among themselves and edge towards the cottages on the far side of the green. Children were less reserved and some even made rude gestures towards the stage before running off, chased in despair by the schoolmistress. Shepherds felt they were justified in returning to their flocks and soon the actors' voices failed when they realised they were addressing empty air. Eventually they wandered off the playing area, the screen was lowered and silence fell.

"I told you we should not finish with a morality play", cried Robin Goodfellow. "We had them eating out of our hands. Now we shall be hard put to it to eat out of theirs."

"They have had a good afternoon's entertainment", said Charles. It is a pity we arrived too late for dinner. But hopefully there will be enough left to give us a good supper. I am going to call at the local inn to ensure we have accommodation for the night. I also need a room where I can work on some material with our new friend here".

With that, one of the two twins spoke up in anger: "Why was he given the part of King Richard. He has only just joined us. He led the crowd. Simply because of the character he shone like a star".

"You were to appear as Equity afterwards", said Charles.

"Yes, to drive the audience away."

"And whose fault is that", said Robin. "This young man had the voice for it. Look at the way he quelled the crowd. You could never have done that".

"Who said I could not. I have enough voice for anything. Listen", and he started crying aloud: "King Richard and England. King Richard and England - ".

As he went on Robin tried to calm him, but others joined in joyfully trying to out-shout him. Eventually Charles managed to quieten them.

"It was an opportunity to see what the young man can do and you must admit he acquitted himself well. We now have a new and useful member of our company."

Still faced with murmurs of dissent he said: "And he has also brought some scripts with him. I want to look at them before we reach Oxford"

"What's the matter with what we've got. The crowd loved Robin Hood and there are *Ralph Royster Doyster* and *Gammer Gurton's Needle*" said one of the twins, with nods from his brother.

"Both Berkeley's and Worcester's men are playing them, sometimes before us. We need something new. The return at Stratford was not what we might have expected. We have only two more stops before London and you know there will be little there for us now that the permanent theatres have been built. So let's have peace among ourselves. We are a goodly company and have had a successful tour. Let's finish it in style."

Charles directed them to go out among the local residents to raise what they could in the way of victuals. Then he told Will to come with him to the local inn with his satchel. There they were welcomed by the landlord and refreshed with beer, although Charles wished he could have the ale other members of the company would be enjoying from the alewives. Charles said he disliked the alien addition of hops to the drink and much preferred the darker, sweeter taste of the traditional English brew. They were also given a dish of various cheeses and bread so fresh it was still warm. They were offered a small room on an upper floor where they could spread out their papers. The landlord said he could not accommodate any of the company overnight, but offered to enquire among the farmers whether a barn could be made available.

When they were settled in their room, with a fire crackling in the grate and a jug of beer on the table Charles said: "I liked your Dream play. The idea of casting a spell on the loving couples is excellent and the transformation of Bottom into an ass is particularly good. I showed it to Robin, who could play it, and he is very enthusiastic. That aspect of the play needs filling out however.".

"Filling out?" asked Will cautiously.

"Yes. Robin agrees with me. More could be made of the character of Bottom. We need some rustics. A group of them could be preparing a play to perform at the Duke's wedding."

There was silence while Will digested this information. He hated the idea of anyone trying to alter his play, but was anxious not to do or say anything that might jeopardise its performance. He decided on a tactful approach.

"That would mean more actors. Where are they to come from?"

"Ah! Now there we might have a solution. We would be presenting this in Oxford, a lively town. There is an active amateur group, attached to the University. Yes I know it is a pain working with amateurs.".

Will was not sure what was meant by amateurs: "Does that mean they won't be paid?"

Charles nodded vigorously: "Oh! definitely yes. They won't be paid".

Something from Will's family business background came to his mind: "How will those in your company like working with them?"

"Oh! they're used to it. They don't have an option."

"Will these amateurs be ready in time."

"Oh! yes. Their scenes will be rehearsed separately. They often have difficulty learning lines, but they make up for that by their keenness."

Will struggled to get his mind round the changes: "It will alter the whole balance of the play. This is meant to be a romantic comedy, with loving couples and – and – fairies."

"Ah! yes. There's another thing. Where did you expect these fairies would come from?"

"I don't know. I think I thought – well – they could be imagined."

"Imagined! Oh! dear no. We'll have fairies all right - a whole troupe of local children."

Will looked at him aghast: "Local children. The play will be ruined."

"Nothing of the sort. You'll see. Children are marvellous, much better than adults. More importantly think what it will do for numbers of audience. The mothers and fathers, aunts and uncles – they'll all come.

And as for the yokels people will flock to see their friends – and enemies – making fools of themselves. We shall be rich from the proceeds. We may even be able to give more than one performance."

"So are plays to be tailored to commercial considerations? Are we to write rubbish into a script so that people will come to see it? I would have been better off as a glove maker."

"But if people don't come to see it, what will be the point of the play? As for rubbish you will be writing it, so I assume it will have quality."

Will got up and went to the unglazed window. A cold wind had risen, blowing a few drops of rain into his face. Charles looked at him anxiously.

"A glove maker? Were you really going to be a glove maker?"

Will shivered. His lovely play, over which he had laboured with care for so many hours, was in danger of being ruined. He thought of the nobility of the fairy king and queen and the subtle irony of her being enamoured of an ass. He thought of the gentle humour in which the young lovers suffered all the torments of mistaken identity. Bottom was intended as a contrast to the nobility, but one who was able to maintain his dignity. What would happen to that dignity when he was surrounded with bucolic buffoons.

He turned and faced Charles: "I cannot do it. I will not do it".

There was a silence. Charles frowned, drank the dregs of his drink and gazed at the empty glass as if it contained the seeds of his displeasure.He filled it from the jug and drank deeply. At length he said: "I wanted you to write it because it is your play. But in fact it hardly needs writing. Given the idea, the group will improvise."

"Improvise!"

"Yes. We do it all the time. I know you think your writing is sacrosanct, but this is professional acting. Although we are individuals we work as a company, for the good of the general effect. And that applies to the man who provides the script as well as to those who speak the lines. You cannot say to your actors, you will do this, or you cannot say that. Would you put an ass's head on all of us? We are not your minions. It is we who must face the public. You either join us or you leave us. Take your choice."

Will struggled to find an argument to help his cause. He went to the fire and warmed his hands, then to the table, where he picked up some of the papers strewn about. He sat down. He had to admit the arguments against him were very strong.

"We will never be able to get it ready in time for Oxford. It took me months to write the play."

Charles looked at the young man's troubled face with sympathy.

"Did it? Yes, well, we work at a different speed in the theatre. If you start work on the new material now it can be ready by tomorrow, which is a Sunday. Our manager will take your script to Oxford and arrange for the parts to be written out. He will also seek out the company of actors I spoke of. They will be rehearsed already by the time we arrive. The children will also have been recruited.."

There was another silence. Charles had a feeling this was a decisive moment in the fledgling playwright's life.

At length Will said: "So you envisage what - play within a play?"

Charles got up with a sense of great relief. He was feeling hungry: "Oh! nothing so grand. Have fun with it. Make fun of the locals if you like. The more you do the better the audience will like it."

Will began to find ideas going through his mind:

"There will be what – a tinker, a tailor?"

"A carpenter, a joiner."

"They will need a plot of sorts" said Will,

"Oh! nothing elaborate. A rustic knockabout, that sort of thing."

Will got up in turn: He was feeling quite excited: "No. I'll provide an extra irony: to see these clodhoppers stomping about. Something from the classics, Roman perhaps, or Greek, Remus and Romulus."

Charles laughed: "No, you can't have my twins".

Will was walking about the room. He stopped by the window and looked out: "I know - Pyramus and Thisbe!"

Charles looked at him with some surprise. He had expected submission, but something creative was stirring in the young man's heart.

"I must go and see how my company is faring and arrange for their accommodation. I will have candles and more of this swill sent up for you and later there will be supper."

"I will need quills and ink."

"You shall have them. Is there anything else?"

The young man did not reply so he left him looking out of the window at the gathering dusk and at a horizon that for Will had just significantly widened.

Chapter 5

The company's next stop was Woodstock, a town Will had heard his father talk of because its principal industry was the manufacture of gloves. They stopped at the Bear Inn, a hostelry yet to achieve the size and fame it later gained as an important coach stop on the route between the north of England and London. The inn yard was, however, already big enough to accommodate the wagon and its trailer, although there were no balconies for the wider audience they usually hoped to attract.

The company member responsible for stage managing was absent on his journey to Oxford and Will was recruited into the business of setting up the preparations for the show. This involved erecting the stage on its trestles, a process he had seen performed in Stratford, but had not before been involved in. It was a more complicated process than he realised and he was made to feel incompetent in his attempts to assist, while the other members of the company – even the children – acquitted themselves with skill and dexterity.

Behind it was what was called a back-drop on which the representation of a castle had been painted, with a curtained gap in the centre for entrances and exits. The wagon, used as a dressing room, was hidden behind this, its side screen raised to facilitate the movement of the actors. Will was initiated into the mysteries of the "properties" table and was berated for not arranging them in the correct manner. It was important, he was told, to ensure they were in a certain position. A sword, for example, must be set with its handle towards the actor, so that he could seize it without delay and not find himself fumbling with the blade. Crowns and coronets always had to be in the same place to avoid the possibility of an actor placing the wrong one on his head and entering as a queen rather than a king.

The same also applied to the costumes, which were many. They also had to be hung on their rails in a way that ensured the actor coming off stage in the guise of one character could speedily transform himself into a different part, sometimes involving the donning of wigs and hats, as well as cloaks and even dresses. The young man absorbed all this and was given to understand that it was such matters, not necessarily the words that were written or even the actors who spoke them, which decided the success or failure of a stage presentation.

Charles Knight had been engaged on his administrative duties with the inn landlord and became angry when he found Will assisting with these arrangements. He demanded to know whether the new parts for the Dream play were ready. He said they were more important than "messing about backstage" as he wanted to rehearse any new material involving the main cast that day. He said he would arrange for Will to have a room where he could work.

Will decided that he would never be able to please everybody and reluctantly left work he did, in fact, find quite enjoyable. The draft of the main scenes involving the peasantry had gone off to Oxford to be copied. He still had to revise other scenes, particularly those involving Bottom and the wedding between the Duke and the Amazon. .What amazed him particularly was that a group of actors who had spent their time since arrival erecting a stage in preparation for a performance to be held that night were also going to fit in rehearsals for a completely new play?

When he mentioned this to members of the company, however, his concerns were met with derision. He would learn, they assured him, how such matters were managed. So he made his way to his upstairs room at the inn and wrote there furiously. The leisurely business of carefully writing and rewriting high-sounding dialogue was a thing of the past. He was now caught up in a maelstrom of activity which seemed to demand that scenes he would have pondered over for days had to be produced in a matter of hours and even minutes.

Then he found himself faced with a situation that might have resulted in his being caught up in a more disastrous sense. There was a loud commotion in the yard and he went to the window to find out what was happening. To his alarm he saw that a motley crew of folk from Stratford had appeared on horseback. It was led by the town's Sheriff, who demanded to see the group's leader. Will moved back from the window quickly and sat shaking. Had they come for him? Should he try and hide?

Later he was told how Charles confronted them and was told that the band was a hue and cry in pursuit of a miscreant who had fled from Stratford to escape justice. He was believed to have taken refuge with the players. Charles had been magnificent. He told them such a person had joined them when they left the town, but had not been allowed to remain. He had stayed with them only so far as Shipston-on-Stour. Then he had taken a horse and ridden on towards London, where he no doubt was.

The Sheriff was not convinced and demanded to inspect the members of the company, to see if he could identify him. Charles suggested they would be better occupied going on to London. The Sheriff persisted and said that as the town's responsible officer he could suffer a fine for his failure to secure the miscreant. Moreover, if he and his companions did not recapture him all the inhabitants of the town could be fined. He also pointed out that if guilty of knowingly harbouring a criminal and not cooperating with the forces of law the company itself was in default and in danger of losing its licence to perform or even travel.

Charles reluctantly agreed to assemble his company. He went behind the screen, took hold of John Pike, thrust a female's gown and a wig into his arms and gave him instructions. Then he led the rest of the company on to the stage.

The Sheriff looked at them and counted. He consulted his notes: "Is this all? I have a list of eleven names. You have shown me only nine".

"There is one – are two – at the inn, working on our scripts."

"I should like to see these men."

"One of them is a woman."

"A woman! You know well that women are not allowed on stage in this country. Do you seek to adopt the lewd practices of the French?"

"Oh! she does not appear. She is an excellent scribe. She writes our parts and she helps with the female costumes."

"A young woman travelling alone, with a company of men. That does not appear to be seemly."

"Well", Charles said hesitantly, "She is not strictly alone. She is – er – with one of us".

"There is no mention here of any married members of your company, male or female."

"Yes, well. It is an informal arrangement."

The man went right up to Charles and placed his face close to him: "You mean she is a whore."

The actors all reacted with mock horror and astonishment.

"No such thing."

Charles hesitated, looking both ways, trying to avoid the accusing stare of the Sheriff. The he faced him again: "She is – well, if you must know, she is my mistress".

The Sheriff took a step back, trying to hide his growing amusement: "I see. Well, I suppose there is no law against that. If there were many of our kings and princes would be guilty of breaking it. Still I would like to see her – and the other member of your company".

"And so you shall, for here she comes now" – and at that moment John Pike appeared leading Will in his new guise. The other company members found it difficult to hide their laughter, turning their backs on the Sheriff, who looked at Will with interest. He went up to him, and peered into his face.

"Well, you are a very lively looking young woman. The worthy leader of your group is fortunate indeed."

He stood close to Will, put a hand behind him and squeezed his rump. Will took a step back and slapped him hard on the cheek. There was a roar of laughter not only from the theatre company, but also from the members of the hue and cry. The Sheriff secretly found this very amusing, even titivating, but decided he had enough of this buffoonery. He went back to his horse, which he mounted with some difficulty.

"Really I must protest", Charles said. "We are an honest group. You have no reason to question us and insult my good lady."

The Sheriff leant towards him, a more serious look on his face: "This miscreant", he said, "comes from a family that is known to have Catholic leanings. It is important that he should be apprehended so that his heretical and criminal activities do not corrupt the general populace. If you encounter him again I order you in the Queen's name to return him to his native town, so that he may be judged according to the law. In the meanwhile I cannot spend more time in the pursuit of this matter, nor can my companions. I will see if I can obtain fresh horses and press on towards London, or return to Stratford."

He led the way out of the inn yard and the company burst into delighted cheers. They clapped Will on the shoulder and railed him for being so convincing a mistress to their leader. The Clown reached behind him and pinched his rump, complimenting him on the softness of his flesh. Will, in turn, fetched him a blow, which the Clown parried. Charles called them to order and told the company to prepare themselves for rehearsal.

When he was alone with Will he asked him first if he had finished the parts. Will told him he had and turned to go and fetch them. Charles stopped him.

"So is your family of the Catholic persuasion?" he asked.

Will hesitated, then said: "We are loyal subjects of the Queen. We attend mass when illness does not prevent us."

"Yes", said Charles, "We all know about the excuses made by Catholics to avoid appearance at the Protestant mass. What I need to know is whether we are protecting a heretic in our midst. It could lead us into disaster and even death".

"I am certainly no heretic", protested Will. "I am well aware of the conflicts that have torn our country and how many have had to revise their views about the word of our Lord Jesus Christ. But I repeat, I and my family have sworn allegiance to our noble Queen Elisabeth and seek only to be allowed to worship as our conscience requires."

Charles took his arm: "We will talk more. I will come with you and read what you have written".

They moved towards the inn and some of the actors who saw them nudged one another and commented on what an attractive couple they made. Charles heard their laughter and hastily let go of Will's arm. Then he looked at him and smiled: "You do appear well in that attire. I think we can offer you occasional parts. You had better keep the dress on for now in case the hue and cry returns. Providing that is", he added with a laugh and a look back at his company, "certain members of our group can restrain their carnality".

Chapter 6

They entered Oxford through the North Gate, past the twin towers conjoined by the Bocardo Prison. Charles was at pains to point out to Will that the gruesome hole had once held Thomas Cranmer while he awaited his execution. No amount of recantation saved him from the fire, Charles said. He was burned by Mary for being a protestant. Now Catholics were burned by Elizabeth. These were dangerous times.

"When have times not been dangerous", asked Will. "But we must still live by our principles".

Charles agreed. "Yes but we must be circumspect and live by them privately. It will not serve any of us on earth or in heaven if our days are cut short by the fiery furnace, apart from its being a very painful way to die".

Will was overwhelmed by Oxford. There was an air of solidity, of permanence, about the buildings, particularly the colleges of the University, some of which had been there for centuries. He felt he had arrived in a spiritual home, under the stones of which, if it were possible to lift them, he would find answers to questions his mind had sought since childhood. The people seemed confident, assured, as they strolled about, laughing and joking with one another, some with papers and even volumes under their arms. In Stratford he could count on the fingers of one hand the number who could understand the words in a book, let alone display one in a street.

They made their way to the Bear Inn, where the facilities were impressive. The inn yard was spacious in comparison with those Will had seen in other towns and surrounded by a three-tiered gallery on all sides. Charles did not allow Will to become involved in the setting up of the stage, but took him off to a private room. The services of a local scholar, skilled as a scribe, had been enlisted to prepare the scripts. He was, Charles told him, a divinity student working as a librarian on manuscripts at Oxford University. He was reputed to be a man of exceptional talents, with a wide and encyclopaedic knowledge.

Will's inbred economic sense led him to suggest that he would expect to be well paid for such a service, but Charles assured him that he had a great interest in the works of the theatre and had agreed to do the work without charge.

Only one full copy had been prepared and members of the cast would receive only those pages relating to the scenes in which they took part. Will found them laid out neatly and it was his task to check them and make any necessary corrections. He was impressed with the meticulous nature if the handwriting and the care taken over the preparation, but he was surprised to find that certain small inconsistencies he had allowed to creep in because of haste had been corrected. There were even places where his work had been amended. This in itself was concern enough, but he was frustrated to find that the alterations were often an improvement. Although not entirely displeased at the results, therefore, he was cross to think that some old fogy – and a librarian to boot – had the temerity to alter his work. He proposed to speak sternly to him when they met. The work of a scribe should be, he thought, to replicate the original exactly, not to make adjustments of any kind without at least consultation.

The parts did not include those for the yokels who were to appear in the play within the play. Will assumed they had been distributed to the potential players, who had apparently already been rehearsing their scenes. He feared the worst. He had seen professional actors make a dreadful fist of playing their parts when their lines had been ill-learned. He dreaded to think what amateurs would make of them. The yokels were rehearsing in a nearby barn and Will hoped to see what they had were making of it, but a dinner had been laid on for the company by the inn landlord and John Pike came up to call him down.

John was an eager young man and his initial antipathy towards Will had turned into something approaching admiration. He had been told the part he would play and was full of enthusiasm. It was, he said, a wonderful play and would make a name for all of them particularly that of the author. Will's pleasure at his praise was tempered when he found it was based to a large part on the scenes the country-folk had been rehearsing. What a wonderful idea, the young man enthused, to have them perform a production of their own before the Duke!

They went down to dinner. The landlord had done them proud. The fact that the actors were to be there had doubled or even trebled his custom for the midday meal. Then there would be the performance of a new play the next day. Moreover, a company of local actors was to be included in the action and there were even to be appearances from local children. All their mothers and fathers, kith, kin and neighbours would attend. It might even be necessary to close the gate and offer the possibility of a further performance on the following day.

So the landlord could afford to be generous in his largesse. There was a saddle of mutton and a good capon, as well as many pies and a large fish caught recently in the Thames. These were followed by sweet puddings, pastries and biscuits and an abundance of seasonal fruits. He was frugal with the beer. There was to be a performance of Robin Hood that afternoon and he was aware that the actors would be expected to keep their wits about them. He had suffered one unfortunate experience in the past when he had allowed a visiting company to be served unlimited quantities of alcoholic beverages, including wine. The result had been a play with little sense or sensibility, which had become so disorganised it had to be terminated half way through and the spectators had demanded their money back.

Attendance at the afternoon performance was poor, but that was anticipated. There was even discussion as to whether they would forego it altogether. The company did, after all, have to find time to rehearse The Dream and new settings to be prepared. Even with the help of local builders (paid for by enthusiasm) the work went on well into the night.

After a few hours' scrambled sleep the company was exhausted and it was only the motivation of a new theatrical production that kept them going. As the time for the performance approached, however, they were invigorated at the crush of audience arriving. The landlord had laid on extra staff to take their pennies and guide those who paid extra to their places in the galleries. Some young bloods joined the throng in the yard and then watched to see where attractive women might be located above their heads. They would then slip extra coins into the palms of the gate keepers to be taken near them.

Sellers of sweetmeats and other popular delicacies moved around the crowd, offering their wares from trays hung around their necks. The landlord did not encourage the consumption of beer in the yard, having had unfortunate experiences with drunken spectators in the past, but wine was sold to the more gentile folk in the galleries, from which he made a good profit. The play was late starting, the business of accommodating and preparing the local cast members backstage, particularly the children, proving a difficult task. The audience began to get restless and Charles decided to start anyway and leave the business of backstage organisation to sort itself out.

With a roll on a drum John strode on to the stage carrying a placard announcing that they were to present a play entitled "A Dream". He then read it out for the benefit of the majority of those in the audience who could not read. This was greeted with applause, which grew when the Duke and Hippolyta entered. They were followed by Philostrate, played by Will, who was late on his cue and was no sooner on than he was ordered off by the Duke.

They listened intently to the exposition, giving sighs of sympathy and gasps of surprise as the lovers' situation unfolded. But when Bottom entered accompanied by his gang of locals they erupted into a veritable volcano of delighted appreciation. Robin, as Bottom, assumed their cries of appreciation related to him and strode to the edge of the stage and bowed elaborately. The others, taking their cue from him and assuming this was what they were supposed to do, performed likewise and the more they bowed the more the audience cheered, until it seemed likely that the play could never proceed further.

Robin's professionalism eventually prevailed and he approached Quince expecting to get his cue, which he did not. Nothing loath he went straight into his first line, adapting it to say: "You were best to call all our company name by name, according to the scrip". When this produced no result he repeated loudly "According to the scrip". The audience, sensing that something might be wrong picked up the refrain and called: "According to the scrip". This brought the actor to his senses and he quickly unrolled a parchment he carried in his hand and spoke his lines, only partly concealing

59

the fact that he was reading them.

After that the scene went quite well, the audience being particularly appreciative of their fellow citizens' performances. There was one disconcerting moment when it was discovered that the actor playing Flute had a stammer. It manifested itself first when he had to ask if Thisbe were a w – w – w – woman and the audience burst into delighted derision at his attempts to utter b – b – b – b - BEARD. This really upset the actor, who strode to the front of the stage and began to harangue them for deriding a poor man in his affliction. Then he strode off the stage in disgust, it being fortunate that he had no further lines to speak in the scene.

There was a great deal of enthusiasm from the crowd when Oberon and Titania entered accompanied by Oberon's train and fairies comprising local children. When Titania instructed hers to skip hence, however, they took it literally and left the stage, causing her to go off and bring them back, thus holding up the action. Conversely, having lullabied them satisfactorily to sleep in a later scene they ignored their leader's instruction to hence away and instead went to the edge of the stage to wave at their parents and friends. This meant that before Oberon could administer the potion into her ear he had to chase the children off, to protests from them and the audience.

As the play went on, however, the audience seemed to become more deeply involved. They laughed at the consternation of the lovers; they were delighted when the fairy queen was seduced by Bottom's ass's head. They sighed with relief and pleasure as the plot resolved itself and applauded unreservedly when the cast eventually crowded on to the stage for their final bow.

Backstage afterwards the players sank exhausted on to packing cases and bundles, but were not able to rest for long. Soon they were besieged by parents and relations to gather their charges, the fellows of the yokels to congratulate them on their astounding performances and many well-wishers and admirers who came simply to praise and to meet the glamorous stars who had shone so brightly, if briefly, in their firmament.

At one point John pushed his way through the throng and said to Will: "The person who scribed your script wants to meet you".

"And I want to meet him", said Will, eager to give the old man a piece of his mind.

John led him out of the wagon into the now almost-empty yard. The sun was low on the horizon and shone across the gateway. Will stood looking for the old fogy who had the temerity to alter his lines, but saw nobody.

"Where is he?" he asked.

"Why here", said John, "coming towards us".

For a moment Will was dazzled by the setting sun. It created a golden glow that suffused the stone and grey thatch of the buildings and cast a gentler hue on the costumes and faces of those members of the audience who remained. Emerging through them was a young man. He was the same height as Will, but slighter in build. His face was calm, yet to Will it seemed to have a radiant quality. The young man stopped a few feet away, raised his hat, and bowed deeply.

"It is a great pleasure and privilege to meet you Master Shivershaft", he said. "My name is Thomas James".

Will thought his voice had a velvet quality as if spoken through fine raiment. Then he recalled the nature of his concern. His pique returned and he responded quite sharply: "Yes, and I am pleased to meet you, Master Thomas James. We need to have a few words".

Chapter 7

The Dream play was so successful and its fame spread so widely throughout the neighbouring countryside that it was decided to give a second performance. To be able to stay in the same place for another day was a rare luxury for the travelling players. It meant they could relax in the morning, with a brief rehearsal to polish uncertain passages in the play. There were also complications with the local members of the cast. One or two of them found it difficult to give the extra time and had to be replaced. There was also much shuffling among the fairies, the mothers of whom were concerned at their charges losing another day's schooling.

Will noticed that the work of coping with these problems and arranging for newcomers to be rehearsed fell upon the shoulders of the man who seemed to be responsible for all the practical requirements of the stage, from the scenery and furniture moved on and off the stage to the smallest item of property used by the actors. Assisted by two of the junior members of the company, he was known as a stage manager and Will, for one, was astonished at the way in which he seemed able to solve a multitude of diverse problems with calmness and efficiency.

Anxious to learn all he could about the technical aspects of the stage Will offered his assistance and was allowed to participate for a while until his inexpert efforts resulted in his being tactfully advised to restrict his activities to script writing. He went to his room at the inn where he spent time going through the Dream play and, in particular, considering the contributions made by Thomas James, which, although minor, caused him a certain amount of irritation.

When the young man arrived Will expressed his anger in no uncertain terms. What did he mean by it, he demanded. It was understood that a scribe's job was to copy the work of a writer, not change it to suit his own predilections. Thomas was immediately contrite. He sat and spread his hands in a gesture of supplication.

"My work involves writing reports for my master, Sir Thomas Bodley. He expects them to be prepared in the best vernacular. I also have to prepare contributions written by other hands and am accustomed to putting them into acceptable prose".

"But this is not prose", Will said. "It is dramatic dialogue".

The man looked puzzled.

"And should that not be correct grammatically?"

Will laughed. After being made to feel incompetent so far in his theatrical work, he was gratified to find himself the better qualified.

"If actors confined themselves to reciting a well-rounded piece of prose, or even verse, they would be hissed off the stage", he said. "The stage is a representation of life, the way people talk to one another, with what you might consider grammatical failings".

Thomas looked puzzled; "You mean we are all talking in verse. In what I believe you call the iambic pentameter".

For a moment Will was nonplussed: "No. We introduce verse because – well because – it's like music. In the same way you might introduce a song and a bit of a dance into a scene".

The young man became quite animated, got to his feet: "Like they do in Italy. I have seen it in books. They call it – they call it – now let me see – the commedia del arte. That's it: the art of comedy."

"You say you have seen it in books. Where would such books be?"

"Why here. In my library."

"You have a library?"

"Well, it's not mine and it's not ready yet. It will not be for many years to come."

It was Will's turn to be excited: "May I see it? And this book about the Italians. Could you show it to me."

"Yes. It is in one of the colleges, only a few minutes walk away".

Will hesitated: "Well, I have to attend a rehearsal".

"It will not take long."

So they set off through the narrow and surprisingly clean streets of Oxford, past buildings that seemed to Will to be exceptionally spacious for their intended purpose, which was merely to educate. According to Thomas their destination was The College of St Mary of Winchester, which he said was larger than all the other colleges put together. It was certainly very impressive, set as it was in wide, well-tended parkland. As they approached it Thomas pointed out the portion of the city wall that marked the College's boundary. It was the responsibility of the College, he said, to maintain it and every three years the City's dignitaries had to "walk the wall" to demonstrate they were fulfilling their duties.

Thomas's own work-place was, however, rather less grand. He led Will to a small room at the rear of the main building, which he reached down narrow stone steps. This contained so many tables that it was quite difficult to move between them and all seemed to be covered with piles of manuscripts in bundles or laid out alongside writing materials.

"This is where I work", said Thomas proudly.

Will was quite disappointed. He looked around him: "This is it? I would hardly call this a library."

"Oh! no. That is through here."

The young man flung open another door and stood aside for Will to pass. When he did the sight that met his eyes astonished him. Every wall, except where pierced by tall windows, was filled from floor to ceilings with shelves containing books. The only furniture comprised a number of high-backed chairs and a large oak table in the centre of the room containing even more books. Will had never seen so many in his life.

"So this the university's library."

"Sadly no. Unlike Cambridge the University has no library. It is Sir Thomas Bodley's lifelong ambition to establish one here. But that will take many a year."

"Where have all these books come from?"

"Some of them were at one time part of a library collected by one Duke Humphrey. Others have been collated by Sir Thomas, brought back from his travels Many have been donated. When it became known that we were going to establish it, there has been tremendous interest mainly locally."

"Where is he now?"

"Abroad on government business. Our Queen has thought fit to entrust him with certain errands that must remain secret. In the meantime I have the task to begin the work of cataloguing and listing all these books and others that constantly arrive from well-wishers."

"It is an immense task", said Will. "But how wonderful it must be to spend your life immersed in such a wealth of learning."

"Yes. I am very privileged. I owe much to my patron."

"You mentioned a book about the theatre in Italy –"

"Ah! yes. It is here somewhere."

The young man opened a folder containing what appeared to be lists. He consulted them and then made his way to a shelf in the far corner of the room from which he extracted a book.

He brought it back to a Will profoundly impressed at such efficiency,

The book comprised mainly pictures and he looked at them in astonishment: "They have masks on their faces. And stand in strange positions with weird gestures."

"Some of it is silent. No words are spoken in some scenes. They call it mime."

Will made a distasteful grimace : "I would not like that. What is the point of a play without words. We playwrights would be out of a job."

Thomas laughed: "And so would we scribes".

Will laughed with him. It was a moment of intimacy between the two and Will began to regret the anger he had felt towards someone who had obviously worked so conscientiously on his behalf.

"I realise now the extent to which we are in your debt for the work you undertook for us".

"I was glad to do it. My whole life is taken up with the art of literature and one of the ways that manifests itself is through the medium of the theatre. To me it is unfortunate that the artistic emphasis in this college is mainly on music, an interest it shares in an *amicabilis concordia* with three other colleges, Eton, Kings and one at Cambridge."

"Is there any dramatic activity in the college itself ?"

"Oh! no. Not here. This college was established for the education of priests."

"So it is your intention to enter the church."

"Well I am a cleric, but Sir Thomas is anxious that I should concentrate on my work here. He insists that working with these books is my destiny. I owe him a great deal. He rescued me from an unhappy life and he is, of course, my patron now."

He looked around at the masses of books: "But

there must be a great deal of material here that will be of help to me in my writing".

"Oh! I'm sure of it", said Thomas, full of enthusiasm.

Will peered along the shelves: "Why here is a copy of Holinshed. We read it briefly at school. We were given transcripts to learn, but only details of dates and successions. And there are such wonderful stories of our Tudor kings, of wars in France, Joan of Arc, Richard Crookback and his defeat at Bosworth, the deaths of the princes in the Tower of London."

"There are lots of other books like that, some of them with more information, greater details of life in earlier times. Then I assume you have Latin."

Will was embarrassed: "Very little, I am afraid".

"Well, here are translations. And from the Greek. They contain stories that can be adapted for modern delight. Then there are fables from Italy. Italy is, I understand, the most wonderful country. I am hoping one day to visit. They have the greatest painters and musicians." Will walked about the room, gazing at the some of the titles, many of which he was unable to decipher. He had always been keenly aware of his educational shortcomings and realised what a wealth of knowledge there was there for him to plunder.

Somewhere a clock chimed.

"Is that the hour?" he said. I must get back. I am expected at a rehearsal."

He gestured at the loaded shelves: "Could I come back here and study?"

"You would be very welcome."

"How will your patron react?"

"Sir Thomas? As I said, he is away on the Queen's business. But even if he were here I am sure he would not object. When it comes to books and learning he is a most liberal and fair minded man. I am sure he would approve of my encouraging you."

"I am bound for London", Will said. "What I shall find there I do not know. How I will progress is in the hands of the gods, but if I can, and if I may, I would like to come back here to Oxford and spend time with you and with your books."

"You could stay in the halls of residence. They are meagre, but will cost you little."

Will held out his hand. The other took it.

"Then it is a bargain", Thomas said.

"It is a bargain."

He was late arriving back at the inn and rehearsals had already begun. He was greeted with grunts of disapproval and Charles treated him to a lecture on the importance of being on time. In the theatre, he explained, one never failed to arrive at the correct time and on cue. Supposing one was ill, Will enquired, to which Charles replied very firmly: "One is never ill".

PART 2

Chapter 8

Gabriel Harvey picked his nose assiduously and examined the product of his efforts before rolling it between finger and thumb and flicking it towards the rushes strewn on the floor. There was a knock on the door. He called out "enter" and looked up to see his servant oozing towards him. The man told him that a mister Poley was there to see him. Harvey was glad to hear this, but knew it was important that he should not be seen to be too accessible to his minions.

"Tell him to wait", he commanded. "Tell him I am meditating".

The servant bowed and left. Harvey knew Poley would bring him word from London and elsewhere in the world outside the narrow confines of Cambridge University. It was important for him to keep abreast of developments in the currently dangerous world of intrigue and conspiracy. Saying the wrong thing at the wrong time, or having dealings with the wrong people could lead one to an extended stay in the Tower, or worse, even conflagration of a most painful kind.

Still the prospect of hearing what was happening in the outside world filled him with a certain nervous trepidation and he calmed himself by reading a letter he had recently received from Edmond Spenser, absent from Cambridge for some ten years and now living in Ireland. The latest one actually included a sonnet addressed to Harvey as the poet's "singular good friend" and he determined that this should be published so that the general public would know the esteem in which he was held by a writer of such repute. For a moment the pedant allowed himself a sentimental reverie in which he recalled the happy hours he had spent with the poet as a room- and bed-mate.

Harvey liked to think that the success of Spenser's poem The Shepheard's Calendar had been due in some small degree to his intimacy with him, although he had to admit that his efforts to persuade Spenser to abandon the use of rhyme had not been successful. Spenser was now apparently working on an extended work entitled The Faery Queen and once again had resisted appeals from the Cambridge critic to adopt his favoured form of the hexameter. Harvey regretted Spenser's move to Ireland, never for a moment considering the possibility that the poet might have welcomed the opportunity to escape from his tormentor's intimidation.

Harvey rapped with a wooden gavel and his servant re-entered.

"Tell master Poley I will see him now."

The servant bowed and left. Harvey adopted a pose of intense concentration and after a short interval Poley entered. He carried with him into the severe atmosphere of the Deputy Proctor's room the air of a wider world outside Cambridge. Compared to Harvey's dark clothes, lacking even a ruff to set them off, Poley's attire was colourful. His hat, for example, although not excessively extravagant, when he doffed it threatened to fly away so adorned was it with feathers. Harvey looked at him with distaste, but reflected that he relied on this man's ability to mix with those whose manners differed so greatly from his own. He returned to the examination of papers on the table before him. Although irritated, Poley knew better than to disturb his concentration. He was content to humour the man's affectations as his influence in the prevailing religious hegemony was one that demanded respect, to his face at least.

At length Harvey looked up, which Poley took as a

signal to begin.

"Well", he said, "your protégé has emerged on to the cultural stage as it were".

"My protégé?"

"Yes. The young Marley. He has arrived at Tom Walsingham's."

"He is no protégé of mine. He was scarcely out of the University gate before he exchanged his cap and gown for doublet and hose and a feathered bonnet not unlike the one you are flourishing."

Poley hastily put the offending garment on to a chair: "It is the fashion", he said, not in any way intending this as an apology.

"Fashion it may be, but you cannot throw off the teachings of our Lord as easily as you can a cap and gown."

Harvey enjoyed the conceit of his aphorism. He unobtrusively made a note and resolved to make oratorical use of it at some future date.

"So he turned up at Walsingham's. Well, he will not be out of place there where his dangerously heretical views may be welcomed. He is a sad case, a sad case. He came to us, you know, on a scholarship, rescued from the stews of Canterbury, and for a while he laboured mightily, gaining his bachelorship with distinction. But from then until his attempts to be accepted as a master his life and his thinking went desperately astray. He produced what some might call poetry, but it is sad stuff, with no form or propriety."

"He has issued a poem beginning 'Come live with me and be my love'" said Poley.

"Well, there you are then. What piffle."

"He presented it to Sir Walter Raleigh, who has written a response."

"A critical one, no doubt."

"Well, no. Very much in the same vein, but satirical.

It has caused much amusement among those who believe that the poem is, in fact, a thinly disguised invitation for Raleigh to live with Marley."

"Surely there is no possibility of that."

"Heavens no! That worthy gentleman continues to aim the arrows of his desire towards fairer prey. There is an amusing tale told of him concerning one of her majesty's chamber maids."

"How disgraceful! To think that such gossip circulates in polite society." Then he added hastily: "But you had better tell me in case it has political implications".

Poley knew his man and his face twisted in a rye smile: "It seems that Sir Walter was embracing the maid against a tree in the royal park. She was concerned for her virtue and said: 'Sweet Sir Walter what will you ask? Will you undo me?' He loved the maid well, however, and persisted in his endeavours. She protested further saying: 'Sweet Sir Walter, sweet Sir Walter'. When she failed to repel him both her danger and her ecstasy increased. As his movements increased so did her cries: 'Sweet Sir Walter, swizzer swalter, swizzer swalter'". Poley ended his story with suggestive gestures. He laughed. Harvey did not. He lowered his head towards his papers in case his face had coloured.

"I assume the young woman was of no consequence."

"None at all I gather – except, of course, to Sir Walter."

Harvey shook his head sadly: "Ah! we live in a licentious world".

There was silence for a while as both men contemplated the scene from different aspects. Then Harvey asked: "Was he at Walsingham's?"

"No. He is abroad on Queen's business."

"Who else was there?"

"Well,Walsingham's man Fritzer, of course, who seems to be omnipresent on these occasions. And some dreadful person called Nicholas Skeres, a cutpurse and a rogue if I ever met one. I know not why Sir Tom tolerates such rascals. And, of course, the lovely Audrey, who continues to ensure the house is run on orderly lines."

"A sainted lady if there ever were one!"

"Oh! and a newcomer. A poet and an aspiring playwright."

Harvey was immediately alert: "A poet you say?"

"Yes, a quiet young man, from the west country, Stratford I believe."

"Not Oxford?"

"Apparently not, although he would have passed through there on his way to London. I gather he came in with a group of travelling players."

"Travelling players! And a poet! How bizarre."

"He has written a play. Something about a Dream. Apparently it was well received in Oxford."

"Well, no doubt it would be there."

"Oh! and Marley has also written a play."

"Some bawdy nonsense, no doubt."

"Well no. It is the story of Tamburlaine. He was an eastern warlord."

"I know who Tamburlaine was. You do not need to update my education, thank you. Well, that will come to nothing. The underlings who attend the theatre do not need to know about eastern potentates. The common people should be fed uplifting stories from the classics, from the Greeks, the Latins, told in good sounding hexameters. I assume it is in verse."

"Iambic pentameter, I believe, but I am no expert in these matters. He was reading out passages and I must admit some of it sounded quite fine. There was one verse that ran – let me see if I can recall it: 'Is it not fine to be a king, Theridamis. Is it not fine to be a king and ride in triumph through Persepolis?'"

"Well, there you are. The thing has no scansion. No rhythm. Well, leave him to his paltry plays. They will come to nothing. What was the talk at Walsingham's?

"I told you who was there."

"Yes, but what was their view of the political scene. Is there any talk of a return to the old order."

"I think not. Surely our protestant beliefs are safe under our blessed queen. We are living in sunny days."

"But the anti-Christ is always there and casts a shadowr. Vigilance Poley. We must have vigilance. We are none of us safe, remember that. We must root out the heretics wherever they are hiding. You do well to keep me advised. It may seem something of a backwater here in Cambridge, but we hold the rich learning of the nation in store. In our school of divinity we train those who will go out into the world and teach the people of this great country how to lead God-fearing lives You would take well to learn from them and from us, Poley, living as you perforce do among the stews and pitfalls of a satanic world, with no greater protection than a feathered headpiece."

Poley decided it was time to leave. He could tolerate Harvey until he became personal. Then he hated the man and tried to think of something that would disconcert him. He rose and picked up the offending bonnet. On his way across the room he said as casually as he could muster: "Oh! that reminds me. There is talk of establishing a library at Oxford University."

He had the door open and was halfway through it when Harvey was by his side.

"What was that?"

"I said there is talk of establishing a library at Oxford."

Harvey closed the door and drew Poley back into

the room.

"Where did you hear that?"

"At Walsingham's. The young man I told you about. While he was in Oxford with this travelling company he met someone who has been employed to begin the work of collating and listing the books."

"A library at Oxford! What nonsense! Theatrical gossip. There is only one library of any consequence and that is here in Cambridge. They had one there you know, but it foundered from sheer apathy and all attempts to revive it have failed."

He went back to his desk and busied himself with his papers as a sign that the interview was over. Poley was satisfied that his shaft had gone home. He reopened the door, but Harvey stopped him again and asked as casually as he could: "As a matter of interest, did this person say who was ultimately responsible for such nonsense?"

"Somebody called Bodley ?"

"Not Sir Thomas Bodley?"

"I believe so."

It was beneath Harvey's dignity to show anxiety, but he could smell a conspiracy as keenly as a vermin remover could detect the presence of a rat

"But he is a member of Parliament, a Queen's messenger. Is he at Oxford?"

"No. I understand he is in the Low Countries on her Majesty's business."

"Then what on earth would he want with a library?"

"I can only report what I have heard."

"So a young man meets in Oxford with someone who is working on the establishment of a library on behalf of a famous Queen's messenger. He then ends up at the Walsingham's. Where did you say he came from?

"Who?"

"This playwright, this so-called poet – what was his name?"

"I can't remember. Something strange – Shakeshaft, Shakescene, or something."

"Stratford is in the west of England. Papistry has always been strong in those parts. He must be watched, Poley, he must be watched. The whole situation must be watched. Look to it Poley. I rely on you."

When Poley left Harvey returned to his desk and began to write an important letter to another member of the Walsingham family, Sir Francis, newly appointed head of her Majesty's intelligence network. From his base in London the job of this dignitary was to identify and, if possible, apprehend anyone who plotted against the establishment. With the country under constant pressure not only from enemies abroad, but also the heretics in its midst these were dangerous times. Francis Walsingham was, therefore, one of the most important officials in the country and Harvey wanted to ensure that he stayed close to him not only for the security of the realm, but also – although he would never admit it – his own self aggrandisement.

Chapter 9

"So you are thinking about writing plays, Master Shakespeare?"

"If I may correct you, Mr Henslowe, I have written plays."

"Ah! yes. The Dream play. I have it here. It is excellent stuff. Quite original. I particularly like the rustic scenes. The play within a play. Very good. Very good."

"Yes, well, the true comic interest lies in the love affairs between the young people, and, of course, Oberon and Titania."

"I see those as romantic, rather than comic – except the ass's head, of course. Good. Very good. But romantic. When writing for the theatre you will find it is important to recognise the various categories : comedy, tragedy, history, romantic, and so on."

"I will remember that, sir, thank you."

Christopher Marley put in a word here: "Will has written poetry, too, Mr Henslowe. Very good poetry."

William had met Marley – or Kit as he liked to be called – when he first arrived in London. The troupe Will had been travelling with put in at the White Hart Inn, a venue, he was told once popular for the presentation of plays. Sadly, due to restrictions imposed by the City authorities, it could no longer be used for that purpose. But the travelling companies liked to stay there when they arrived from their country-wide tours.

The first thing that struck Kit about London was the smell – indeed it was an actual physical impact that caused him to put his hand to his nose in an attempt to ward it off. He had encountered similar stenches in neglected cattle sheds, or in stables that had not been cleared out for a long time, but even there the odours seemed cleaner, redolent of the corn and grass consumed by the animals. In the city it was putrid, coming as it so obviously did from the open sewer that was the river and from the ordure festering in the alleyways and streets. He mentioned this to Kit, who dismissed it with a wave of his hand, saying one quickly got used to it – and indeed Will found this was the case.

The next thing that impressed him was the size of the place, the number of buildings, the throngs of people, who all seemed to be in a constant state of rush and turmoil. They went about their business with their eyes fixed straight ahead, paying no heed to passers by, or even those they jostled and pushed. Kit strode through them with similar urgency and Will noticed that most made way for him even when he found himself shouldered out of the way.

He had been immediately attracted to Kit, who was the opposite of himself in almost every particular. Where Will was quiet and softly spoken, Marley was flamboyant, to the point of excess. Words seemed to tumble out of his mouth almost without his stopping to consider them. Sometimes that led him to make statements that were thoughtless to the point of being seditious.

Kit also took to Will, clapping him on the shoulder and tweaking his beard in the lightest and most affectionate manner. He had taken him to meet friends of his in neighbouring Kent – the Walsingham family – where he met a strange and varied collection of individuals, some of whom were actors, others aspiring writers like himself. Now he was in the process of introducing him to Henslowe, manager of the splendid theatre that had been built on the south bank of the Thames. Things were more spacious on this side of the river, which Kit explained was not part of London proper. The building was set among other places of pleasure and entertainment, as well as many crude houses hastily built on the mud flats. Henslowe owned much of the property, Kit told him, including the bear bating rings and brothels.

"He is an old rogue", Kit told Will in advance, "but do not be deterred by that. He is as shrewd as a street of Jews and the best businessman in the theatre. If he likes you and, more importantly, if he likes your work, you are a made man."

So, here they were, behind the scenes in the Rose, and here was the man himself clutching the script of a Shakespeare play.

"You also write poetry, Master Shakespeare. Yes, well, I would encourage that. It is like the tennis player who exercises his limbs in private, but what really counts is what he achieves on the court. I have room for writers of talent. You can become part of our team."

"Your team?"

"Of course. You do not think it possible for one person to create something as complex as a modern stage play on his own. You will work with others."

"Initially, perhaps?"

"We shall see. We shall see. Your friend Marley here has produced a very fine play entirely on his own and if it is successful he tells me he will produce a sequel. Then there is a writer called Thomas Kydd. You will meet him no doubt. He has produced a play called A Spanish Tragedy. You should read it. You will learn a lot from it. Bristling with action. Full of fire. Action is what the theatre is all about, Will. Action. Remember that. It is what the groundlings expect."

"But surely there is room in a play for poetry, for thought, for exchange of ideas?"

"Ideas? Ideas? I don't know that the theatre has

81

much room for ideas. Kit here was a divinity student at Cambridge. I am sure he had his fill of ideas there. In the theatre we are dealing with several hundred inattentive, generally brainless spectators, who have left their farms, their trades, their wives, sometimes their husbands and paid their penny at the door to be excited, invigorated, entertained. If they have any minds they leave them behind as well. I don't think they will take kindly to being presented with ideas. Now I have a play -"

He rummaged among the piles of manuscripts on his table top.

"– well I say I have it, I have the script of it, but I do not actually *own* it. That is the trouble. It belongs to a certain Mr Burbage. He has a theatre north of the city. It is an excellent comedy and I would dearly love to present it."

"So why not do so?"

"Because I would have to pay a fee, or be accused of plagiarism. Then although the plot is good, the dialogue is poor, stilted. There is, however, no copyright in ideas. It can be rewritten, with perhaps changes and additions to the plot. Then there could be no objection to our presenting it."

"What is it about?"

"It is about a termagant of a daughter, who must be married before her younger sister can. But her father is in despair because no one will take her, she is so shrewish. Is that not good?"

He found the script and waved it in the air: "Would you like to work on it?"

The idea of reworking someone else's play was repugnant to Will.

Kit urged his friend: "What do you think Will? A comedy. That will be novel. I have no skill with humour, but it is very popular".

Will took the script and glanced at the opening scene, which introduced the father then the shrew herself, but the dialogue was stilted and lacking in poetry.

"We will need to provide variations on it, of course", said Henslowe. "I have an idea that we could add a prologue, involving young courtiers who persuade a rustic he is ennobled. That will put the original writer off the scent. If you agree you will become part of the team, with a small stipend. Then I understand you have some competence as an actor. You could play the occasional part, for an additional consideration of course.

"Let me speak for my friend", said Kit. "I brought him to you Mr Henslowe, because I know you are the principal theatre manager in London and you have here built a wonderful arena to present your plays. Will is new to London. He comes from a small town, hardly more than a hamlet, and has no knowledge of the world, or of London, which let's face it is the centre of the world. He has no way of making an informed judgement and I am going to ask if I can make it for him".

Henslowe turned to Will: "Do you agree?"

Will was still unsure, but felt that faced with pressure from both the distinguished theatre manager and his new-found friend, he had no option. He nodded, then said: "Yes. Yes. Mr Henslowe. I will take whatever you have to offer."

He rose and held out his hand, which Henslowe shook warmly.

"Good", said Henslowe, "I am sure we will have much good work from you. But remember there are a dozen or more writers out there all clammering to have their achievements shown to the public. You will have to fight to have anything of yours included. It will be down to you. Take the script and work on it. Let me have the result tomorrow"

"Tomorrow!"

Henslowe laughed: "We have to work swiftly here, Mr Shakescene. But you will get used to it. Show him the ropes Kit. We'll say the day after perhaps".

The two got up and started to leave when Will turned back: "How did you know I had been an actor? I did not mention it to Kit."

"Ah!" said Henslowe, "Your fame has gone before you. One of those you have been touring with, by the name of Edward Alleyn, has spoken very highly of you."

"I do not think I know anyone of that name."

"Then perhaps you would recognise him as Charles Knight. He has now assumed his proper name and will be one of my leading actors. I have taken on others from the company you came into London with, including a fat man who is the most wonderful character actor I have ever seen – and a great trencherman into the bargain. I met them at the White Hart, although sadly I was unable to see them perform there."

"It seems unfortunate", said Will, "that the Inns are no longer able to present plays as they do in towns outside London."

"Not unfortunate for us dear man. We are the future. The inns would be competition for us. As it is I have only that shyster Burbage to worry about. So long as he stays north of the river I don't mind, but there is talk he is coming to this side of the Thames and that could mean trouble for me. But so long as I have a talented team and young people like you and Kit to write my plays I don't think I need to worry. Now I have a season's plays to plan and prepare. I must bid you good day and God be with you."

The two left the tiny partitioned space at the back of the stage apparently used as an office and made their way on to the stage at the heart of the auditorium. Will stood and gazed around him in wonder. The sun was high in the heavens and shone through the round O above their heads, bathing the two writers in an astral limelight. Will looked across the pit where the groundlings would stand and up at the towering galleries that would be filled with lords and ladies, bedecked in the finery of their costumes. He was aware of being overwhelmed by a sensation he had never experienced before. It was a sense of belonging, of standing on the threshold of his spiritual home. There was a curious aroma in the air, a combination of human sweat, of the costumes the players had worn, of paint used on the scenery. It was something he had never known before.

The place was like a sleeping body, quietly waiting for the call to rise and come to life, to exhibit the frailties of the human experience, to laugh at its predicament, to become aware of mortality, to fear death and the prospect of the after-life. He felt at once inspired and humbled. He desperately wanted to be part of it. As he stood there his chest swelled and he had an urge to recite, to burst into song. He opened his mouth and gave a great cry. It seemed to come from the very depth of his being, from his stomach, from his groin. The sound echoed around the arena. It bounced off the balconies. It came back to him and he took it in and cried aloud again. As the vibrations died there was a silence and Will, who had never been a religious man, suddenly felt himself near to God.

Then he felt a touch on his arm. Kit was looking at him strangely, but not unkindly. Will gave him an embarrassed smile.

"Shall we go?" his friend asked. "There is an

excellent hostelry near at hand and some good fellows I want to introduce you to."

They made their way off the stage and through the auditorium, Will turning his head as they went so that he could observe the building from different angles. He stopped at the main exit and looked back: "It is very fine", he said. "It is quite unique".

Kit took him by the arm and guided him out.

"Oh! no. Not unique. There are several like it", he said.. "They are all located outside the London wall, since they were banned by the City authorities. Mr Burbage has a very fine one at Shoreditch."

"Burbage? Oh! Yes, Mr Henslowe mentioned him."

"Yes, there is great rivalry among the managers. But there are customers enough in plenty – for the right kind of play. And that is where you and I come in, my friend. I have one I want to discuss with you. I am too busy to work on it myself, but if you were prepared to take it on – it is about a Roman tyrant, Titus Andronicus. Others have worked on it, but it needs pulling together. It is full of horrors and is regarded as having potential after the success of The Spanish Tragedy"

"The Spanish Tragedy?"

"By a friend of mine, Thomas Kydd – a great writer. We lodged together for a while."

. He went silent and Will thought his face looked sad for a moment. Then he said: "Come on. We will cross the river".

They walked towards London Bridge. To get there they passed between cottages recently built alongside the Thames, flowing brown and sluggish towards the sea. The river bank was inclined to be marshy and they had to watch their step, walking as far as possible on the firmer surface higher up towards the houses. These were generally workers' dwellings, poorly built, mainly of clay and wattle, with unglazed windows and holes in the roofs through which smoke could be seen curling up in the grey sky.

Will paused for a moment and looked towards the far bank, where the major buildings of the city rose in an uneven prospect of roofs and towers and spires.

"It is a fine sight", he said. "Surely the greatest city in the world."

"But not the largest", said Kit. "There is Paris and Rome and they say there are cities in the Far East that will make this look like a hamlet. But just the same I doubt if there is a more impressive spectacle anywhere in the world. Those great houses along the bank are where the noblemen live, with their gardens leading down to the Thames and berths for their transport on the river."

"I noticed on our journey into the city the scene was disfigured in many places by ruins of monasteries and even churches."

"Well, good riddance to them", said Kit.

Will looked at him in surprise: "You speak like an atheist, Kit. Surely that is dangerous these days. It could be regarded as mortal sin."

"Then what is mortal sin? Our worthy King Henry destroyed the monasteries and now the latest queen forbids allegiance to some of the churches. And meanwhile we are not entitled to speak our minds even among our close friends, which I hope you will be Kit. As for the danger, we all of us live between the Tower on the right, there, and the palace of the Archbishop in Lambeth over to the left. If we offend the one we are as like as not to finish up in the other! But what are we to do? Are we not men and according to the churchmen, God's children? And if he gave us minds and tongues to express what is in them, surely we serve his purpose better on earth by speaking without fear of retribution, whether in this world or the next?"

He stood looking down the river to where the buildings on the bridge obstructed the view. Will looked at him anxiously, feeling that his new-found friend might have a troubled soul. He reached out a hand a touched him tentatively on the arm. Kit turned and smiled at him. He seemed to relax and his mood changed: "Come let us find ourselves a watering hole to fill up our bellies with good ale and exercise our minds with good fellowship. We'll cross the river by the bridge. There is a tavern I know on the Strand."

They made their way to London Bridge and went through the southern gate. Will marvelled at the huge wooden drawbridge that Kit told him had not been raised in anger for over one hundred years.

"It held back the Lancastrians from the north and before that repelled Jack Cade's rebellion from the South. God grant it may never be used again."

The bridge itself was built up on either side by the tiny houses of tradesmen whose stalls plied their trades with the hundreds who crossed every day. It was exciting for Will to find himself among the shouts of the traders, the hurly-burly of their customers, the to and fro of the barrows piled high with produce. It was like nothing he had experienced before, even surpassing the great markets held annually in and around Stratford. Somehow the people seemed more alive, their concerns more urgent as if the whole population was in a haste to move the world along and ensure that their business was concluded before the end of the day, or perhaps the twilight of their lives. To a country dweller like Will the people he passed among seemed like a different nation, an alien breed almost. They collided with one another, scowled at their fellows and directed spittle and worse towards the gutters.

On the other side of the river the roads were more

firmly surfaced, but still presented hazards to the unwary walker. There were ruts and holes beneath the feet and detritus frequently jettisoned from the windows above their heads, not to mention horse traffic travelling without concern for the lowly pedestrians. The buildings themselves seemed to jostle one another as they competed for space and allowed little room for ingress and egress, or even Will thought for the occupants to breathe.

Narrow as the main streets were, the little alleys leading off them were hardly wide enough for a human being to pass between the houses, the upper floors of which almost met overhead. It was while they were negotiating one of these that they encountered a man who seemed determined to maintain his right of way and expected Kit and Will to back away out of the alley so that he could pass. The roughly dressed man was tall and broad, with his shoulders hunched and his head low. Will started to retreat down the alley, but Kit refused to give way and collided with the man, who swore at him and pushed him. Not to be outdone, Christopher also swore and pushed him back.

Whereupon the other drew his sword and cried out that he was an officer of the City and would arrest Kit for assault. Kit also drew his own sword and hurled abuse at him, telling him that he didn't care if he was the Lord High Admiral himself. The two began to thrust and parry. The action took them out into the main street and a crowd of spectators began to gather. They took sides, some of them urging on the ruffian, others siding with the smarter young man. The man had the advantage of weight and size, but Kit was more skilled. As they fought both became angrier and Will was concerned the situation was getting out of hand. He filled his lungs with as much of the fetid air as he could bear and shouted in his best stage voice: "Hold.

In the name of the Queen. Put up your swords."

The attacker seemed surprised at this and lowered his sword. Kit on the other hand was in the middle of a lunge and seemed unable to check it. The blow caught the man in the shoulder and he dropped his sword, clutching the wound with a cry of pain. At the sight of the blood Kit raised his sword in the air and it appeared to Will that he was about to cut the man again. He stepped between them and held his friend's arm. Others passing by joined in, helping to restrain Kit and tending to the other man.

"The man is wounded Kit", cried Will. "Come we must leave him to find his own apothecary".

He dragged him away up a narrow alley, followed for a while by a few bystanders. They soon fell away and when Will felt they were alone he stopped and made sure Kit was all right.

"Why did you stop me", demanded Kit. "I would have cut his ears off".

"Yes I thought that's what you were going to and much good it would have done you. You would have been hauled up before the sheriff and spent the next few years in the Tower, or worse. I just hope you haven't killed the poor fellow and that his wound can be treated."

"Poor fellow indeed! The man is an oaf and a ruffian."

"He said he was an officer of the city."

"That's hardly likely."

They had emerged from the narrow alleys around the end of the Bridge and into an area where the streets were wider and the buildings larger. Will looked around him and cried out in wonder: "What a splendid city this is to be sure".

Kit said: "Yes, we have reached Blackfriars, so called because of the black robes worn by the Dominican *freres*. When King Henry closed the priories theirs was turned into a playhouse. There's an irony for you. Can you imagine that? Plays presented under cover. With a roof. No need to worry about rain. Sadly it is closed now, of course, but there is talk that Richard Burbage's father, John, is trying to buy it and then one day perhaps all plays will be produced like that and we will no longer have to rely on daylight to light them, or fine weather to attract an audience."

"How will they be lit?"

"Lanterns, candles – oh! you have no idea the ingenuity that can be used to light a play when you do not rely on the sun. And, of course, you attract a different class of audience. This is an area where rich people come to play – tennis, walks in the gardens. You could charge what you liked for entrance. You don't have to write down for the underlings. Think of it – perhaps even playwrights will be rich."

"You live in this part of London?"

"What me? Gracious no. This is an area for the aristocracy. That large house there, for example, that's where the French Ambassador stays. No. We writers could not afford such luxury. Most struggle to make a living, even well established writers like George Peele, Robert Greene and Philip Massinger. We tend to gravitate nearer the city wall. Several live in a district called Depford - hacks like Anthony Munday, Robert Wilson, Richard Hathwaye, Henry Chettle."

They started to walk westwards, leaving behind the area with splendid houses and entering a city scene that quickly changed from opulence to poverty. The sense of euphoria that had gripped Will since he entered the city began to fade. Kit's talk of so many other writers made him realise how much competition there was and what a difficult path there was for him to follow if he was to make a success in this strange new world..

"So there is not much hope for a writer struggling to make his way is there."

"Oh! Some seem to make a living, not by writing plays I fear Then there is a market for works in prose, philosophy perhaps, or science, but not too serious. They have to be aristocratic in tone of course. There is no market among the lower classes, most of whom cannot read. I met a man in a tavern who does very well writing books. His wrote a very successful piece called Euphues – the Anatomy of Wit. Did very well out of it".

"I know that work. There was a copy going the rounds in Stratford. It was wonderful. John Lyly. So you know him? I'm very impressed."

Kit smote him on the back: "Don't be. He's a hack like all of us. He takes the work where he can find it. At one time he even acted as some kind of secretary to a noble lord – Edward de Vere, the Earl of Oxford. He soon learned his lesson there. That's a man to avoid if you can. He'll cut out your liver and feed it to the dogs."

Will laughed at the description: "Why should he need a secretary? What does he do?"

"He tries to write poetry and even plays, but can't be bothered to knock them into shape. He needs someone else to do that. Then he gets actors to put them on, amateurs mark you. There was talk he was going to be involved with the Blackfriars, but I believe that came to nothing. I believe it all fell through because he wanted to put plays on by a company of boy actors and you can imagine what lay behind that!"

Will looked at his friend in concern at what appeared to be slanderous comments about a peer of the realm. He looked hastily about to make sure they were not overheard. But nothing seemed to daunt the flamboyance of his companion, who even gave a little dance along the street calling; "Edward de Vere – a man to fear; don't meddle with Oxon, you're safer with the oxen".

Kit returned to his side and they walked for a while in silence. Then Will said: "I am also able to make a little money by acting. Perhaps that will lead to fame and fortune one day".

His companion laughed: "Fame and fortune! As an actor you are little more than a beggar. No offence dear friend, but you have just been travelling the country as a vagabond. What do you think distinguishes you from the minstrels, pedlars, fortune tellers who frequent the markets and hold out their hands for a few pennies from the public they try to entertain?"

"Well I would hope we are better than they."

"You might, but the government does not. Oh! you are being given some respectability by being associated with an aristocrat, like the Lord High Admiral, or the Lord Chamberlain, but you are still only his servant. People who write for the stage are not much better."

"What shall I do then Kit? Have I wasted my time and efforts in coming to London."

"Not at all. You are a poet. You must find yourself a patron."

Will thought of his friend Thomas in thrall to his lordship."

"Won't that mean becoming subservient to one man's demands?"

"Not at all. There could be nothing more than an exchange of coin for a few lines of verse. Now here is a sight you will have wanted to see."

He stopped and Will looked around. The narrow pathways they had been following had opened out into a wide area dominated by the walls of a commanding church. Will wanted to be impressed, but he was sadly very disappointed.

Chapter 10

Will had been anxious to visit St Paul's. Although not a strongly religious man, he admired the works that had been wrought by Christians, the splendid churches with their amazing vaults and colourful windows. He had heard tell of London's wonderful cathedral. They could see its tower as they walked westward, but he was surprised to see it had no spire.

"I understood it was the tallest in Europe", he suggested to Kit.

"Collapsed into the nave", explained Kit.

"And the nave – it is I believe immensely long."

"Oh! yes, it is that."

"And the colourful windows – they are, I believe, wonderful to behold."

"Were. Destroyed during an early Protestant uprising. You'll see."

He did and was even more shocked. They made their way through buildings that would once have been used for ecclesiastical business, but were now occupied by tradesmen of various kinds. There were more of these inside the church itself and he was astonished to behold the throng of people who seemed to be engaged in nothing more mundane than strolling do and fro, talking among themselves, exchanging badinage with the trades people.

He remarked on this to Kit.

"Yes. They call it St Paul's Walk. It was much grander in earlier times, when lords and ladies would perambulate just to be seen. Now the practice is falling into decline, like the building itself."

Will allowed himself to be led among the jostling crowds, looking up at the sightless windows and eventually the gap where the roof of the tower had been. As they retraced their steps they were accosted by two females, whose attire seem to have been thrown carelessly on to their bodies. They linked arms with Kit and Will on either side and strolled along with them.

Kit stopped, turned to the woman on his side, thrust his hand under her skirts and said: "No. There is nothing there to attract me."

She made a jocular attempt to slap his face, but he held her arm.

"See if my friend is interested", he said.

Will had already freed himself from the grasp of his assailant.

"Thank you no."

"They will be cheap", suggested Kit encouragingly.

"I have a loving wife for whom I intend to remain chaste."

Kit laughed: "Every man to his own inclination".

The women went off in search of more favourable trade.

"I am astonished", said Will. "How can such things be allowed in the temple of the Lord."

"There is no law against it."

"Christ drove the money-lenders from the temple."

"Now they probably own it. Come on. Let's find a tavern. I'm starved and I expect you must be."

He took them to an ale-house close to the church. It was crowded and Kit was greeted by several of the motley crew gathered there. One of them came across and bowed low. Kit met him coldly and introduced him as Richard Baines. The newcomer's attitude seemed quite unctuous to Will, who disliked him from the first. He fawned on Kit as a "rising star", whose plays, he said, would one day light the world. He brushed aside Kit's protestations that his play had not yet been actually presented to the public.

"But you read it to us with such style, such bravado. It is", he said turning towards Will, "about one Tamburlaine, of whom I had never heard, but is apparently famed throughout the orient. You will see – it will rival The Spanish Tragedy, and talking of that, your friend Thomas Kydd is over there. Come and join us."

"I think not. Tom has little time for me."

"Never mind. He is coming to us."

Kydd was a small man, fastidiously dressed, with a small beard and piercing eyes. He came up, not to Kit, but to Will and spoken to him directly.

"You are not thinking of sharing your life with this miscreant, are you?" he asked.

"Well, no", Will replied. "Kit is being kind enough to help me in my introduction to London and, incidentally, its theatre".

"Then beware. He will want to draw you into his devilish fellowship."

Kit took the man's arm and drew him aside. He spoke quite seriously: "We are good friends, Thomas, and always have been. I do not know why you regard me thus".

"We were friends so long as I did your bidding, in and out of bed."

He released his arm and moved away, spitting on the rush floor as he did so. Then he turned back: "I have papers of yours at my lodgings. I would be glad if you would come and take them away. They are full of heretical statements. Their discovery could lead me to the Tower and worse."

Kit replied contemptuously: "You are full of fears and fancies. I wonder you can even live with your own shadow. Who would want to investigate a failed playwright who has not been able to fulfil the promise of one modest success."

"Modest success! The Spanish Tragedy is a masterpiece as well you know. I've no doubt you are already seeking to emulate it with your – what is it – Tamburlaine?" He looked at Will: "Take my advice. Do not listen to his atheistic ideas. He will lead you so near the fire it will scorch you. And those are only the flames you will feel on earth. They will be nothing to the fires of eternal damnation."

He rejoined his group. Baines returned to them with tankards of ale and the three of them sat around a table near the window.

Kit asked Will if he had read or seen The Spanish Tragedy and told him it was full of bombast, death and destruction. It would be outdone by their Titus and urged Will to begin work on it as soon as possible so that it could be included in the first season of the Rose Theatre.

"The man Kydd is a fool", he said, "and a bigot. He would like to be an unbeliever as I am, but lacks the courage. We lived together for a while and I thought we had like minds, but he was too full of the teachings imbibed from the church. Something you must beware of, Will. It is essential to see through the fallacies spread by our religious masters."

"What do you mean by fallacies?" asked Will.

"All this claptrap about a bearded god in a white nightshirt creating the earth and parenting a son."

Baines half rose, looking around him alarm: "You mustn't say things like that here".

Will was becoming accustomed to Kit's outspoken ways, but even he was concerned at this latest outburst: "Surely you do not deny God and his son Jesus Christ?"

"I had the dubious pleasure of reading divinity at Cambridge" replied Kit, "where the finest minds of the land sought to instil the word of God as it is supposed to have been handed down to us by various dubious witnesses."

"Well, yes, Moses for one", suggested Baines, resuming his seat.

"Moses? Moses was a juggler, who used trickery to bend the will of the people in his direction. Sir Walter Raleigh's man Herriot can perform better. Moses kept the Jews wandering in the wilderness for 40 years so that he could subdue them to his tyranny. They could have made a similar journey in one year."

He had raised his voice and others in the bar were beginning to listen. Kit looked around and realising he had an audience addressed them generally: "The first beginning of religion is to keep men in awe. Christ was a bastard, the son of a carpenter and with a mother who was dishonest to put no finer point on it."

"Christopher you are denying the divinity of Lord Jesus Christ", cried Baines anxiously.

Kit emptied his tankard: "We shall need more ale and I need the privy. I will find a serving wench, just for the ale you understand." – and he made his way uncertainly towards the rear of the bar. Kydd came up to Will and Baines: "You see what I mean. The man is dangerous, dangerous. He will have us all in the Tower."

"But surely there are many who hold atheistic views. It is not as if he were a Catholic."

"Oh! but he is", said Kydd.

"How can that be?"

"I have heard him say that if there is any good religion it is papism."

"But if he is against all religion, how can he support papism?"

"It's the ceremonies, the masses, the singing, even the shaven crowns of the priests. He says it is like theatre."

Then Kydd lowered his voice and looked around

him as if concerned that someone might attribute such views to him personally:

"He says – he says that all protestants are hypocrites."

"Well, you know", said Will reflectively, "Roman Catholic rites do have a certain substance that sometimes seems lacking in protestant church. Their priests, too, appear to have greater authority. I have met some who formerly practised in the west of England. They were impressive figures. In comparison some ministers of English churches present themselves very poorly. Ones I have known seemed no more than parochial morons"

"In foreign countries, such as Italy", Baines said, "Catholic priests often assume the status of statesmen in addition to their spiritual role".

"You see", said Kydd. "Baines you are already corrupted by this man".

A serving wench arrived with three tankards of ale, put them on the table and waited expectantly. Baines looked at Will and both peered over their shoulders to see whether Kit was in sight. He was not so Will drew a coin from his pouch and handed it to the girl. She flipped it into the air, tossed her skirt at him and went off without offering any change. He did not object to paying for the drinks. Kit had been very kind to him since they met shortly after his arrival in London. He had introduced him to Henslowe and was providing an opportunity to work on scripts with him. Will was prepared to return kindness with generosity.

He was on his way back to them now, stopping to greet acquaintances with much laughter and slapping of backs. Will watched him with a certain amount of admiration, wishing that he could be so ebullient, so popular with his fellow men. Kit was well built and despite the fact that his clothes were obviously not of the best quality wore them well. The softness of his face belied the sometimes coarseness of his talk although when he was aroused to anger his expression could turn from the gentleness of a smile into a snarl of displeasure.

Seeing him, Kydd hurriedly left. Kit arrived back at the table, picked up his tankard and drank deeply.

"Am I indebted to you Will?" he asked. Will waved the question aside. "Then it will be my pleasure next time. Well, Baines, and what have you two been conversing about in my absence? Affairs of state? The nature of religion?"

"It is not safe, Kit, to discuss such matters so openly", said Baines.

"Why? In case there is a spy who will carry tales back to the Privy Council. A pox on them. I would rather die an honest man than live a hypocrite."

"Surely it is not the dying, but the manner of it that is of concern. The idea of a slow death by torture or fire is not to my liking. Nor is the prospect of being consumed in the eternal flames of hell", said Baines.

"I'll have none of that. The body is a finite object. Once it is burnt it is burnt. You cannot go on suffering eternally. What the hell is eternity anyway?"

Baines got to his feet. He looked quite angry: "You should not talk so. It is heretical. I cannot speak for Will here, but I fear for my immortal soul."

"Yes. You often talk about your immortal soul, Baines. I'm more concerned about where my next meal is coming from. If I do have an immortal soul I'll let god worry about it – if there is a god".

Baines rose and picked up his hat.

"Well, in that case I will seek other company. Forgive me". He bowed to Will, put his hat on his head and, without another word left to join Kydd and his group.

Kit waved his hand dismissively: "Let him go. He is a phoney. A person of no account. He will hang on to any company with an intellectual content, although he won't find much where Kydd is. Baines will be in good company there."

He drank in silence. Will looked at him speculatively. This man seemed to treat his friends with little respect. Would he suffer the same effect?

"You were quite close to Kydd then once? You shared a room with him?"

"Yes – and a bed. Well, you know how it is. It is a much better and cheaper way of eking out ones slender resources than living alone."

He drank deeply again, then banged his tankard on the table: "You must come in with me, Will. No. I insist. At least for a while. I must confess my funds are in a parlous state and I could use assistance in that direction. Also I would welcome your companionship. There is so much we could do together. We could work on Titus and, if you needed it, I could help on the script Henslowe gave you."

Will thought about the proposal. His own room was a poor one, near the Ald Gate, and he had felt lonely since his arrival in London. Sharing with a fellow writer would not only be financially advantageous, it would surely assist with creative output. The ultimate aim was to ensure his plays received public performances, but if to reach that goal he had to work with others, well so be it. As for the man's character, Will felt confident he could deal with that.

"I would need to give notice to my present landlord", he suggested.

"Let him rot", said Christopher. "He would not hesitate to throw you out if it was in his interest."

"Nevertheless", said Will "I have a commitment to him".

"Oh! very well. Let us say the end of the week. We could make the move on Sunday."

"On the Sabbath?"

Kit laughed: "It's my way. If you are going to live with me you will have to accept it"

Will said very calmly: "I don't see why. You might just accept mine."

Kit looked at him in surprise, then laughed: "I promise I will not draw my sword on you, will not lead you into temptation – unless you want to be led. We will just be two fellows enjoying life. What do you say, eh? Will you join me? We shall be two penniless playwrights starving together, but perhaps making a name for ourselves in the process?"

He held out his hand and with only a slight hesitation, Will took it

"But a week today. After I have given notice. Oh! and I must warn you, I have a tendency to snore."

"Oh ! I have a way to stop that!" cried Kit . Then he stood up: "Come, I'll show you where it is."

He finished off his drink and waited. Will drank his more slowly before allowing the other to lead him from the tavern. Then, side by side, they made their anonymous way through the crowds in the noisy, stinking London streets.

Chapter 11

The first night of Tamberlaine was a momentous occasion. Word had gone round that it was a new type of play, with an exotic plot, written by an author who was reputed to rival such popular playwrights as Kydd, Greene and Peele. It was shown at the first playhouse to be opened south of the River. The area had been reclaimed from marshy land and spawned such offspring from the lower levels of entertainment as brothels, gambling houses and bear baiting arenas. In promoting the event the wily manager Henslowe had ensured potential audiences knew they would be able to experience the building's new developments in theatrical design, such as the sloping floor of the pit, called a rake. This obviated the disturbances caused by late-comers who found they could not see the stage over the heads of early-arrivals and sometimes reacted violently by shouting and even throwing missiles. He also promoted a catering facility built alongside the theatre, providing an opportunity to eat, drink and carouse during intervals and even while the play was progressing if it failed to hold the audience's attention.

As it turned out there was no danger of this happening during Tamburlaine. From the opening scene, when the players entered, their Elizabethan dress augmented by exotic eastern costumes, and began to deliver lines of such resonance and colour, the audience was gripped. From groundlings to lordlings they entered into the concept of intrigue, treachery and general back-stabbing that was, anyway, a feature of their own political scene. They were particularly delighted to find a humble shepherd could aspire to become king and emperor and express himself in such high-flown language:

"Is it not passing brave to be a king, Techelles?
Usumcasane and Theridamas,
Is it not passing brave to be a king,
And ride in triumph through Persepolis?"

It was not only the sentiment that moved them, it was the manner in which it was declaimed, the foreign sounding names of people and places, the glowing vowels that rolled off the actors' tongues and the staccato consonants that received emphasis from a stamp of the actor's foot or the wave of a hand in a majestic gesture. They roared with delight, clapped and threw their hats into the air. The reaction was more restrained, however, at the notion that to be a king was more glorious than to be a god. Most had been brought up to believe that, whatever hardships they had to endure on earth, awaiting them in heaven above were pleasures that would only be mitigated in judgement of their sins below. To suggest otherwise was a mite too close to the concerns of conscience and personal safety they all experienced in that dangerous age.

However, when it was over they roared their approval and the actors gloried in the acclamation, reluctant to leave the stage until the applause had completely died. Will, who had played a very small part in the play, stood on stage with the others and felt once again the exhilaration of a shared experience between audience and players. He knew then that all he wanted in life was to be involved in such acclaim. How much greater, he thought, would it be if he was also the play's begetter, at least in part.

Afterwards the company gathered and enjoyed tankards of ale and even a little wine especially imported from France for the occasion. There was something of a stir when a newcomer arrived, in a flamboyant manner with much bowing and doffing of hats. Henslowe seemed perturbed at his arrival and would have confronted him, but he was constrained by others. Will was standing with Kit and asked him who the newcomer was.

"It's only Henslowe's deadly rival, Burbage. He has a face to come here tonight."

"So that's Burbage. It is a name I have heard frequently."

"And well you might. He and his father represent a kind of royal lineage in the theatre. He even gave it the name. You know, after the Greek word for place."

Will did not know, but did not like to show his ignorance.

"Here he comes", said Kit. "Henslowe will not like this".

Henslowe did not like it. He pushed aside members of the company and hastened to join them at the same time as Burbage.

"What do you want Burbage? Have you come to poach my writers and actors, or plagiarise my plays".

"I came to congratulate you, Henslowe", said Burbage coolly. "You have a magnificent play on your hands and a great playwright".

"And they are staying there", said Henslowe.

"They may, so far as I'm concerned. I have quite enough to content me north of the city."

"That's not what I hear. They tell me your father has taken a lease on Blackfriars."

"Forward thinking, Henslowe, forward thinking. The authorities will have to relax their restrictions eventually and when they do the future will be found in plays performed inside."

"People will always prefer the open air. They don't like being enclosed, with all those candles and lanterns, it's not safe. You'll see. You might get a few aristocrats, but my audiences, the real people, they will come here."

"Oh! I am not turning my back on them. Indeed, I am thinking of building a new one. Possibly here in Southwark."

Henslowe began to get very angry: "You keep to your own patch north of London. Don't you start trespassing down here."

"I had not heard you have taken ownership of this part of London, Henslowe."

"I don't need ownership to make it mine. You are not welcome here. You may drink a tankard of my ale, but that's all you are getting. Then I hope you will leave".

The two stared at one another with increasing animosity and Will wondered if they would come to blows. He was struck with the resemblance between them, both about the same age – 40 he would judge – the same height and build, both a little portly. They must be, he decided, characteristic of theatre managers. Then Henslowe left them without another word. Burbage towards with a gentle smile and addressed Kit.

"I much enjoyed your play, Mr Marley. You have a fine way with words. I must confess I was a little surprised at some of the phrases uttered."

"By the characters, not necessarily by me."

"True, but that can be misinterpreted by some authorities. Perhaps you should strive to be a little less - er explicit."

"I write as I feel", said Kit.

"Yes I gathered that."

He turned towards Will: "And you, sir, I believe I saw you on the stage".

"You did, sir, briefly. But my real interest is in writing for it."

"Is it? And have I seen any of your works."

"I think not. I have only had one presented. It was called The Dream, but has assumed the title of A

Midsummer Night's Dream."

"You wrote the Dream play. I know it by repute. An actor who was recently joined my company told me about it. He was touring with a company that produced. It was it a great success in – where was it – Oxford?"

"It was well received there, sir."

"Lot's of yokels and children running about the stage as fairies. Very original. Well, if you find you do not get on well with Mr Henslowe you must come and visit me north of the city. Excuse me gentlemen".

He left them to talk to other actors, some of whom seemed to know him well. Then the party began to break up. Will felt the euphoria of the show beginning to wane. He thought longingly of bed and perhaps an extra hour there the next day. This hope was sadly dispelled, however, when the stage manager reminded him there would be a rehearsal at eight in the morning. Will had arranged to stay at Marley's place for the first time that night and they called for a lantern to light their way across the river. Although the play had been scheduled to start mid-afternoon the sometimes prolonged involvement from an excited audience meant it continued until sunset. Then the celebration afterwards continued long after nightfall.

They made their way over the bridge where Will was surprised to find the traders were still peddling their wares. The city seemed never to sleep. The lights through the windows, combined with the lanterns that were hung outside many of the houses, meant that their own torch was hardly necessary. There were still many people abroad, some going civilly about their business, others obviously the worse for imbibing strong drink at the many taverns still open. Bawds hung about outside brothels, attempting to entice the two young men as they passed. Marley would have none of them, cursing them for pox-ridden whores and jostling them aside when they approached too close. Their pimps were also importunate and Will was concerned that they would once again become embroiled in a brawl. Kit had been drinking heavily and as he had already demonstrated would not hesitate to draw his sword if the occasion arose.

Although the life and movement in the city excited him, as they passed from the larger buildings and wider streets of the centre he was saddened to find when he looked up he could not see the sky through buildings that pressed closely upon one another and often rose to a height of three storeys and more. Even where there were gaps between them the firmament he loved to gaze upon at home was obscured by a haze caused by a combination of smoke issuing from a multitude of chimneys and the lights from windows and torches.

Kit's room turned out to be an attic at the top of a three-storey building. It was sparsely furnished. Several bare wooden tables were completely covered with papers, books and writing materials. The chairs were upright, stark and looked very uncomfortable. It was a place where a man could work and sleep, but offered no element of comfort whatever. It lacked the amenities Will had been accustomed to at home and even the room he had just vacated was better furnished. He was relieved to see the bed was generously wide. He had shared a bed with siblings and with his wife, but never a stranger. He was unsure how to adapt to the present situation. He stood uncertainly in the centre of the room. Kit looked at him.

"I take it", he said, "we both sleep there".

"Of course", said Kit. "Is that a problem?"

"Well, no, it's just – "

"Surely it is not the first time you have shared a bed."

"With my wife, yes, but – "

"But perhaps not with a male companion eh? I don't think I have ever slept otherwise. It is no novelty to me I can assure you".

Will felt he had to make his position clear: "I must let you know that I do not – I mean, I have never had relations with a man. I would not like you to think – "

"My dear fellow – that is perfectly all right. I take my companions as I find them. We can curl up under the covers and get a good night's sleep. I gather you have to rise early."

"Yes. We are called to rehearse at eight. Oh! where do I go if I need the privy?"

"Through that door and down the steps outside. And if at any time you feel the need to bathe there is a wooden tub, but it is difficult to obtain hot water. I am hoping it will not be necessary to use it until the warmer weather. Of course there are always the stews."

"The stews? I thought they were – well – brothels."

"Yes, but you don't have to use the women. I don't filthy hags they are. But every so often they fill the baths with hot water and send young lads around the town to announce it. That way you can enjoy the luxury of a hot soak – providing, of course, you keep the women away."

Later as they lay side by side in the darkened room Kit said: "You will need to find yourself a patron".

Will's first thought was of Thomas in Oxford and the restrictions placed upon him by Bodley.

"Is that really necessary? Doesn't that mean you are restrained by his wishes?"

"Or hers. No. The only exchange is in the form of money – and perhaps fame. I made an approach to Sir Walter Raleigh, which was only partly successful."

"He is a very great knight, an adventurer and a warrior. They say he has the ear of the queen."

"And much else according to repute. I wrote a poem

to him."

"You wrote it to him?"

"Yes. Ostensibly it was from a shepherd to his love, but it was really an invitation to him."

"An invitation?"

"To live with me and be my love. Oh! it was couched in satirical terms, offering him silk and laces, you know the sort of thing. But it was a forlorn hope".

"He obviously declined."

"Yes, but he responded very courteously, in the same form, with a poem. Sadly without financial reward. Sadly, sadly."

"Did you expect one?"

But he did not reply and Will realised he was asleep. He lay in the dark thinking what strange turns his life had taken. London was so different from the towns and villages that had formed the background to his life hitherto. At home one set one's clock by the sun. Here people lit torches and lanterns so that they could live through the night. There were noises even now in the street. He got up and felt his way to the window to see what was happening. Shafts if light shone through the cracks in the shutters and when he opened them he was delighted to see that it was an almost full moon. Somehow it was reassuring. There were some things that remained the same, whether it was in a big city or a tiny hamlet.

From the bed came the sound of a faint snore and a rustling of rugs. He was glad to have met with Kit. Despite the differences outlook he felt they could be good friends and hoped he had made it clear enough that he did not share the others sexual predilections. Sharing a bed was not entirely to his liking and perhaps he would have to find a time when he could tactfully move to other accommodation. Meanwhile, he had to try and get some sleep. He closed the shutters and made his way back, making sure as he climbed into bed that he did not wake his companion.

The next few weeks were full of frenetic activity for Will. He was engaged in a constant merry-go-round of work and excitement. He would rise early. Have a breakfast of ale, bread and cheese and go to the theatre. Although the parts he had to play were small (sometimes little more than walking on stage with a banner or a sword), he was expected to attend rehearsals and usually found himself involved in what was known as backstage activity. Performances would take place on most days in the afternoon and he would then go home to write until late into the night, meeting the ever-persistent demands of Henslowe for scripts.

He was not happy working on Titus Andronicus. It seemed all it had to hold it together dramatically was war with all its attendant horrors. He persisted with it, however, because he thought it could establish him as a solo playwright in the eyes of Henslowe. He derived greater satisfaction with his work on the play he called The Shrew. This was closer to his own experience as a married man. He loved his wife dearly, but saw elements of her character that he was able to draw on for Katharina. The original he had been asked to adapt had made the husband a buffoon, lacking in any kind of human sympathy. He tried to suggest there was a gentler side to his nature and that he could genuinely fall in love with her.

Will quite enjoyed writing the prologue suggested by Henslowe. He could see that much might be made of Christopher Sly by the actor he knew as Robin Goodfellow and kept him in mind when evolving the character. He drew upon his own country life for a scene involving hunters and found himself recalling his married life when writing the dialogue between the two protagonists. He showed the finished result to Kit, who laughed immoderately and congratulated him, saying that he was astonished at the naturalness of the dialogue both in the prologue and in the verse passages between Kate and Petruchio. He admitted to Will that he found it impossible to write humour and asked him how he achieved it.

"I simply see the event in my mind. I can envisage it happening on the stage. Do not ask me how."

He showed the first draft of the Shrew to Henslowe, who expressed himself delighted with it and proposed to produce it immediately. Will protested that he had not had time to refine it, but Henslowe said that such work could be safely left to the actors. Will also pointed out that he had not written an Epilogue showing what happens to Christopher Sly, but Henslowe dismissed this as unimportant.

"The only purpose for introducing him was to disguise the play and avoid the charge of plagiarism. Nobody will worry about what happens to him at the end".

Will continued to protest, but Henslowe would have none of it and his view eventually prevailed. The play was produced with great success. Will apologised to the actor playing Sly for not developing his character, but that worthy clapped him on the shoulder and said he was delighted not to return to the stage as it gave him more drinking time.

Henslowe also produced the Dream play with great success. Changes had to be made to suit the different casting situation in London and Will agreed the title should be extended to something more fanciful, perhaps relating to mid-summer, which was imminent. There was general agreement that nothing like it had been seen before. Pundits compared it with the comedies of ancient Rome. Others thought Shakespeare had drawn his inspiration from a wonderful work that had recently found its way into England from Italy. Will insisted, however, that he had never heard of Boccaccio, or his Decameron. This reminded him once again that he not only lacked a formal education, but did not have the opportunity of remedying it.

He felt a desperate need for books and often thought longingly of the time he spent in Oxford. There were booksellers around St Pauls, but sold what seemed poor stuff to Will, often little more than leaflets, treatises designed to suit the popular demand for sensation, legends, relating the deeds of Robin Hood, King Arthur and his knights of the so-called round table. Generally Will had no time for them, although he was taken with some fanciful tales of early kings of England and Scotland and even the stories of witches and their impact on human behaviour.

Somewhere he managed to fit it in visits to taverns, where he would eat and drink in the company of Kit and his lively companions. The success of his plays was beginning to result in a certain degree of fame, which he enjoyed, but avoided the egoistic displays of his friend Kit. In his relative naiveté he expected his success would beget an empathetic relationship with his acquaintances in the theatre and the taverns. Far from being the case, however, it seemed to engender an antagonism from actors who resented his playing parts they might have filled and from fellow writers who seemed prepared to overlook their own shortcomings in the envy they felt towards him.

One writer in particular took every opportunity to denigrate his work and even cast aspersions upon his character. Will did his best to avoid him if he encountered him in a tavern, but the man, whose name was Greene, seemed to make a point of sitting where his remarks on the younger man could be overheard.

Will mentioned this to Kit, who dismissed it with contempt.

"The man is a poor fellow", he said, "who had lately left his wife in favour of a mistress, who then discarded him, so that he was left with nothing but his regrets to feed his frustration upon."

"Then why feed upon me?" asked Will resentfully.

"Because you are there", replied Kit with his customary laugh. "Will, my dear young friend, you have nothing to fear. You have obviously done enough to make these fellows envy you. One day you will produce work that will far out-pass them".

Despite his early fears life with Kit became very agreeable. The ebullient playwright also involved himself deeply in his work and both writers found it constructive to discuss their plays with one another. The success of Tamburlaine led Kit to write a sequel. Although he was effusive in his praise for the quality of his friend's verse, Will secretly had reservations about the play, which did not in his view make the most of the mental struggles and striving that such a character would suffer in his rise to power.

Only once did Will find himself uncomfortable in their relationship. Kit was drafting scenes for a play on the life and death of Edward the Second, king of England. It was, he said, a tragic tale of a man prepared to put his love for another above the exigencies of state. Love, he suggested to Will, should be rated above all else. In saying this he looked deep into Will's eyes. Will turned the discussion into a consideration of historical plays generally, something he said he was greatly interested in.

"I admire the work you are doing on this play, Kit, but I am at a loss to know how to proceed with something of my own. I have thought of writing a series of plays about the Tudor dynasty, but I am reminded of the old saying about bricks without straw."

"Then you must find some, Will."

"But how? Where?"

"I cannot help you there. I have enough material from my Cambridge days for a dozen plays. I went there to read divinity, but took advantage of the opportunities it gave me to broaden my mind. I learnt there a wonderful story about a man who sold his soul to the devil. Then there was another about a Jew on the Mediterranean island of Malta. I read the work of Greek and Roman playwrights and many books dealing with the history of the English. The tale of Edward II, for example, came from a book written by Hollingshead. Have you read it?"

Will admitted he had not, although he seemed to remember seeing a copy while in Stratford.

"Where can I find such material?" he asked.

"Well, I would not recommend Cambridge. The emphasis there is on divinity. I was glad to escape the malign influence of Gabriel Harvey. There are other places – Winchester perhaps".

Will had a thought: "Or Oxford".

"Oxford? Does that have a library?"

"No. But it had one and another is in course of preparation. I saw it during my journey from Stratford. And there was a young man there. His name was – " he thought for a minute – "James, I think, Thomas James He is gathering material together, manuscripts, books – you never saw so many books. He invited me to return."

"Well. There you are then. Except – er – you are not thinking of leaving me."

"Well, you wouldn't want to come with me?"

"To Oxford? No. I think not."

"Well then. You have so many acquaintances here in London. You would hardly miss one."

115

"Acquaintances, yes. But, Will, you are my friend."

He seemed very dejected and Will looked at him in surprise.

"Why Kit, it would not be for long. We could write to one another. Lots of friends do. Sonnets perhaps."

"No. I'm afraid the garden of roses is not for me. My verse lives more happily in a wild meadow. But as for you – what are you waiting for?"

And he busied himself in his work.

Yes, thought Will. What am I waiting for? His current work was holding the stage. He felt sure Henslowe would excuse him, particularly if he relinquished his meagre stipend. He wrote to Thomas James and letters he received in reply assured him he would be welcomed.

So it came about that one summer's day he hired horses, packed his few belongings and turned his back on a city that had provided him with so much excitement and success. He left it with regret, but with a feeling that he was taking one more step on the road to fame and fortune.

PART 3

Chapter 12

"This Richard is a villainous character. He seems to have little or no redeeming feature."

Will looked up at the young man's comment.

"I'm sorry to hear you say that. I am trying to present him as a rounded personality."

"Rounded! Well yes he is that, with a rounded back and a rounded – or rather warped view of men."

Will laughed. His new friend could be very direct, but he had found it very useful to show him the early drafts of his labours. He had a way of noting inconsistencies in both grammatical details and the wider spread of the narrative.

"What made you decide to write about him", Thomas James asked him.

"I did not intend to. Henslowe had given me an earlier play about Henry the Sixth to work on, but I was finding it a chore. It is an old play and a badly written one. Henry seems to be a contemptible character and there is an execrable section devoted to the burning of the French heretic Joan la Pucelle. There is so much material that it may take up two plays, perhaps even three. Then I remembered a suggestion by an actor in the company that I should write about Richard, perhaps because he liked the idea of playing a crookback. Anyway, I looked him up here and found him much more to my liking – dramatically, I mean."

"Will you then consider writing plays about other kings?"

"Oh! yes. I have found so much material here. They all have stories to tell, from Richard the Second to Henry the Eighth. Not Edward the Second. My friend Marley has already done that. It is a strange play", he added reflectively, "and I don't think he has got it quite right. So yes. Possibly a whole series of plays about the Tudor dynasty."

"Why do you only write about kings and princes. Surely there are interesting stories to be found among the lives of the common folk."

"You are right. I very much want to do so. It would help me introduce a comic element into my work. The trouble is the records of the common man in those days seem to be non-existent. Writers like Holinshed seem concerned only with royalty or the nobility."

"Now there I think I can help. There is one group of papers, comprising mainly letters, that illustrate the life of one particular person who served during the French wars. His name was John Fastolf and he wrote much to a friend named Paston. He was something of a character and may suit your purpose well."

"Tell me about him. Where can I find these papers?"

"Many of them are here. I can let you see them. Fastolf was branded a coward for leaving the field of battle, but that account is contested. I suppose you could call him a nobleman, but he was very much a man of the people, spent much of his time at an inn he owned called the Boars Head."

"He sounds exactly right for me. I may have to change his name, in order to avoid any problems with surviving relatives. There is someone I have been toying with. His name is John Oldcastle, but he lacks colour. I will use one man's character in another's name."

"Are you allowed to do that?"

"Who is to say me nay?"

"Surely though Will writing comedy is not a worthy aim for a serious playwright?"

"Writing comedy is a serious business. You reflect life, true life, but in a humorous way. That makes it doubly difficult – and doubly interesting. There is a young playwright I have spent time with in London. His name is Jonson, Ben Jonson. He is determined to write humorous plays about common people. He is younger than me and has a great future I believe."

"So you are going to introduce comedy into your plays about our country's history."

"And also plays that exist simply for their humour. The Greeks did it and the Romans. Among your books I have found a play by Plautus, but my Latin is very poor and I have only been able to discover the gist. Perhaps you could help me. It is all about identical twins. Two of my children are twins you know. And in the company with whom I travelled from Stratford to London there was a pair of twin brothers – you could not tell them apart. What a wonderful opportunity for mistaken identity!"

Thomas found himself laughing at the very idea.

"You see. It is funny and I haven't even written it yet."

The two men went back to their respective tasks. Since he came to stay at Oxford Will had been writing fluently in what he found was the fertile ground of a future library. He worked at such speed that it had even been necessary to employ a young student to keep pace with him in the supply of quills and ink. The sad fact that the plague had returned to London and the theatres were again closed, worked to his advantage and he felt justified in remaining at Oxford.

After a while Thomas lay down his quill: "Why do you always write in verse?" he asked

Will looked up, puzzled by the question: "I do not always write in verse."

"Most of the time", Thomas said. "I would have thought prose was a better medium for expressing someone's day-to-day thoughts."

Will wondered if he was having a joke with him.

Thomas did have a wry sense of humour. It was one of his more attractive characteristics.

"All great dramatic dialogue is in verse."

"Yes, but why? People do not converse in verse. Why do you try to fit their talk into iambic pentameters?"

Will laughed: "As a matter of fact I am not trying to write in iambic pentameter. I am trying not to. It is expected of us, by the literati. But it becomes such a jog trot, which is fine if you are writing an epic poem, or a sonnet, but it holds up the dramatic action. That's why I do use quite a lot of prose, particularly in the comedy scenes."

"Yes but you seem to confine it to the lower orders of society. Is it because they would not understand iambic pentameter?"

"The lower orders of society don't understand the prose, let alone the verse. It's the action on stage that appeals to them, that and the rhythm of the words when they are declaimed. That's why Marley is so popular. Great big sounding phrases, like – like a drum beat in music."

He declaims: "'Is it not passing brave to be a king Techelles, Usumcasane and Theridamas, and ride in triumph through Persepolis?'"

Thomas looked at him in admiration: "You speak the lines very well. They resonate."

"They need to in order to fill the space. But you notice how he uses the names, how they scan in the verse. Marvellous. I doubt if I could do that. But then according to my theatre manager most of the audience is only there for the action. They want to see Richard the Third brought down, they don't care if it happens in verse or prose. In real life he would be staggering speechless about the field of battle waving his sword before he dies. He would never cry: "A horse, a horse, my kingdom for a horse!" I get him to do it in iambic pentameter. Then the intellectuals are also pleased – well some of them, anyway."

"I gather there are those who disapprove of what you present in the theatre, whether it is in verse or in prose."

"Yes, if they had their way they would all be closed, as they have succeeded in doing within the city walls."

"And at the moment because of the plague."

"Which they regard as an act of god, anyway, bringing the justice of the almighty on Satanic practices. Kit Marley has told me of one Gabriel Harvey, a Cambridge pedant, who works all the time covertly and overtly to bring about their permanent closure. He approves of poetry, providing it is composed in a strict hexameter. I cannot think of anything more boring."

Thomas looked up at the sound of the name: "Gabriel Harvey? Yes. My patron has mentioned him. He is, apparently, a man who likes to involve himself in matters not only academic, but political as well. Sir Thomas does not speak well of him. It appears he opposes the idea of a library being established in Oxford."

"Why would he do that?"

"At Cambridge the emphasis is on divinity. Harvey would like to ensure that readers have access to books only under strict liturgical control. He uses that as an excuse for not supporting the establishment of a library in Oxford. In fact he is probably afraid of the competition. Bodley's idea is that everyone should be able to read the great literary works of the past. It would be a library for the whole public, something that has never existed in this country."

"But could this man prevent the library from opening?"

"I doubt it. Sir Thomas is a Queen's messenger and

has great influence. He is also very determined. He looks ahead and plans for years to come. That's why I am here. To prepare the ground for the library and I believe – and hope – to become librarian."

"Would you enjoy that?"

"It would be a wonderful opportunity. I love books and working among manuscripts like this seems to satisfy a spiritual need."

Hw was silent for a moment then added: "The situation does, however, have its drawbacks."

"What might they be?"

Thomas hesitated before replying. He looked almost regretful. Then he said: "Sir Thomas is rather strict in his requirements. He has made it clear that anyone who undertakes the role of librarian will have to give his life to the work. It will have to be someone who is unencumbered."

"Yes. I think you told me. You would not be allowed to take on a ministry."

"It goes beyond that, I fear. I will not be allowed to marry."

Will looked at him in astonishment: "Not allowed to?"

"If I did so, Sir Thomas would not allow me to remain in his employ. In addition to the effect it might have on my work, he points out I am a cleric and sworn to celibacy. He is very strict in such matters."

"Surely that is a situation hard for a young man to contemplate?"

"I am content."

"I assume he has never married."

"Oh! yes. Quite recently in fact. His wife is a very charming woman."

"So he gets married himself, but will not allow you to? How can he sustain it? How can he inflict such a destiny on another man? It is a situation I could not tolerate."

"You have a wife, no doubt."

"Yes and three wonderful children."

He felt the need to justify his position and became pompous: "It is very gratifying to me that I have been able to contribute to the perpetuation of the human race."

"Yes. I know the arguments and understand them. I fear I shall not have the joy to enter the realm of what I believe is known as conjugal bliss."

"Well it's not entirely that, but I cannot imagine a life that does not involve the enjoyment of a woman's company and the procreation of children. Surely that is man's destiny. He was born with sexual urges. What is the alternative? If man is denied a relationship with women there is a danger of falling into the heretical practices of the Bulgars. Why does he think being married would adversely affect your work here? Being married and having a family has not encumbered me?"

"Well, you don't know. It might have done. Perhaps by now you would be a famous playwright, even a rich one."

That silenced Will and he had to think about it. Would it have made any difference if he had not married the lovely Ann so early. He thought of the happy times he had enjoyed with her and with the children and the warmth and excitement of sharing her bed, but he was also uneasily aware that it was only since he had left such joys behind that he had begun to make his way in his true vocation.

On the other hand mankind was put on earth to reproduce. He could not exist without society and his duty to society was to ensure the perpetuation of the race. So, whatever his success or failure in his chosen profession, the importance of his marital experience could not be denied. He looked at the young man, who sat gazing unseeing at the papers before him, a troubled look on his face. It was one thing, Will decided, for someone to make a vow of celibacy and live by it out of conviction, but it was quite another for it to be imposed by an employer. He wondered how strong his feelings were.

"So is there nobody who might change your mind. You live in a society here with many fair examples of the opposite sex. Do none of them persuade you that perhaps you are suffering something of an injustice by having celibacy forced upon you?"

"Oh! I don't regard it as being forced upon me. And yes, of course, there are those I become aware of as I go about my daily duties. When you meet her you will see that my lady, the wife of his lordship, is a very beautiful woman and it is easy to see how he would be attracted. And she has a handmaid, who is not beautiful in that way, but very – er very – "

"Pretty?"

"Yes. I suppose you could say that. I hope you will in time meet both of them. I am arranging for you attend dinner one day."

"That is kind of you."

"They are both called Ann, the younger one, she is Anne with an e."

He returned to his work, but not before Will noticed with a smile that his face was suffused with an embarrassed blush.

Chapter 13

Before he met Sir Thomas Will decided he was not going to like him. The idea of someone trying to impose his will on a younger, impressionable man was anathema to him. He keenly remembered his own experience with his father. Here was a statesman of position and authority who had decided somewhat late in life that he should marry, attempting to deprive his protégé of the same conjugal satisfaction. The young man had lived a sheltered life. Born in the relative remoteness of the Isle of Wight, he had early gained his scholarship to Oxford, where he was cloistered, living the life almost of a recluse, surrounded by books and manuscripts. From these he had gathered an astonishing degree of learning that fitted him for a scholarly and ecclesiastical role. But, Will argued, that did not mean he should be deprived of a man's full enjoyment and fulfilment. Under the edict of his master he would never know the satisfaction of married life, the love and care of a woman, the knowledge that his offspring would carry on his family's name.

Additionally, Bodley had even decreed that he should not take on the work of a ministry in the church, something he had been trained for as a divinity student and would give him a settled income with the possibility of independence from his patron's dominance. Thomas was inexperienced and thus easily influenced by a man not only much older than he, but one with a wide knowledge of the world.

Thomas had told Will something of Sir Thomas's life and work, although much of it was shrouded in secrecy. He had travelled widely, in France, Italy and Germany and was able to speak learnedly on the wonderful cultural renaissance he had encountered particularly in the Italian cities, such as Rome, Florence and Venice. He was for a short time a Member of Parliament and then held a Court appointment as gentleman usher to Queen Elizabeth. In this position he was entrusted with diplomatic missions to Germany, France and the Netherlands. He was about to be sent to represent his country in the Netherlands with ministerial status, a position of great importance in view of Spain's imperial ambitions towards that country. He was, however, becoming increasingly frustrated with the politics of power and would prefer to settle down to a quieter life, in his new home, with his new bride, Ann Ball, a rich widow from Bristol. The pressure of his official duties had already led him to consider resigning his Fellowship of Merton College, although his many friends at the University were urging him to stay. He was also anxious to give more time to developing his dream of creating a library.

Will received an invitation to visit the Bodley household with some trepidation. Apart from his reservations about the man as a person the prospect of meeting such an important and distinguished statesman was daunting. Nevertheless, one fine summer morning he and young Thomas James rode up to the portals of an undistinguished house, which had yet, the young man told him, to be named. Their horses were taken off them with due deference by servants and they walked up the stone steps to be greeted by two women, totally different in age and appearance.

For many months Will had led a life that was almost totally male orientated. There were no women in the theatre groups and even the taverns he frequented in London seemed to be dominated by men. The occasional women met there were hardly of a type that would appeal to Will's romantic ideals and he was happy to join Marley in eschewing their company.

Now Will found himself confronted by two women who, each in her different ways, personified all that the poet in him venerated. The older woman was tall, as tall as Will himself, with a crown of rich dark hair, gathered high on the forehead. It was swept away from the face, revealing clearly the high cheekbones and aquiline nose that betokened a woman with a strong will and forceful character. Her dress was in the height of fashion, the cambric ruff, with its lace edging standing up high at the back of the neck, accentuating her air of authority. There was also a wide ruff of a type Will had not seen before, pinching in the waist and giving dramatic emphasis to the wide-spreading farthingale. Her arms through the hanging sleeves were folded loosely across her bosom. Her whole appearance was stern and forbidding until, as the men approached, she let her glance rest on Will with a smile that lit up her face and her whole person. To Will it was as if the sun had burst through threatening storm clouds.

The other was little more than a girl. She stood a little behind the lady presumably to betoken her position in the household, keeping her head declined and her eyes fixed on the ground. She was dressed more simply than her mistress, her garment making no attempt to hide the gentle curves of her immature body. She was, thought Will, exceptionally pretty, presenting a striking contrast to the handsome, sterner features of the lady. He became aware of a chemical charge emanating from the young man at his side and looked at him to see that Thomas was gazing open eyed at her. Manners decreed, however, that he should pay due deference to the mistress of the house and there was a moment's silence as their smiling hostess waited for the men to introduce themselves. It began to be embarrassing until Will nudged his companion, who

129

seemed to recover himself. He swiftly removed his hat, bowed and said:

"Lady Ann, we have met, but you may not remember that I am Thomas James, a protégé of your husband."

"I do indeed remember you, Master Thomas, and my husband speaks very highly of you. You may kiss my hand."

He did so then glanced towards the young lady. Will nudged him and Thomas remembered his manners: "And this is my good friend the playwright, William Shakespeare."

Will doffed his hat and bowed low.

"You are very welcome, Master Will. You must tell us news from the London theatre. We are so provincial here in Oxford and I fear have little opportunity to attend such pleasures."

She held out a jewelled hand to Will. He took it, lowered his lips to it and received in return a delicate aroma of a kind he had not encountered before. She did not draw her hand away immediately and Will eventually released it, looking up and finding himself the subject of intense scrutiny from eyes that seemed as dark as her lustrous hair. She then turned towards the young woman at her side.

"And this", said the lady, "is my confidante and willing helper, Anne Underhill."

Thomas made an unnecessarily low bow and said: "Your servant." something Will thought was inappropriate to a serving girl. He also noticed that as Thomas made his way into the house he allowed his gaze to remain on the girl, although she modestly kept her eyes firmly downward.

They went first into a reception room and sat on wooden settles with young Anne on a little seat in the bay window. The room was gaunt, with an unfinished, almost unfurnished look. Ann seemed aware of this and mentioned that they had recently moved in.

"With my husband being away so much there has been little opportunity for us to give much time to the house. He is about to return abroad, but we are hoping it will be for the last time and that he will soon be able to stay in England and perhaps give his attention to creating a more home-like atmosphere."

Will struggled to find an appropriate response: "It is an excellent place of residence, your ladyship", said Will, "and I am sure you will both make it a comfortable place for yourself and – er – and your family".

"My family? I fear I have no family."

Will was embarrassed: "I apologise. I meant – well, you will no doubt –" he stopped realising he was making things worse.

She laughed. It was a pleasantly musical sound from someone who seemed outwardly so severe. He noticed that her teeth were quite dark and wondered if this was a sign that she had an expensive addiction to sugar.

"I think we might both have left it too late to be contemplating children", she said. "When it comes to decorating the house, however, I could do more on my own, but there will only be my husband and I – and Anne, of course – so it does need participation from him. But I am neglecting my duties as hostess. We will be having wine with our meal. My husband brought some fine bottles back from France on his last journey. Or you gentlemen might prefer ale."

"You are very kind", said Will. "For my part I am quite happy to wait until dinner."

"Then let us go to the table", she said and rose. She led the way into the large dining room, where a long oak table had been laid. "My husband will sit at the end there and I suggest you Thomas and Will sit at either side. Anne will join me at this end."

They sat and servants came in to pour wine and place copious dishes on the table until Will wondered how they could manage to consume so much food. There was a capon, a leg of mutton and what Ann explained was a spinach pie. There was even a large dish of oysters, which she suggested they might begin to eat before Sir Thomas came down. Will had never eaten oysters before and he was astonished to see Ann pick up one by the shell and slurp its contents between her lips.

"You would be wise to allow the teeth to sink into the oyster before you swallow. If it tastes bitter do not hesitate to regurgitate it."

"What would happen to me if I did not?" asked Will.

She laughed: "You might die".

Then Sir Thomas appeared. He struck an imposing figure, tall and only a little portly around the middle. His dress was quite formal, with a ruff framing his face high above his ears. His beard was closely clipped and small moustache followed the line of a firm mouth. The eyebrows were held high, giving a haughty expression and Will was amused to notice that his thinning hair ended in what he had heard described as a devil's peak on his forehead.

The men rose as did young Anne. He went to his wife and kissed her on the cheek. He bowed briefly to Anne, then went up to young Tom and embraced him warmly.

"You are looking a little pale. I hope I am not driving you too hard."

"I am pleased to work assiduously on your behalf Sir Thomas."

"I'm sure. You are a good lad and will go far."

"May I have the pleasure to introduce Master William Shakespeare, the playwright whose work I mentioned to you."

Sir Thomas approached and held out his hand. Will took it and became aware of the magnetism deriving from a man who had travelled far, seen much and been party to the great and powerful of the world. Although the other was not tall he felt quite dwarfed by him.

"Master Shakespeare, you are very welcome."

He took a step back and bowed. Will returned his bow

"You are a playwright then?"

"I do have that privilege."

"A privilege eh? And you think it is also a worthy aspiration for a young man of letters?"

"I believe so, sir. We have opportunities of communicating with the populace in a way and to an extent that has never been achieved before".

"Then I hope what you communicate is worthy of their attention – and yours."

He turned away and took his seat, gesturing to the others to do so. Then he reached across to pick up bread and break it with a certain formality. He continued to address Will:

"My protégé here has spoken most warmly of you. He tells me you have worked with the Admiral's men at a theatre in London."

"That's true, Sir Thomas. It was the Rose, managed by a man named Henslowe. I am in process of writing scripts for his players to perform."

"That must be a very difficult discipline. I envy you the skill."

"I merely write to manipulate actors on a stage, answerable only to a rabble of an audience. As I understand it you have the much more onerous task of manipulating the statesmen of the world, answerable to a much higher authority".

"Prettily put, sir, prettily put. But your work may

133

have a greater significance than you think. There are those in high places who are watching the progress of the theatre. Indeed, I have it on good authority that the Queen herself takes an interest in it."

"May one ask what authority that is?" ventured Will cautiously.

The great man smiled: "Why the Queen herself, no less. The queen herself".

There was silence as they ate and Will absorbed the significance of his situation, dining with someone who had the ear of Queen Elisabeth.. They picked at the food mainly by hand, using a knife only to cut pieces from the joint of beef and the bird.

"You notice, Master William", remarked Sir Thomas "that we do not adopt the French fashion of using a fourchette. I hope it does not embarrass you".

Will was, in fact, more embarrassed by the question. He felt his host was being patronising.

"I am country born, sir, and spent most of my early life in a small town far from the centre of fashion. We ate with knives and our fingers. But I have been introduced to the use of the fork at the house of the Walsinghams."

"You surely do not mean Sir Francis Walsingham?"

"No sir, I refer to Sir Thomas Walsingham, of Kent. It is a place much frequented by playwrights and poets."

"And thieves and vagabonds too, I understand. Present company excepted of course."

Once again Will felt embarrassed, even belittled, and did not know how to respond, so he kept silent.

After a while, Sir Thomas said: "You will also notice that our fair lady companions eat but little. They are waiting for the dessert, when I am sure the table will groan under its load of sweet dishes. Am I not right, my dear?"

Once again Will thought the man was being patronising and this time towards his beautiful wife. She soon answered for herself, however: "Apothecaries tell us, Sir Thomas, that sugar is good for the complexion and helps to keep us ladies soft, warm and pliable, which I am sure is entirely to the liking of our men-folk"

"Then long may you do so."

"And of course we are fortunate in having the riches necessary to keep us supplied with such luxuries and that, of course, is thanks to your industry."

Will admired her answer greatly. She could easily have returned his comment with asperity, but instead she chose to pay him a compliment.

"Not only my dear. Your contribution has been substantial, which is perhaps just as well. I am as you know deeply anxious to be excused my more onerous duties. When that happens there may be fewer funds available to indulge you."

"But I hope you will always feel able to indulge your dutiful wife, my dear."

Will looked at her quickly and thought he detected an irony in her words. He thought the exchange between them cool and lacking the kind of affection he would have expected in a couple so recently married. They sat at opposite ends of the table. Sir Thomas smiled as if at an inner secret, eating his capon leg with relish. Ann seemed to be paying more attention to the young lady at her side, occasionally whispering in her ear and then joining with her in quiet laughter. Sir Thomas turned back towards Will.

"And what do you hope to gain from your stay in Oxford."

Will was glad of an opportunity to enthuse on a subject obviously close to his host's heart: "Oh! sir there is so much information here, a veritable cornucopia of knowledge. Thomas has been very helpful in guiding me."

"I hope he has not been filling your head with unworthy tales. There are many such to be found in our little collection."

"No, sir. I have been mostly interested in the history of our great country. The lives of the monarchs and great people in the past contain much dramatic material. I am presently working on what I hope will eventually be a whole series of plays on the Tudor dynasty."

"The Tudor dynasty indeed. That is an ambitious project. But surely it encompasses generations, centuries even. Are you proposing to travel from William the First to Henry the Eighth. Our present noble Queen even?"

Will laughed: "Well not quite that far. As a matter of fact, for practical reasons I am having to start near the end, with the Sixth Henry, but I shall certainly take in other Henries and Richard, of course."

"First, second or third?"

"Perhaps all three."

This produced laughter from all those present and Will was gratified to find himself the centre of attention. He noticed that the lady Ann looked at him admiringly and even the young Anne glanced in his direction with interest.

"I also hope to write on classical subjects from the ancient Greek and Latin.

"You are proficient in those languages then "

"Sadly no. I have to rely on translations."

"No doubt young Thomas can help you there. He is something of a linguist, aren't you Thomas."

"Only in a literary sense", said Thomas. I lack the experience you have had with travel in foreign countries. I would dearly love to visit Italy, for example.

The stories you have told me of the artistic wonders there have filled me with longing."

"Well, it is not given to all of us to have such a privilege. As I have often said we have to accept our station in life and our destinies. My dear wife here has to look after a household. Yours Will perhaps is to write plays. Mine is to travel and to deal with authorities both in this country and abroad. It is not, however, the pleasurable experience you may imagine. To tell the truth I am sometimes sick to the heart with it, with the constant move from country to country and all the inconveniences of transport. I would wish for nothing better than to put my feet up before a fire in the grate with my wife at my side and a dog's head in my lap."

"Would you not rather have your wife's head in your lap and a dog at your side", suggested Ann. Sir Thomas roared with laughter at her sally and the men felt safe in adding theirs.

"In fact I believe I have another destiny, which may seem insignificant compared to affairs of state, but in my mind is much more important in the longer term. I refer, of course, to my hopes for establishing a library here in Oxford, but not any library. It will contain knowledge of the widest diversity, and will be one all people may have access to, not just the privileged few. Knowledge is a precious commodity, possession of it will help to rid mankind of so many ills, so much ignorance. There was once a great library in Alexandria, Egypt, perhaps the greatest the world has ever seen. The Romans destroyed it and I believe in doing so presaged the end of their empire. With a library such as I envisage I believe this country can become greater than ancient Rome. With the help of young Thomas here I believe it can be achieved."

A silence fell as each of those around the table considered the impact such a development would have on their lives. Will thought how wonderful it would be if such a facility were open to all; Ann wondered what the impact would be on her life and the household she ruled if her husband was constantly present; young Thomas allowed his eyes to wander on to the younger Anne and began to regret his involvement in the proposal would preclude the enjoyment of what might be an earthly paradise; the young lady herself picked daintily at the savoury food before her and hoped the sweetmeats would not be too long arriving.

Ann broke the silence: "Are you married, Will?" she asked.

"I am my lady."

"And you have children?"

"I do."

"So where are they now ?"

"Sadly in Stratford, where I had to leave them."

"That is sad. It must be wonderful to have progeny and to find it necessary to turn one's back on them would be hard – for the children, as well as for you and your wife."

"I do miss them, your ladyship, but as Sir Thomas says, I have to follow my destiny."

Sir Thomas turned to his young protégé: "There Thomas you see what happens when you venture into married life. This young man has to leave his loving wife and his children behind him while he makes his way in the world. If he had stayed behind to fulfil his conjugal duties he would never have achieved what he obviously regards as his destiny."

Will could not resist: "But surely sir, it has not prevented you from marrying".

The others around the table looked at him in surprise that he should challenge the great man, who sat silently for a moment while he considered the question.

"But I have waited until I can see the end of my

journeying before entering that happy estate. I know it will not be too long before the saddle of my travels is hung up."

He looked at his wife and his face briefly relaxed into the semblance of a smile: "Except perhaps to ride out foot on foot with my dear wife."

Ann did not at first respond and her expression remained unchanged, until perhaps realising that some response was expected from her, quickly said: "Amen to that".

Thomas rose: "Well, my dear, I must ask you to excuse me. I will leave you ladies to consume the sweetmeats. I have papers to deal with before I leave again tomorrow".

All except Ann rose as he went towards the door. A servant held it open for him, but he stopped and turned, a thoughtful look on his face. Then he came back and stood quite close to Will, who had resumed his seat.

"Young man, we may not have another opportunity to talk together and as you are going to participate in the activities of this household in my absence there is something I must say to you. I spend my time in the real world, where such people are in a constant fight for power. There are factions afoot that you may not be aware of. I have told you of the Queen's interest in your work, but others are less sympathetic. You say you are writing about the kings and nobles of the land and uttered on the stage may be nothing more than bombast, but there are those who will take them very seriously."

"They are not my words, sir. They are intended as the utterances of the character."

"Others may not see them as such. I do not have time or opportunity to visit playhouses myself, but I have heard there are those involved in the theatre whose views are so far removed from our holy church they may even be regarded as heretical."

He was standing close to Will now, looking down at him with a fierce expression on his face. Will felt very intimidated by the man and was uncertain how to respond.

"Why sir", he managed at last. "there is no-one of my acquaintance who can even remotely be regarded as heretical".

"Indeed. And is not this Christopher Marley, or Marlowe, of your acquaintance?"

Will was astonished: "Why yes, but I hardly think – "

"You hardly think indeed. That is the trouble, Master Will Shakespeare, so many of you hardly think, until perhaps you are faced with the gallows or the fire".

Will began to get up startled, but the man placed a hand on his chest and held him firmly in his chair.

"I understand this man has uttered heretical statements in the hearing of others. His plays contain characters who deny the existence of god and dialogue that defames the Christian belief. It is rumoured he holds Roman Catholic views. And you share his room, his bed and even his heretical beliefs?"

Will forced himself to his feet and challenged his accuser.

"No, I do not deny I share his room and his bed, but there is nothing to that for poor folk who cannot afford a grand house and – " he gestured to the remains of the dinner – "a sumptuous table, for which please accept my grateful thanks – but he is no heretic and neither am I."

The other placed his face only inches away from him and called: "Can you prove that, eh? Tell me. Can you prove it."

"Indeed. I cannot and I don't see why I should. I

thought the law said a man was innocent until proven guilty."

"If the law said that it was an ass and so are you to believe it. Christopher Marley is a heretic. Can you prove he is not?"

"No. No."

From being the participant in a pleasurable social occasion, Will felt he had become the victim of a fierce inquisition. There was a power to the man confronting him he had not experienced before. The eyes were cold and the beard bristled with anger. Even the widow's peak seemed to point at him accusingly. There was silence as Will tried to hide the fact that he trembled.

"So you understand my concern that people of that kind should not enjoy the hospitality of my household."

At that the lady Ann rose to her feet. In a voice strident with authority she called to her husband that it was no way to treat a guest. She asked – nay she demanded – that he desist.

For a moment Thomas did not relent. He looked at his wife and the ghost of a smile once again haunted his visage. Then as suddenly as it arose the storm subsided.

"I am sorry to disturb your dinner table, my dear, but if you think I have been hard on our young friend, just consider how much harder the Inquisition would be if it decided to ask him the same questions."

He clapped Will on the shoulder: "Sit down lad and enjoy the rest of your dinner. I am certainly not going to have you sent to the tower. I have no thumb screws to apply. This sumptuous board as you call it is no rack. But there are those who are only too willing to drag you to their invidious banqueting table. Even I, who have a position of some authority and influence, am not immune from the predations of envious men. You probably think it strange that I should be so well versed on the activities of theatre folk, but it is with good

141

reason. If you are a friend of this man Marley you may have heard of a man named Gabriel Harvey".

"I have indeed."

"Then you will know that Marley, a former student of his, comes in for his particular vituperation. This man sits in the University of Cambridge, each of his six feet attuned to receive the vibrations of the cultural and political world. He sniffs out heresy as a pig might some delicacy in the ground. More importantly for me he is opposed to the idea of establishing a library here in Oxford. It might be in competition with Cambridge, where he likes to dominate the minds and hearts of our countrymen. Who knows what he could say in my absence about me and those who enjoy my hospitality. Fortunately, I have good friends at Court and that is something he can never gainsay. So, young man, you are welcome here."

He turned towards his wife: "Well, I have said enough to disturb the equanimity of our dinner table. Apologies my dear."

He went towards the door; "I may not appear for supper."

"I will arrange for something to be sent up", she said as he was leaving.

Upon his departure the table was cleared of residue from the first course and in its place there appeared an amazing assortment of sweetmeats, cakes, buns and biscuits, which the two ladies consumed greedily. A sweet cordial was served, although both Thomas and Will excused themselves and asked for ale. To accompany that they were provided with cheeses from several different parts of the land, until Will felt his stomach could hold no more.

Afterwards, as it was a fine afternoon, Ann suggested they should stroll in the grounds of the house, apologising for their meagre extent. Will was surprised when she took his arm. Her hand felt warm and firm and he greatly enjoyed the sensation of a woman's touch after such a long abstinence. Thomas took the opportunity of further acquaintance with the lady's young companion and lagged further and further behind until they were almost out of sight.

"You are staying at the University?" Ann asked.

"No. I have lodgings."

"They will not be very comfortable", she suggested.

"They serve, but as you say, are not very comfortable."

"We are still settling in here and there are many empty rooms. You would be very welcome to lodge here during your stay."

Will stopped in surprise and turned to look at her.

"Your ladyship! You hardly know me. That is a generous offer to a comparative stranger."

She smiled at him: "I hope you do not regard yourself as a stranger, comparative or otherwise. The recommendation of your young friend carries sufficient weight. After all he will be staying here as well."

She squeezed his arm in an affectionate gesture and continued to walk: "I will speak to Sir Thomas about it, but I do not think he will object. He may be absent for some time and it would be an advantage to have male guests in the house."

"It will mean travelling to the University every day."

"Surely not every day. You could bring your books back here." She gave a little gentle laugh. "It appears Sir Thomas will be turning the house into a library anyway."

They reached a stream bordering the estate. The sun sparkled on the water, although a slight breeze had brought a chill to the air. The lady shivered and released his arm and struggled with her shawl.

Feeling very chivalrous he quickly helped to adjust

the shawl round her shoulder and found himself enjoying the physical contact. She stood for a moment looking into his eyes.

"Thank you. What a gallant young man you are", she said, "and handsome".

He turned away, feeling sure he was blushing.

Then she laughed, kissed him gently on the cheek and said: "We must find the others".

She led the way back towards the house, where they found Thomas and Anne deep in their own intimacy.

Chapter 14

The room was silent except for the scratching of Will's quill across paper, the rustling of parchment at Thomas's table and the occasional movement of their chairs among the rushes on the floor. Then Will heard what he thought was a sigh from his companion. He looked at him and saw the young man had leaned back in his seat, a hand to his face, and was gazing towards the light from the leaded window.

"Something is troubling you", he asked.

There was no reply for a moment, then Thomas rustled the documents on the table, picked one out and looked at it, shaking his head.

"I have a confession to make Will. I have been trespassing on your territory. I have tried my hand at writing poetry – not original, I must admit, but in translation."

"The territory, as you call it, is free to all, Thomas. You have only to open the gate and stroll in. But you seem doubtful about what you have written."

"Well I do not have your skill with words, Will, but that's not where my doubts lie. No, they are with the subject matter. It is all about love, something I have no experience of, something I find difficult to understand."

"I can assure you Thomas that even those who do experience it usually fail to understand it. What have you translated? Something from the Italian?"

"No. The French."

"Ah! Ronsard perhaps. He has written some splendid sonnets."

"No. He wrote in the French of northern France. This was an earlier tradition of poets in the south of the country, Provence and places adjacent to it."

"The Troubadours perhaps, or the Trouveres as I believe they are now called."

"Even earlier. These poets wrote in a culture that no longer exists. It was completely obliterated by the Albigensian Crusade."

"But the crusades were directed against the Muslim infidels when they occupied Jerusalem in contravention of holy scripture."

"Not this one. This was not Jerusalem. It was southern France, Languedoc – the land where yes is pronounced 'oc', instead of 'oui' as in the North. A whole civilisation once existed there, with a culture to match those of Greece or Rome. It was exterminated, the innocent as well as those who might be regarded, rightly or wrongly, as guilty."

"Guilty of what? It must have been a great evil to have brought such punishment upon their heads. What did they do that was so antithetical to Rome?"

"They committed heresy. They taught a variation of Christianity – decrying some of the biblical texts. They claimed that Jesus Christ was an angel and not the son of god. They worshiped the virgin Mary and venerated women. It is said they encouraged unnatural practices between men, although that seems to have been introduced by immigrants from eastern European lands, the Cathars, the Bulgars, from which we derive a word that will be well known to you. The Pope preached a crusade. Their northern neighbours marched against them, motivated it seems less by Christian spirit than by greed, a desire to take over their lands. They were joined, I am sad to say, by some from this country who also saw it as an opportunity to increase their wealth and power. With the result all we are left with from a once living civilisation are the verses of their poets."

"I am astonished, not only at the story, but also that it is so little known today. How came you by it? Is it well attested?"

"Oh! yes. Sir Thomas brought it back from one of his journeys and I can assure you he is totally reliable in such matters. His thirst for knowledge and for its preservation is unquenchable. He brought back many examples of the Languedoc literature - poetry of marvellous simplicity and beauty. It has a great diversity. The poets would argue in verse, what they called a *tenson*. But it is their love poetry that is so wonderful. It speaks directly from the heart. Much of it was written to the great ladies of the court and lordly estates by young squires and followers, who had no other way of showing their feelings. A tradition grew up of courtly love in which a poet would praise his lady perhaps in the absence of any physical or sexual relationship between them. Can you understand that?"

Will thought he could. From his own experience he knew that poetry did not necessarily arise from the physical act of making love. He had never been inspired to write a poem to his wife, much though he loved her. It was usually the frustration of loving without consummation that would result in a kind of music in his mind. It found its way on to parchment in the form of a sonnet or was absorbed by the dialogue when he was writing an amorous scene for the stage.

"Has any of their poetry been translated?" he asked.

"I have tried my hand at it, but I am not a poet. I lack your genius in that regard. I can only interpret the words as I have understood them. Also, it appears that the poems would probably have been sung to a music accompaniment.

"Nevertheless I would like to hear something you have written. Please read me something."

Thomas demurred at first, but Will persisted and eventually the young man recited:

The gentle thought
That love can bring
To my heart brought
A song to sing..
The one above
Whom I desire
Would doubt my love
Nor trust my fire.
And yet I promise make
If I appear untrue
It is for her dear sake
All caution I eschew
To beg her mercy all my days
All nights give only her my praise.

To hate may turn
The love you bear,
If you discern
I love elsewhere
You took from me
The joy I know –
How can there be
Joy, but in you.
I could not love her more
Yet I have to deny
The one whom I adore
And hope she will descry
All this I'm bound to do from fear
And trust me whether far or near.

In memory
I hold her face
Worth more to me
Than wealth or place
Such faith, if I
To God could show,
Then when I die
To heaven would go.
To give my heart to her

I would not hesitate
Nor ever be untrue.
How could it compensate
That I could with another sleep
And lose the heart that she might keep.

The sunlight shone through the leaded window, throwing a faint angular pattern on the table with the dusty books. The young man had read the poem with feeling and Will looked at him sensing that he was applying its sentiment to feelings of his own. Once again he wondered at the conflict that his emotions must be arousing and was concerned for his future.

"That is beautiful Thomas", he said, "I love the simplicity and the changes of rhythm from stanza to stanza. It seems to tell the story of an unfaithful lover who is trying to justify having slept with someone else. There is also the irony is that he is not be sleeping with his mistress, which would make her more angry and his remorse the greater".

They laughed together and enjoyed the pleasure of sharing a male concept. Will looked at his young companion and wondered if he should raise a subject he had thought about a great deal in relation to his friend.

"You read the poem almost as if it reflected your own feelings", he said cautiously.

As Will feared, Thomas responded quite indignantly: "My feelings! I am not aware that I have amorous feelings for any lady, let alone two".

Will hastily apologised and the two men returned to their work. Something Thomas said, however, stayed in his mind.

"You said that in this land there was a tradition of courtly love. That poets would write in praise of an unattainable woman, perhaps an older one."

"Yes, a squire perhaps, who would have no hope of consummating his love for her ladyship, even though he knew his feelings were reciprocated."

Will said no more and appeared to immerse himself in his writing, but his thoughts were on the lovely mistress of the house, whose presence filled his waking hours with pleasure. When near her his feelings were so strong that he often found it necessary to turn away. And when he looked back he would see of a kind that reflects those inner secrets women keep so effectively and disconcertingly from a man.

He was considering this when he recalled with a start that he had offered to give her lessons in the use of the long bow. He had been boasting of his own prowess and told her stories of the chase and of the encounter with brigands on the journey. She had asked if he would help to increase her skill. The house was, she said, fully supplied with the necessary equipment.

So he lay down his quill pen and told Thomas where he was going. Thomas asked whether the young Anne would be there and when Will said he thought it was possible, the young man got to his feet over eagerly. .The two made their way downstairs where they found Lady Ann and her companion sitting by a window with needlework in their hands. She put down her work and stood.

"You are tardy, Master William", she said, wagging an admonitory finger at him, but smiling at the same time. "I had begun to fear that you did not relish the possibility of being my tutor today".

"Nothing will give me greater pleasure", said William.

"And you, young Thomas, are you prepared to leave your books long enough to accompany Anne?"

"If that is your pleasure, your Ladyship."

"I don't think my pleasure comes into it."

She led them into a walled, grassy area at the rear of the building, where a targe had been set up at the far end and mats placed at strategic distances from it. Two little marquees had been erected, providing cover for refreshments. Two maids were in attendance, in addition to the young Anne, and the gay colouring of their clothes combined with the marquees to provide a festive air. Will decided he would be able to enjoy a welcome relief from the constant burden of bending his head over books, having the feathers of an arrow in his hand rather ones shaped into quills.

Ann indicated the scene with a wave of the hand: "You approve of the arrangements?"

"They are excellent, your ladyship."

"I am hoping to develop this as a rose garden", she said. "You see over these, against that wall, where it catches the sun".

She stood close to him and pointed. He became uncomfortably aware of her bosom pressed against his chest and edged slightly away. She looked at him and smiled: "I am told that the Amazon women remove their right breast so that they might more skilfully draw the bow in battle."

He attempted to laugh off his embarrassment and said: "The story is certainly apocryphal and anyway I am sure it will not be necessary in your case".

She also laughed: "I hope not Will. I certainly hope not."

She moved away with a little twirl of her skirts: "Do you think I am appropriately dressed for sport". She had dressed down for the occasion, discarding the elaborate ruffs and wide farthingale in favour of a simple gown that set off her full figure and softened her somewhat angular features. He felt it was not his place, however, to offer a view on her appearance and she did not seem to expect one.

There were several bows and a quantity of well-fletched arrows and although Will regretted the absence of his own bow was surprised at the quality of those provided. He wondered when Thomas Bodley found time to engage in the sport of archery and whether it was against targets or in the hunt.

Her ladyship was not backward in seizing a bow and arrow, striding up to a mat and placing herself in what Will was amused to see was a very aggressive stance. She tested the hempen string on the bow, put an arrow in the nock and stretched it. Will watched her and drew near to examine her grip. She relaxed the bow and turned to him.

"You look at me critically, Master Shakespeare. Are you an expert in the sport of archery as well as shooting down deer in the hunt or brigands on the road?"

"Not an expert, your ladyship, but I do have some skill in the discipline."

"And do you have advice to offer me in my technique?"

"I was interested in your grip. It appears to be one used by a relative novice, what we call a pinch draw. If you would allow me I will demonstrate the Mediterranean draw and release."

"Please feel free."

"It would give you much better control."

He joined her on the mat and took the bow and arrow off her. Once again he found her closeness disconcerting, becoming aware of the strong odour from perfumes she had obviously used in her bath that morning. He demonstrated the way he thought she should hold the forefinger above the fletch and the middle and ring fingers below.

"This will enable you to draw the bow with the least effort and will lead to a more accurate shot."

"Yes, I see", she said. "Like this?" She placed her

right hand over his on the arrow. Her arm went round his shoulders so that she could hold the bow. Their cheeks were touching. She placed her fingers as he had directed: "Like this?"

"Yes. Yes. That's good"

He disentangled himself very gently from her. She took the bow and arrow off him and pointed it at the target.

"But when you fletch the arrow and before drawing the bow, you should point it at the ground. That will ensure that it is not loosed off at a dangerous angle. Then you may lift and point it at the target."

"Like this?" she asked. She lowered the arrow towards the ground, drew the bow then raised it. The arrow flew towards the target, which it struck just off centre.

"That's excellent, excellent", he said, unable to keep the astonishment from his voice.

She motioned to one of her maids, who brought a quiver of arrows and stood by her side. She fletched the arrow, raised the bow and shot an arrow unerringly to the target, where it hit the bull. Will scarcely had time to take in her achievement before she had drawn other arrows from the quiver and shot them in a close pattern to the first. She lowered the bow, turned to Will: "Did I do it correctly?" she asked.

She laughed at his astonishment. He looked at the boxes of equipment, then back at her.

"This archery equipment is yours, not your husbands?"

"My husband's? Good gracious no. He has no time for such frivolities."

"And you have practised it before?"

"A little. Oh! I'm sorry. I should have said. My former husband was a skilled bowman and we practised it constantly at our house in Bristol. What you described as the pinch draw was, in fact, a variant known as the Mongolian. He saw it used during one of his travels and taught it to me. You see, the thumb is under the forefinger, not over it. It apparently has advantages when firing from horseback."

"Perhaps you would have preferred to have this exercise on horseback", said Will with a trace of bitterness in his voice.

She laughed: "Oh! you mustn't mind. When I lived in Bristol our friends and neighbours joined us in the sport. We had many competitions, including those they call roving. Women can be every bit as skilled in the art as men."

"I do think you might have told me. You must have thought me very foolish."

She placed a hand on his arm and smiled sweetly at him: "Oh! please don't mind. I was having a little joke with you. Please".

He was quite unable to resist her blandishment. He smiled in turn.

"Of course Lady Bodley. It was my fault for being aggressively male."

"Oh! I'm sure you could never be that, Master Shakespeare."

"There is no reason why women may not be as skilled as men in such an art, although of course they lack the strength to shoot as far and as strongly as a man".

"I disagree. I can fire an arrow further than you."

"I would challenge you in that."

"Very well, but first let me see if you can better my score on those four arrows."

A fresh quiver of arrows was brought and Will took his place on the mat. Taking great care with his aim he placed four arrows in the bull."

Ann clapped her hands: "Well, you certainly win that

round. But now let us see if I can better you for distance. You go first."

He drew the string of the bow to the furthest distance and released an arrow that went several yards past the target. Satisfied that she would be unable to do better he handed the bow to her. Unlike Will she did not point the arrow at the target, but into the air. On release it achieved an exceptionally high trajectory, arching so that its flight was almost lost in the sun. To his astonishment and chagrin Will saw it land beyond a hedge at the far end of the field a long way ahead of his.

There was silence for a moment, then everyone except Will, burst into applause. She looked at him and smiled, something he could not resist. Grudgingly he acknowledged her achievement: "Another little trick your first husband taught you?"

"Yes, I'm afraid so, but you deserve a little compensatory reward" and with that she kissed him full on the mouth. Will felt he should respond to her familiarity with his own gallantry. He bowed low and said: "I could not have been better graced if I had been rewarded with a golden trophy.

She inclined her head: "What a gallant speech, from a gallant loser".

"But if that is what the loser gains surely the winner deserves something even greater", and saying which he put his hands on both her shoulders, pulled her towards him and kissed her firmly on the mouth. She made no attempt to resist and he was gratified to feel it open gently and the tip of her tongue touch his. He released her and she stood silently for a moment then she turned to her maids, who stood hiding their grins behind their hands.

"I think we have had enough sport for the morning" she said. "I am quite fatigued. Let us have some refreshments".

They sat in one of the marquees and were served pastries and biscuits, with sweet cordials to drink. The summer fruits were in season and Ann amused herself by placing a strawberry into Will's mouth, making it necessary for him to meet the gaze of those disconcertingly dark eyes. Anne sat a little apart with Thomas and Will reflected that he had never heard the young man laugh so much. It was a charming, intimate scene and Will thought it was many years since he had found an occasion so enjoyable.

After a while the young girl asked her mistress if she could go for a walk with Thomas and she was given permission to do so. They took themselves off towards the distant river. Will suggested that perhaps he should follow them and act as chaperon, but Ann replied that she thought her protégé was quite capable of looking after herself. Then she said: "I see young Thomas has taken her hand and I wonder if he is aware what a jewel he is holding."

"She is certainly very pretty."

Ann gave him a searching look.

"Like most men it is the outward form that most attracts you."

"I would not say that."

"And a young one at that."

He laughed and looked at her very directly: "For my part I am not particularly enamoured by unripe fruit".

To his surprise he saw that she was blushing. She put a hand to her cheek and turned away.

Then without looking at him she spoke very firmly: "I must make it clear that I am a married woman and would not consider in any way jeopardising the sacredness of my marital vows".

"Madam I would not have it any other way. As a married man myself I would expect your behaviour to be that which I would hope for from my own wife".

Then glancing round to ensure that he was not observed, he went quickly to her chair and knelt on one knee beside it: "But I must confess to finding your person of the greatest attraction and I hope you will allow me to admire you, without asking for, or anticipating anything in return".

She smiled down at him and passed her hand softly over his hair.

"Your behaviour is that of a gentleman and exactly what I would expect from so good and kind a person."

"Then I may be your friend?"

"Of course. I will be flattered."

"And your lover?"

She placed a finger on his lips: "Hush. Do not hurry me. There may time for that but, more importantly, a very strict limit".

She kissed him lightly on the forehead.

"I must attend to the kitchen. They will be preparing for the midday meal. Perhaps you are right. You should go and find where our young friends have gone. I trust them, of course, but it does seem as if love is in the air!"

Chapter 15

Thomas asked Will if he could come to his room when they retired that night. He had something he wanted to discuss with him, a personal matter on which he needed advice. Will thought the younger man looked troubled and was glad he had chosen to confide in him. He thought of his relationship with Thomas as avuncular. The gap in their ages was not great, but there was a considerable difference in the extent of their life experience. Thomas had told him something of his background, his birth and childhood in the remote island of Wight, his opportunity to come to Oxford where he had lived a sheltered existence under the tutelage and patronage of Bodley. Will, on the other hand, although he had not travelled extensively or been involved in matters of state, had nevertheless married at an early age, fathered three children, travelled to London, appeared on the stage there and been involved in what was, after all, the cultural activity of the day.

He was happy to act as a father-figure to the younger man. It was the least he could offer, anyway, in return for the inestimable benefits Thomas had bestowed on him. The young man's knowledge of books was quite literally encyclopaedic. It had helped Will to fill his plays with detailed historical information he would not have been able to obtain elsewhere. In addition to studying the history of the English monarchy there were translations of Greek and Latin literature which filled his head with stories for future plays.

So he spent his time very agreeably, divided between research for his plays, conversation with his young friend and enjoying the company of the Bodley household, particularly, he admitted to himself, the mistress of the house. He was very flattered by the attention she paid to him. She was discreet in all her dealings, but he would have been less of a man had he not been aware of the chemical charge that seemed to emanate from her whenever they were together and particularly on the rare occasions he found himself alone with her. The wit and wisdom of her conversation was also stimulating and helped him when he came to delineate his female characters.

He particularly enjoyed their walks in the pleasant countryside, with its soft pastel tones of green, yellow and brown, beside a river that flowed with such charming music past hedges fertile with berries and fruit and through woods furnished with ash, maple and elm. It reminded him of the forested countryside around his home, although sometimes it served to increase the uneasy sense of guilt he felt at his failure to visit his family. His wife and children became more and more remote. It was as if he had found a new family among people he cared for and even loved.

There was a timid knock on his door and when he called "come in" Thomas entered, wearing only a doublet and hose. Will was already in bed, sitting up reading by the light of a candle. A small fire burned in the grate and the room was warm and welcoming. Putting his book aside, he motioned Thomas to sit in a small armchair by the bed. Then he tucked his legs under his long nightshirt and pulled the bedclothes up around him. He turned towards the young man and hoped he was about to unburden himself. He was not disappointed.

Thomas said he had been meaning to speak to Will for some time. He regarded him as an older man with greater experience of personal matters and someone whose judgement he could trust. He was, he said, in something of a dilemma. Indeed, dilemma was too mild a word to describe the turmoil in which his mind had been racing for weeks and even longer. He paused, placed his chin on his hand and his elbow on his knee, presenting himself as someone with the most perplexing problem to be solved. Will waited for to say what was on his mind in his own time.

"As you know", he said at last, "I was born and spent my early childhood on an island called Wight. This is a relatively remote part of the country, sparsely populated, but very beautiful and desirable in all aspects. It really is a most beautiful place, separated from the country's mainland as if some providence had decreed it should retain its charm and innocence.

"However innocence, like beauty, is only skin deep and beneath the outward appearance of sanctity and purity there lurked the sins and perversions tradition might more properly associate with the slums and depravity of a city environment. My parents lived lives of honest conjugal bliss. They were born, met and were married in a town called Newport in the west of England. When they moved to the island, by coincidence it was to a town of the same name.

"My mother had many children, so many I have lost count, but I believe it was about 15 in the space of some 20 years. Some of those are still living. Others died in childbirth or soon after. I was born in 1571 and, as you see", he added with a wan smile, "I am still alive".

Will wondered where all this was leading. The fumes from the logs burning in the grate were beginning to make him feel drowsy. He had had a long day and, although he was happy to advise the young man, he did wish he would come to the point.

"At an early age I apparently began to manifest evidence of what my parents saw as exceptional mental ability and it was agreed I should be put to school. I was sent to stay at a boarding school in the north of the island, which had lately been heavily fortified against the threat of invasion. I felt I was living in one of those fortifications. It was a time I hated. We were treated badly, ill-fed and punished for the slightest indiscretion. We slept in large, unheated dormitories and sometimes for warmth and comfort and to try and achieve some relief from the cold and our unhappiness we would creep into another pupil's bed. This was strictly forbidden and being caught resulted in severe chastisement. One master in particular delighted in waiting until late at night and then surprising us in another boy's bed.

"He called me out one night and took me to his room. There I was made to bend over his desk, lift my nightshirt and expose myself to the lashing of his rod. He then regaled me to the evils of what he called the ultimate sin. I was told I was a perversion, that I would never know a woman, but go through life seeking to satisfy my unnatural longings in evil practices and distractions.

"I cannot tell you how much distress this caused me and many was the time I was tempted to throw myself off one of the school's high walls and end it all. Then one wonderful day I was rescued from my ordeal when the man who was to become my patron visited the island and expressed an interest in taking on a protégé. He was looking for someone, he said, whom he could train to work on a particular project he had in mind in Oxford. That man was, of course, Sir Thomas, who has since been very kind to me and offered me the possibility of a fulfilling professional career."

"Why do you think you were chosen – of all the children at the school, I mean?"

"Well I think I did show a certain exceptional ability, in literary matters. Then it is likely that the predatory schoolmaster suggested I would grow up to be the sort of man Sir Thomas was looking for – someone who would be content to be a cleric and all that involves."

"You mean to remain celibate?"

"It was a *sine qua non*. Sir Thomas wanted someone who would dedicate his whole life to the project he had in mind, who would not be distracted by marital complications and would be content to live a life of abstinence. After all, it not at all unusual for any man intending to become a priest."

Will burst with indignation: "Yes, from choice, but nobody has the right to dictate to a young person at such an early age and under duress. Whatever made you decide to accept such a proposal?"

"I would have said or done anything, I am afraid, to escape from that appalling place. And what Sir Thomas offered seemed very attractive. Indeed, seems so still."

"Seems? You seem to have doubts."

Thomas was silent for a while and seemed to be struggling with some inner torment. A burning log fell from the fire and sparked in the hearth. Will got up and attended to it. Then he turned and waited for the young man to continue.

At last, Thomas burst out: "Oh! Will I believe – I believe - I have fallen in love."

"Don't you know?"

"How should I? How can anyone know when you haven't experienced it before?"

"Oh! you would know. If I were not so tired I would present you with a catechism to establish the fact beyond question."

"Then do so. Please do so."

Will sighed. "Oh!" very well, but first I must know the young lady's name."

"It is Anne, of course."

"Is that Ann with or without an e?"

162

"How can you tease me so – you must know it is Anne with an e. Young Anne. Anne with an e Underhill".

"Well, we seem to have established that: Now, Primo before you go to sleep at night who is the last person you think about?"

"Why Anne, of course."

"Anne with an e."

"Yes, yes. Anne with an e."

"Secondo when you wake up in the morning whose is the first name on your lips?"

"Anne."

"Anne with an e."

Thomas did not reply. Will went on: "Tertio when you are working and something or somebody distracts you who is it most likely for that something or somebody to be?"

"Who do you think?"

"Assuming the somebody is that of Anne, what effect does the somebody of Anne have on you? Does it disturb you? When you are close to it – or her – do you react in a particularly masculine way?"

"Of course I do. That is what I find so wrong."

"I can assure you there is nothing wrong about it at all. Indeed I would have been very disconcerted if you had said otherwise. "Quartus do you regard her as being superior to all other beings in the world – male and female – except me, of course."

"Of course I do."

"Thank you very much" – and he climbed back into bed and pretended to sulk.

Thomas got out of his chair and sat next to Will on the bed: "She is the most marvellous creature I have ever beheld. When I am with her the whole of nature takes on a different aspect. Birds sing a different song, flowers seem to glow with more vibrant colours. Even

163

the breeze blows more gently in my face. When we walk in the fields and forests I want to sing."

"I hope you do not. It will frighten the birds and may even deter her."

"We sit by the side of a river and the waters express the words I cannot bring myself to say to her. When she speaks her voice is like music and it is always to the point. She is wise beyond her years and is so full of affection for all those around her, even the animals on which she seems to lavish particular care".

Will turned away from Thomas and picked up a tablet and quill: "Permit me to note what you have just said. It had a certain poetic quality".

Thomas left him and walked about the room impatiently: "Oh! you are just teasing. I hoped talking to you would help to resolve my problem".

"But it will. Have I not just completed a catechism?"

"And what is the result."

Will put down his tablet and looked at his friend seriously and with affection: "Oh! goodness me Thomas. Yes. You are obviously, hopelessly, idiotically head-over-hose in love."

Thomas hurried back to kneel beside the bed: "I thought so. I felt I must be. Nothing else would distract me from the work I have in hand."

"So you see your patron is right. You are already affected adversely."

The young man looked startled: "I am? Perhaps I should – "

Will laughed: "I was joking. Being in love will not affect your work, providing it is reciprocated. Does the young lady returns your feelings?"

"I am certain of it."

"Has she said so?"

"Oh! no, she is much too refined. But I know it from every look she gives me. When we are alone

164

together our hearts go out to one another. I am sure of it."

"Then what is your problem? I cannot imagine the Lady Ann objecting to the match. Indeed, she seems to encourage it. When Sir Thomas returns home you will ask his permission to marry and that will be the end of it."

Thomas hung his head despondently: "Sir Thomas will never agree."

He got up slowly and went back to his chair: "Will, what am I to do?"

Will looked at him with sympathy: "I cannot help you in your relationship with your patron. But I do not see how you can avoid speaking to him about it."

"I will do it. Next time he comes home."

"Good. Glad I was able to help. Good night Thomas. Sleep well, or as well as a frustrated lover can".

Thomas went towards the door, then stopped and turned back. Will looked at him anxiously, wondering why he did not leave him in peace."

"There is something else that concerns me", Thomas said.

Will stifled a groan and leant up on one elbow. Thomas came back to the bed.

"Remembering my experiences in Wight, how can I be sure - I mean will I be able to fulfil my duties in the marital state? Surely my sexual proclivities will prevent it?"

"Oh! pooh. What sexual proclivities? If they are as you suggest, you would not find yourself attracted by the pretty young maid. You would in fact be repelled by her".

"I would?"

"I guarantee. Now it seems to me that there is very little that you, or she, can do until Sir Thomas returns.

So enjoy your courtship. Find a suitable opportunity to express your feelings for her and ensure they are reciprocated. More immediately, please take yourself off to your own bedroom so that I can sleep."

Will punched his pillow and was about to settle his head on it, when the other threw his arms around Will's neck and kissed him firmly on the cheek. Will pushed him away.

"What the hell did you do that for? If you are worried about your sexual proclivities I suggest you refrain from any such demonstrations of affection so far as I am concerned and reserve them for your lady love."

"But Will do you not realise – one of my perplexities is that I really do feel something for you. Is it possible that I love you? Was that master right in Wight to give me a good thrashing?"

Will sat up, took Thomas by the hand: "But of course you love me", he said gently ,"and I love you Thomas. There is no reason why two men should not have affection for one another. That doesn't necessarily mean they want to get married and have children – even if that were possible. I hope we will always have gentle feelings for one another and when I go back to London I hope to write to you. But I have a wife and three children. You will marry and perhaps have many more. Now let me get some sleep, or you will find that any love I feel for you is likely to decline rapidly into sustained dislike."

Thomas looked as if many of the world's problems had been lifted from his individual shoulders. He thanked Will and almost danced from the room. Will put out the candle, checked that the fire was safely dampened in the grate and lay on his pillow in the dying light. He thought back to his own courtship and the happy days of winning a woman's affections, even though in his case she had been rather older than he and had not waited for him to demonstrate his intentions before making hers plain. He was however becoming increasingly aware of the pressures abstinence was placing upon him. Disconcertingly, as he fell asleep he remembered the catechism with Thomas and found the last image in his mind was of another Ann, older, more mature and to him infinitely more desirable than the pretty young Anne.

Chapter 16

Time passed very pleasantly. Winter came and went with little disturbance to the smooth life of the household. Ann bestrode her domestic realm like a monarch, or to Will's admiring eyes something akin to a goddess. When his day's work was done he was very content to sit by a fire in the great living room and listen while his hostess or her protégé played on the spinet especially imported for their enjoyment. Sometimes he would look up from a book and find Ann's eyes on him in what seemed a meditative way. He would smile and she would smile back. Then she would return to her needlework. She was handsome rather than beautiful. Her nose was somewhat large and her lips too full, but the sexual attraction he felt towards her made for a sweet tension between them. He would not have been without it for worlds, but it troubled him and he knew it was one that could never be consummated. The religious conflicts still dividing the country had left him with conflicting views towards accepted doctrine and he was not a devout Christian, but he was still guided by the strong moral environment if his upbringing.

He also had an ambivalent feelings towards young Thomas. There was no doubting the young man's physical attraction and Will was aware there were men who found such beauty irresistible, but once again he would not allow such considerations even to enter his mind. He loved Thomas, certainly, but because of his clarity of mind, universal knowledge and youthful eagerness, which he applied even to the mundane occupation of reading, classifying, annotating and recording the ever-growing mountain of books and documents that rose around him and even threatened to obscure him from the sight of others. Will laughed at this and said one day he would be missing and eventually found buried under a paper and parchment landslide.

His relationship with those around him inspired a need to express his thoughts and feelings in verse, although the intensity of his dramatic work left him little time or even aptitude for poetic expression. He made notes of phrases that came to mind and he found they fitted happily into sonnet form. It was the custom of the age for men with a close affinity to one another to correspond through this medium, but he felt there was something overtly gross in revealing the secrets of one's innermost thoughts and desires. So he refrained from communicating the verses even to the objects of his affection. He recalled the contemptuous reaction of his friend Marley to the exchange of sonnets between Gabriel Harvey in Cambridge and the poet Spenser in Ireland and thought how sad it was that such poetic sentiments should receive public scrutiny and even critical comment.

As a mild winter lapsed into a mellow spring Shakespeare faced with regret the necessity of returning to London, where the theatres began to risk re-opening their stages to the weather. He had produced a body of work he felt sure would satisfy the esurient Henslowe. He explained to Thomas that he had discovered a new way of presenting historical tales to an audience. In the past they had tended to comprise scene after scene of factual, political, heraldic information. To maintain the interest of the audience and give a wider picture of the social environment he was adding something else – the lives of the common people. The history of a nation should be delivered, he decided, not only through the thoughts and actions of the monarchy and peerage, but those who served them.

"Among the books here I have discovered a character called Sir John Oldcastle in a play about Henry the Fifth", he told Thomas. "He was a rebel , a Lollard, who sadly suffered martyrdom. I have introduced him into a play about Henry the Fourth as a link between the king, his son who later becomes Henry the Fifth and the common people. There are scenes of comedy and low-life and an interesting tension between the king and his son. Do you not think that is a splendid idea?"

"Yes. No doubt. But if this character was a genuine historic figure will not his descendants object."

"I doubt that. He may not even have any descendants. He died nearly two hundred years ago."

And so he bid a sad farewell to his friends and surrogate family, who released him only with his promise that he would return as soon as possible. He was received by Henslowe not exactly with open arms, but with only the mildest of censure for his protracted absence. He lost no time in producing Henry the Fourth, which was an instant success. Will was mistaken, however, when he thought the descendants of Sir John would not react. They did so very strongly and there was a threat to have to play taken off. Will was alarmed and asked Henslowe what they should do. In his typical perfunctory way he replied: "What's in a name? We'll change it"; and so he became Sir John Falstaff.

Audiences clamoured for a sequel, which Henslowe insisted Will should supply. Will told him he needed the seclusion of Oxford to produce it at speed and such was the commercial success of the first part that Henslowe agreed with some reluctance to release him from his commitment to play occasional parts without withdrawing his stipend.

He was received back at Oxford with great pleasure by his friends and began to settle into a routine again. One morning he awoke rather later than usual to find the household in a state of noisy commotion. It was customary for everyone to be aroused and about the day's business before six, but on this day there seemed to be more than the usual level of activity. He pulled on some clothes and went out of his room to the top of the stairs leading down to the great hall, in which there was a scene of chaotic bustle. The great tapestries decorating the walls had been removed and men with a multitude of ladders were in the process of hanging replacements. Maids were wandering around engaged in the seemingly pointless work of removing cushions, giving them a flick with feather dusters and placing them on other chairs. A man encased in an impenetrable level of dirt was standing in the huge fireplace and bawling instructions up the chimney. After a few moments a cloud of soot descended upon him, followed by a small boy with an even greater degree of grime on his tiny, half-naked body. He said something to the man, receiving in reply a curse, a slap round the head and a kick in his rear to send him staggering out of the front door.

Will saw Ann approach the man, confront him and, with an imperious wag of her finger, address him with words that practically had him almost grovelling on his knees. Then he followed his acolyte out into the garden. Ann directed two of her maids to clear up the mess the chimney cleaning had caused. Little Anne bustled into the hall, went up to her mistress and gave her news that was obviously of some urgency for Ann hastened out towards the rear of the house followed by Anne and one of her maids.

At this point Will was joined by Thomas, who looked down at the scene of confusion with some amusement.

"His Lordship is returning home", he explained. "She received the news in the early hours and you see the result".

"I thought he was away on extended business for the Queen."

"He has been, in the land of the Danes. But presumably that is now concluded. He has landed at Portsmouth and should be here within two days."

In fact it was several days before he actually arrived. He travelled via London in order to have an audience with the Queen. There were rumours that he was about to be appointed to high office and Ann was greatly concerned that this might mean he would be despatched abroad again on diplomatic business. She was hoping at least for a brief respite from his constant absences so that he could deal with pressing matters regarding the estate.

Because of his delayed arrival, once the business of cleaning the house had been completed, all its occupants sat in near silent, anxious anticipation. The tension was palpable, even to Will and Thomas who both tried to hide from it in their respect havens of literary activity. When they emerged, at meal times, or to fulfil the requirements of social courtesy, they found the mistress of the house, her protégé and most of the servants pale of face and ill-tempered.

At one time Will attempted to lighten the mood by suggesting what a joyous occasion it would be when the master of the house set foot in it after so long an absence. The response from Ann was acerbic to say the least.

"Oh! yes. He will no doubt deposit his dirty laundry on us and will scare us to death with his tales of treachery in high places and the fear of living always in the shadow of the gallows - or worse."

"Is there any worse?" Will asked, once again hoping – and failing - to introduce a lighter atmosphere into the conversation.

"So I am told, but I will certainly not go into details around this dinner table."

So he held his peace and allowed his mien to match the doleful countenances around him. One day, however, as they dispersed after the midday meal she touched him on the arm and said: "Stay a while, Will, and talk to me".

He was glad to do so. He had felt something of a gap, almost a gulf, had opened between them since they had received the news of her husband's return. Thomas went off to his study and Ann sent her protégé away on an errand. The maid servants cluttered with the crockery on the table until she chased them too and was alone with Will. The weather had turned colder and a fire had been built in the huge grate, on either side of which they sat. Unable to tuck his legs under the solid front of his chair, Will stretched them out towards the welcoming blaze. She gazed at the fire, a mournful expression on her face as he waited with some trepidation to find out why she had sought a private audience with him. Suddenly she turned towards him and smiled, her face lighting up as she did so in the glow of the fire.

"Tell me Will", she said, "about your work. I know so little of it. I know you write and the results of your writing are presented by actors on the stage, but how you achieve that and what form it takes I have very little idea."

Will was immensely relieved. Of all the subjects she might have wanted to talk about his writing was likely to be the least troublesome. He was happy to expound at length on the way he expressed the story of a play through the dialogue of his characters, with a few indications of the movements they might perform on the stage.

"Do you mean they eat, drink, fight, engage in the sort of actions we perform in our daily lives?"

"Well, as for fighting, that has to be limited. One can hardly have a full-scale battle, with only half a dozen combatants on a tiny stage."

"They make love perhaps."

Will laughed: "Hardly. As with the wars any question of making love is restricted to words."

"What sort of words. How can one describe such encounters?"

"One does not describe the encounters so much as the feelings the lovers have for one another."

"Such as?"

Will began to feel discussing his work was not as innocuous as he had envisaged.

He attempted to excuse himself: "I have written little of love so far".

"But if you did. How would you present the act of love?"

"The act of love? If by that you mean the physical coupling of two bodies, I find little of virtue in that. What is of dramatic interest is what passes between two people when love overtakes them – either before their copulation or perhaps in retrospect. You cannot reproduce in dialogue the grunts and groans that may or may not form part of the sexual act, nor even the shouts and cries of ecstasy that might accompany it."

"You seem to denigrate the sexual act. That seems a shame in one still so young."

"I do not denigrate it. It can be among the greatest satisfactions mankind can experience. I only think it is not fit matter for stage presentation. No doubt the partakers in Roman orgies, or those who witnessed them, derived satisfaction from them, but the purpose of the dramatist is to touch the intellectual, or even spiritual, lives of his audiences."

Ann got to her feet and strolled to the window, through which the afternoon sun shone weakly, lightening her hair and showing her full figure to advantage. It was one of those moments when he thought of her as a very beautiful woman. Partly out of courtesy when she stood, but also so that he could see her more clearly, he also left his chair but stayed by the fire gazing at her.

"And how would you describe the absence of love? When there is nothing between two people, not even those intellectual or spiritual experiences; how can your actors express that?"

"Ah! that must be the most difficult part of a writer's job. Indeed, I do not know if it has been successfully presented. I certainly have not. The business of the stage is action, physical or mental. I do not see how you can demonstrate inaction."

She turned to him: "So a marriage like mine would not be a suitable subject for dramatic presentation. It is, you know, one that might be described as convenient".

He did not know how to respond and waited for her to continue.

"Here was a man who had never married, who had significant commitments in the public arena, who needed somebody to run his estate, and perhaps be a partner for him as he retired in later life. It would also be an advantage if she was spectacularly rich, which I happened to be."

"But surely", Will ventured, "there was love between you."

"Love? Oh! well, I suppose so. More respect, I believe. Respect and a belief that we could cohabit amicably. And I think we do that – well, when he is here, of course, which I fear is not often."

He tried to relate the conversation to his own work as a writer: "Sad to say such a marriage would only be of dramatic interest if something happened to disturb the equanimity."

"Infidelity perhaps. Particularly if the wife strayed."

"Why yes. One could imagine a husband becoming enraged."

She shivered, left the window and came to the fire, where she warmed her hands.

They were closer now and once again he was aware of the chemical magnetism that affected him so keenly in her company.

"Although of course it is not something one could imagine happening in such an ideal household as this", he said drawing on all his reserves of tact.

She glanced at him with a little smile: "Oh! I think I am a little too old to be thrashing about on a bed with a young man, however attractive he might be. But a women wants to be admired, wants to feel a man is attracted to her, that he has a shoulder she can lean her head on in moments of distress, who holds her in - what was the word I heard you use one day when describing one of your characters? – veneration."

Will felt he could contain himself no longer: "Oh! madam I hold you in the greatest veneration. To me you are all that is excellent in womanhood. You are proud, yet gentle, you care for the people around you and, particularly, I think you care for me. How could I feel anything but a tender love for you, as my benefactress, my idol, my goddess."

"Your goddess! Ah! William how little you know women. Most of us would exchange a lifetime held in such veneration for just a few moments of more earthly bliss."

She put both hands on his shoulders and gazed into his eyes. He felt himself overwhelmed by her closeness, her breasts pressed against him. Everything told him he must try to resist the desires she had awaken in him, that it was for him to behave responsibly in the face of what his upbringing and tradition had told him was the weakness of a woman. But they were alone in the room and unlikely to be disturbed. There was fresh carpeting on the floor and a warm fire in the grate. Would the fire burning in him consume them both, or would it warm the hearts of two lonely people, who sought only a little human warmth and happiness? What was to prevent him from accepting the gift she was bestowing upon him and taking advantage of the opportunity that was offered?

And possibly he would have done so, but at that moment there was a great commotion outside and the door to the room burst open. Young Anne rushed in, closely followed by Thomas. The girl stopped when she saw her mistress, who hastily pushed Will away.

"Why Anne. Master William was just showing me how to actors would rehearse a scene in a play. Whatever is it?"

"Madam, I'm sorry, but a messenger has just arrived. The master is only an hour or so away."

"Heavens! We must be prepared. Summon all the servants. Have them assemble in the hall."

As she hurried from the room, Thomas put out an arm to stop young Anne. She turned upon him in a manner that Will thought was unnecessarily abrupt.

"Not now Thomas. There is work to do."

She followed her mistress.

"We had better hide ourselves away while the women are busy", said Will to Thomas.

The young man looked totally downcast and Will took pity on him: "What is it Tom?"

"She is so angry with me. I can't help it. I told her there is nothing I can do until I have spoken to the

Master. And she just rounded on me. She said he would never agree to our marriage. She said I was weak and hopeless. I love her. I am in despair, Will."

"It's a lover's tiff, Thomas. It will pass. You'll see."

At that point Anne returned: "Thomas my mistress is asking for you. She says there is a man's work to be done."

He started to leave the room, but stopped to talk to her. She waved him away, however, and said: "Although in that case why she sent for you I cannot imagine".

He waved his arms in despair and left the room. Anne turned to Will and gave a little curtsey.

"You must excuse me, sir. My mistress needs me."

He held up a hand to stop her.

"Anne. You should not be unkind to him. He loves you dearly."

"Much good it may do me. You do not know Sir Thomas. He will be adamant. He lives in a different world from us. To him duty comes first. First, last and always. A personal matter like love between two people does not even enter his head."

"But he must talk to him, explain how you two feel about one another."

"Oh! sir he must not do that. Think what it will do for me. He may even banish me from the house."

"Surely not."

She was now in a state of some panic: "What will happen to me then? What will I do? Go on the streets. Live in taverns as a troll, a slut, for any man to take".

"You would never do that Anne. I don't believe it."

"A girl has to live. And do you not think I could. Do you not think me attractive?"

She went close to him. He caught the whiff of a cheap, but attractive scent.

"Would the men not want me?"

"Of course they would, but that's not the issue."

"Do you find me attractive? Do you want me?"

"Anne, you are Thomas's girl."

"But I'm not Thomas's girl, am I. And will never be. I will never know what it is like to be with a man."

She burst into tears and ran from the room.

There was the sound of horses' hooves and the light of lanterns through the windows. He did not relish mingling with the new arrivals so he went to his room, where he stoked the fire, lit candles and settled down to read. After a while the noise from elsewhere in the house subsided. He undressed, pulled on a nightgown and, still clutching his book climbed into bed.

He must have dozed off to sleep. The candle was burning low and there was little light or heat from the fireplace. He heard a light tap on the door and, surprised, called: "Come in". He was not expecting any visitors, but thought it might be young Thomas. To his astonishment the visitor was the young Anne, dressed in a long gown, her hair falling over her shoulders and almost to her waist. She came up to the bed and stood gazing at him with what he thought was a challenging look in her eyes.

"I hope I am not disturbing you, Master Will", she said.

He looked at the beautiful young girl, with the evidence of her youthful figure showing under the gown and thought – yes you are disturbing me, but not in the way you think. Then she disturbed him even more. With a sudden movement she lifted the gown and pulled it over her head. She was naked underneath.

"Well", she demanded. "Do you not find me attractive?"

"Yes. Yes. I do. You are very beautiful."

"Well then."

With another abrupt movement she pulled back the

bedclothes to demonstrate that he did, in fact, find her not only attractive, but extremely desirable. He clutched himself in his embarrassment.

"Is there something wrong, Master Thomas?" she asked.

"Of course. You should not be here. Like that."

"Let's put it right, then, shall we."

And with that she climbed in beside him.

When it was over he stroked her gently and whispered: "I hope I did not hurt you".

"A little, a little, but oh! it was beautiful, beautiful."

The candle spluttered out. The light from the fire dimmed and as he lay there, holding the warm young body in his arms, he thought: "I must go home. I must return to my wife and family, and soon".

Chapter 17

With the arrival of Sir Thomas the house took on a completely different atmosphere. It was as if a small port, hitherto a haven only for boats and pleasure craft, had suddenly received a visit from a large ocean-going man-of-war. For a start, he brought with him his own entourage, including a secretary and man-servant, as well as the servants who had attended him and his horses on his journeys, all of whom required accommodation.. This meant that the rooms occupied by Will and young Thomas were no longer available to them and had to be given up. As a temporary expedient Will moved in with his friend, but it was understood that both would have to move out as soon as that could be arranged.

The master's presence also required changes to the household routine. Lady Ann quite firmly insisted that meal times were not altered so that dinner was still taken in the middle of the day, with lighter repasts for breakfast and supper. New faces appeared at table. In addition to the senior members of Sir Thomas's party, there were occasional visitors, particularly from the University. He had resigned his Fellowship at Merton College, but was still held in high esteem among the doctorate and his opinion was often sought on matters of policy.

Shortly after his arrival a banquet was held at the College in his honour and he returned from that event in a state of great excitement. Young Thomas later told Will he had been given assurances that his proposal for a library would be welcomed and supported. Sources were already being sought for additional funding. When he had been asked about a suitable candidate for the post of librarian he had expressed himself greatly pleased with his protégé's work during his absence. He assured Thomas that when the time came to appoint one he would not be looking elsewhere.

Will assumed Thomas would be delighted at this news, but he now seemed even more certain that Sir Thomas would oppose his liaison with Anne. He had been unwittingly privy to a conversation between Sir Thomas and his wife, from which it appeared he had become estranged from his sister, a young lady he had at one time dearly loved. Against his advice and firm instruction the girl had eloped with a commoner. Sir Thomas had disowned her and wanted it understood that she would never be welcome in his house.

Although dominating and even magisterial, however, Sir Thomas's influence on the household was, however, far from malign. He was for the most part a kind and genial man, whose humour made itself evident even when he was describing incidents relating to the most important affairs of state. He could obviously not reveal the details of his dealings with English statesmen or foreign potentates, but his stories of his travels in foreign countries were full of amusing anecdotes, revealing an essentially humanistic view of the sometimes diverse communities through which he travelled and the peoples with whom he had dealings.

He was knowledgeable on matters relating to the development of public theatre and confirmed that Her Majesty was continuing to evince a keen interest in its development. A number of noblemen were vying for opportunities to patronise theatre companies. One day when the whole household was gathered round the table for dinner he asked Will what contributions he was making to the dramatic scene. Will told him about his historical plays, the first of which had been well received. After that he admitted he was uncertain what

182

direction to take.

"Look abroad young man", Sir Thomas said, "Go to Italy, the home of the narrative. You will find more tales to turn into dramatic presentation in one city state than in the whole of the rest of Europe. They have a most diverting theatrical form known as the *commedia del arte*. It is a little frivolous to my taste, but very diverting. Then there are Greece, France, Spain. Even Denmark has its share of stories to tell. I heard a tale there of a king who was murdered by a kinsman, who then took not only his realm, but his wife as well. The murdered king's son is driven to distraction by his loss, swears revenge, and they all die in the end."

There was silence while the rest of the company digested this tale with their venison. Sir Thomas looked round at the solemn faces, laughed and said: "I thought it most diverting."

Will found it difficult to believe such a congenial man would react adversely to his protégé's desire to lead a normal married life. He had urged Thomas to confront his master and when he looked across at his friend he thought from the look of determination on his face that he was about to take his advice.

Sir Thomas was recounting the praise he had received from various high-ranking members of the establishment for his work in foreign diplomacy on behalf of the Queen. There were indications that, if his next assignment proved as successful, he would be granted employment among the highest offices. He might even be appointed Secretary of State. Regretfully, this might mean a further extended stay abroad, possibly in The Hague, but once that was over he was optimistic the Queen would grant him leave to return to England and remain in the bosom of his family. If that happened he was determined to give as much time and attention as he could to his over-riding ambition, that of serving his beloved University, its Colleges and, indeed, the country generally, by establishing what could be the first public library in Europe. He turned towards his namesake and smiled.

"And when I do, it is my intention to appoint our young friend here as the first librarian."

There was a little murmur of commendation and applause around the table. Young Thomas bowed his head and looked both pleased and embarrassed.

"You do me great honour, sir. Your confidence in my ability and desire to further my advancement and happiness are a source of constant gratification to me. I will always do my utmost to justify your trust."

"Well spoken young man", said Sir Thomas and turned to his wife in order to carry on a private conversation with her. Then Thomas took the unusual step of standing while his master and mistress were still seated.

"There is one thing, however, on which I venture to seek your sympathy and support."

Will, anticipating what he was about, looked up at him and smiled encouragement. He gave a little nudge of his head to urge him on.

"There is one thing, however, on which I venture to seek your sympathy and support."

Sir Thomas stopped talking to his wife and turned to him in surprise. He waited. The young Thomas seemed to be screwing up his courage to the utmost and eventually blurted out: "I refer to the question of my marriage."

At this a silence fell upon the table. The individual conversations ceased. Everyone stopped eating. All, without exception, turned their gazes upon Sir Thomas to see how he would react. He himself lowered the portion of food on the end of his knife and looked at his protégé in surprise

"What was that? Did I hear you say something about marriage?"

"Well, yes, sir." Thomas now spoke bravely, although his lips trembled and it was obvious he was in a state of parlous fear. "I know you have always indicated that you would prefer me to remain celibate, but I thought since your own marriage – "

"My own marriage? My marriage! What has my marriage got to do with you, or anybody other than myself and my dear wife?"

"Well, nothing really, only – "

"Good. Then let's have no more talk about marriage, shall we? I thought we had agreed about that from the beginning of our arrangement."

Obviously regarding the matter as concluded, he carried the portion of meat to his mouth and chewed with relish. The chatter around the table resumed and with it a notable easing of the tension.

Will was not sure whether to be disappointed or relieved. He had begun to fear he might have advised his friend wrongly. The danger appeared to have passed, except that the young man was still on his feet. He gestured to him as subtly as he could, indicating that the matter was closed and he should resume his seat. Thomas ignored him and spoke again.

"As you wish, sir. It is just that I thought your concern would relate only to the situation I was then in with no attachment, or prospect of one. Now I am older and have found myself drawn to a particular party."

An involuntary cry came from Lady Ann: "Thomas no".

Her husband looked at her in surprise, then at young Thomas.

He put down his knife and stood slowly. His voice was cold: "A particular party?"

185

This was an age of beards, which at times of wrath could be said to bristle. On this occasion not only Sir Thomas's beard, but his whole demeanour bristled. His form took on a new dimension, enlarged into a shape both threatening and alarming. One could imagine him facing down recalcitrant statesmen from foreign lands, even kings and princes who had dared to question the might of the sovereign he served. Now he was confronting a mere acolyte. Lady Ann thought it an appropriate moment to intervene.

"I think, my love, this is something better discussed between ourselves in private."

"Nothing of the sort. I do not think there is anything private here. The young man seems to suggest that he has become involved with someone. If that is the case the sooner we know about it the better. Presumably it is some girl from the neighbouring village who has set her cap at him. If so, it will be necessary for her to take her head gear back and shake it at someone else."

"I really think we should – " Ann began, but young Thomas seemed determined on self-destruction.

"It is not a village girl", he said.

Will wanted to run round the table and put a hand over his mouth to stop him saying any more. But he was powerless. His friend had placed his head upon the block and nothing could stop the executioner's axe from falling.

"It is the young Anne, your wife's protégé", said Thomas "I do love her most devotedly and believe she – "

Sir Thomas held up a hand as he might have done to demand silence from an obdurate foreign emissary. It was effective. Thomas stopped his avowal in mid-sentence, his mouth still open. His patron turned to his wife: "Did you know about this?"

"I thought there might be – "

"You thought there might be what?

"The beginnings of a liaison, but – "

"A liaison! In your own household. You were not taking care."

Ann bridled : "Well as for that – ", but her protest was unavailing.

"And how long has this been going on in my house, during my absence, while I have been involved in affairs of state at the highest level. I have a traitor in my midst, one who meddles with females who are under my care."

Young Thomas had the temerity to protest: "It was nothing like that, I assure you".

"You can assure me of nothing, my good sir. You can go to your room. I will deal with you later."

He turned to the young Anne, who sat with a handkerchief held to her face, her eyes staring wide in fear and dismay.

"As for you young lady, I hereby banish you from this house. I never want to set eyes on you again."

At this the lady Ann got to her feet: "Sir Thomas, I must protest. Anne is my protégé. She is here under my protection. I can vouch that she has not been involved in any wrong doing. I will not have her ordered from the house and I insist that you discuss this matter with me as the head of your household."

"I, madam, am the head of this household."

"No sir, your very absence from it for sometimes years on end deprives you of that responsibility. You delegate it to me and I have conducted its affairs with devoted care. I am responsible for this girl and I will not have her placed in jeopardy, which would certainly be the case if she were banished."

Sir Thomas started to respond, but to the astonishment of the others around the table, Ann asserted an additional degree of authority. She held up

187

her hand as her husband had with the same imperious impact:

"We have said enough in this relatively public arena. I am sure there comes a time in your dealings with international affairs when the main protagonists find it necessary to discuss matters between themselves. That is also the case in our small domestic crisis."

For a moment they faced one another, then the magisterial demeanour Sir Thomas obviously adopted before foreign potentates seemed to diminish: "I do not like to think of ourselves as protagonists, my dear", he said. He turned to the others around the table and dismissed them with a wave of his hand: "Get out all of you. My wife and I have to discuss affairs of state".

Everyone was more than anxious to leave the troubled scene. They got to their feet even overturning chairs in their haste. Anne rushed away to hers, choking back her tears. Will accompanied Thomas back to their room, and they remained there, not daring to leave, only occasionally venturing a head around a door to hear the muffled sounds of a discussion that went on for hours. Eventually maids were sent to summon them and they gathered round the table in the dining room. Sir Thomas had a meeting at the University and did not join them. Ann told them that Anne to would be allowed to remain, but would be permitted no further intercourse with Thomas, who would return to his accommodation at the University. It would also be necessary for Will to make way for the new arrivals in the household.

He decided, however, not to go back to the University, but to take the opportunity to pay his belated visit to his home in Stratford. Messages had reached him saying that his son was not well. Both his wife and his mother were urging to return, at least for a visit. So it was that a few days later Will bade his sad farewells to a household that had given him so much comfort and support. He travelled light, leaving his effects and his precious manuscripts behind with Thomas, who promised to take great care of them.

Will's feelings were mixed as he made his way towards Stratford. On the one hand he looked forward to seeing his children, who must have grown out of all recognition. On the other he was anxious about the reception he might receive from his wife, whose letters had not contained any intimation of affection and who might justly feel aggrieved at the prolonged absence of a husband who contributed little to the family's welfare.

The passage of time meant he need no longer fear any retribution for his former misdeeds, but he did not relish a confrontation with his father. He had turned down the prospect of a prosperous future as a glove-maker on the presumption that he would make a fortune in the professional theatre. He had not succeeded. Indeed, he appeared to have spent a great deal of his time in relative idleness in Oxford, while his family faced an uncertain future both financially and in terms of parental support.

He would not be able to stay long in Stratford. His funds were almost exhausted. He could hardly rely on his mother's generosity to support him further. It was essential that he return to London as soon as possible, with the anticipation that he would continue to be employed as an actor and, more importantly, that his scripts would be bought and performed. Life was very uncertain and, as he rode towards his home, his only consolation was in observing the beauties of the countryside that revealed themselves at every horse's stride. It was spring and his poet's mind drew inspiration from the fresh green foliage sprouting on trees and hedgerows and the glimpses of yellow and blue from daffodils and bluebells he could glimpse in the woods.

The sense of space and fresh air was something he had missed in London, for all that city's human attractions. Even in Oxford the environment seemed to enclose him and drive his spirit down to a demanding page, the four walls of a gloomy room, or a limited view through a window. As he travelled he breathed deeply an air free from either the pollution of a metropolis or the atmosphere of intellectual restraint. Even his horse seemed to relish the freedom, trotting at an easy pace and bearing his rider with a jaunty step.

He did not hurry, spending a night in Woodstock and guiltily aware that he was in no haste to return home. When he did arrive he was greeted coolly, his wife curtseying deeply and avoiding his eyes. He in turn bowed and wondered whether he should advance and embrace her and the three children clustered around her skirts. Instead she ordered them to him. The two girls obeyed, but the son remained with his mother, gazing at him with uncertain eyes and clutching her skirts. He looked pale and thin and was obviously not in good health.

A servant came and took his horse away. His mother came out of the house and embraced him warmly. His father was at work all day. She looked in concern at the sparse luggage he carried and asked if his effects were following. When told that there were none she expressed her concern that he was not staying long.

He did not respond and his wife led the way into the house, which he found much as he left it. He had, however, a sense of alienation. He felt he did not belong in this house where he had once spent so many happy years. As he sat with his family at a welcoming repast he looked around him at what had once been familiar sights and could not see in them aspects of his present life. Since he had left them behind he had travelled with strangers, had spent time in the hurly-burly of the London theatre and had become involved in the much grander surroundings of a large house, with expensive draperies on the walls, fine furniture and servants to wait on his every wish.

He looked at his wife, who still avoided his gaze, and thought that it would be necessary for him that night to revive their intimacy. His children still regarded him with something approaching suspicion and he wondered what he could do to regain their trust and perhaps, he thought, their love. He had not intended to stay long, but felt he owed it to them all to make an effort with them as well as with his wife. Perhaps, he thought, there would be opportunities alone with her when he could explain what it was he was seeking to do and his hopes for the longer-term future.

His father, when he arrived in the evening, was formal to the point of coldness. He took an opportunity when the women were otherwise engaged and he was alone with Will to question him upon his intentions. He suggested that Will's future lay in Stratford, with his wife and family, perhaps in the glove making business. He seemed perplexed at Will's description of life in the theatre world and asked pertinent questions about his ability to earn enough to pay his way. He pointed out that he and Will's mother were housing his wife and children and made it clear he did not regard this as a situation that could continue indefinitely. Will reassured him the future held a promise not only of a steady income, but also of patronage from those in high places who supported the theatre and those who wrote for it. He even went so far as to mention the interest the Queen herself was taking in theatre companies like the one for which he worked.

As for his wife, the possibility of a quiet sympathetic word with her was doomed from the moment she made it clear that, although she would continue to acknowledge him as her husband and the father of her children, from now on they would sleep separately and be no more to one another than strangers in the same household.

After Will had been at home a few days, there was great excitement in the town. A touring theatre company was setting up on the green. Will asked his wife to come with him to see them prepare for their show and, although she refused at first, eventually he persuaded her. It was a scene he knew well, He could not see anyone he recognised, but he introduced himself to the leading actor, who greeted him with astonishment and acclaim.

"What an honour! Master Shakespeare! We are presenting one of your plays. Richard the Third". He formed himself into a grotesque shape and quoted: "Now is the winter of our discontent".

He called to the members of the company, who were busy preparing the stage: "Gather round everybody. We have a celebrity. The greatest playwright in the land."

The others did gather round and there was much hand shaking and back slapping. Will felt, for the first time in a long while, supremely happy. This was where he belonged. This was his true home. Not the domestic hearth in Stratford, although he did love his wife and his children, nor the more luxurious household in Oxford, despite his love for those who lived there, but here among these strangers who created a kind of reality for him on stage, which turned into a home for him when he occupied it as an actor, or wrote for it as a poet. He must try and make his wife understand. If he explained she would see. He would explain he did not love her the less for it. He turned to speak to her. But she had gone.

PART 4

Chapter 18

Philip Henslowe was not having a good day. In the first place he was dealing with the accounts of his various enterprises and, although he regarded himself as a man of business fully capable of earning money from even the most unlikely sources, the effort of writing details of his dealings in what were known as his books proved almost too much for his poor numerate skills. Then he had quarrelled with his wife, a not exceptional event, but on this occasion one that concerned his step-daughter, for whom he had developed a sincere and filial affection. The principal actor in the theatrical company currently occupying his theatre had begun to pay court to her. Her mother approved, no doubt influenced by the glamour emanating from the actor's theatrical standing. He, however, believed the girl, extremely pretty and not without wit and intelligence, should save herself for a worthier suit. Although he was quite prepared to employ actors, make money from their performances and lend some of it back to them at quite exorbitant interest, he did not wish to find himself the step-father-in-law of one.

Then he had had an argument with Will Shakespeare, the most promising in the group of writers providing material in what so far had been a crowded and successful season at his Rose Theatre. He hated arguments with members of his company. He expected people who worked for him to do what they were told. After all, if it wasn't for him they would not have the work. The playwright had not long ago returned from one of his extended visits to Oxford, although he had compensated to some extent for his absences there by returning with scripts for plays that were proving very popular and successful.

His first play, A Midsummer Night's Dream, had been well received, as had his reworking of The Taming of the Shrew. Then there had been the three parts of Henry VI and an astonishing play about Richard Crookshank. His two parts of Henry IV had introduced an entirely new aspect of historical drama. He had included characters and scenes from low life, although the controversy over the character identified as Sir John Oldcastle had created certain legal difficulties until Shakespeare had agreed to change his name to Falstaff.

Now the playwright was saying he had run out of inspiration and did not know where to look for further sources. Henslowe did not care a fig for inspiration and so far as he was concerned a writer's sources were in his own head. He suggested Will should collaborate with other playwrights in his team, such as Barksted, Barnes, Fraunce, Pickering, Rankin. Will rejected this with scorn and pointed out they were journeymen writers, incapable of producing anything but run-of-the-mill dramas, unworthy to be ranked alongside Marley and Kydd, or, he added, himself.

Henslowe retorted that Kydd had managed to write only one really successful play, The Spanish Tragedy. As for Marley, he was an exception, a poet of great power and authority, in a league far ahead of Shakespeare. At this Will started to become abusive and asked Henslowe why he thought he was an authority on what constituted a well-written play. He was, after all, only a businessman, responsible for purely commercial enterprises. He might have been successful in establishing a theatre, but it appeared that he was even proposing to use that as a venue for bear baiting and fighting.

As if in confirmation of this view Henslowe had parted from him on fighting terms. Will said he would be returning to Oxford to begin work on another play, but did not at the moment have any idea what the subject might be. Henslowe let him go without demure. He certainly did not intend to allow the playwright to escape his clutches. He might be an uncultured businessman, viewing the theatre as a mining enterprise, but having uncovered the pure gold of a talent like Shakespeare, it was important to sieve it gently in the pan and not allow it to be scattered for some other prospector to garner

He looked out of the window of the room he used as an office in an upper storey of the Rose Theatre and let his mind dwell on the aspect of cottage roofs and cluttered streets that represented his fiefdom. Down there were the inns, lodging houses and brothels that brought his wealth. He could allow himself the indulgence of a risky investment in the cultural development that was gripping London. The exploitation of young women in his houses of low repute, rich though the pickings were, often brought bring him a certain notoriety, but running a theatre, and perhaps more than one, with the approval of the great ones of the age, could result in fame and even glory.

The bright spot in his current horizon was the expectation that he was about to receive a visit from someone who occupied a most august position among the realm's nobility and who in addition ranked high among the poets and playwrights of the age. He had been astonished to receive a message from no less a person than Edward de Vere, Earl of Oxford, saying that he wished to visit him and view his theatre. Many stories circulated about the dissolute life of this young nobleman, but Philip knew better than to heed what might be no more than malicious gossip. The Earl, descended from a family that had crossed the sea with William the First, with a castle that was the wonder and envy of all those destined to spend their lives in humbler dwellings, could bring to him and his theatre a degree of wealth and lordly influence.

Only one matter relating to the forthcoming visit concerned him. The Earl had sent for his consideration and possible performance the scripts of plays he had written. They had, it appeared, been performed by de Vere's own company, the Oxford Men, apparently with some success and his lordship wanted them to receive a wider audience. Henslowe had shown them to his leading actor, Alleyn, who had described them as poor stuff, well-enough written, but full of scholarly allusions and obscure phrases. He had heard of the Oxford Men, who were mainly amateurs. There had also been a group known as the Oxford Boys, but following an unspecified incident, it had been disbanded. Alleyn's advice was to take as much of the Earl's money and patronage as he was prepared to offer but tactfully reject suggestions he should produce them. Henslowe decided that if the Earl was prepared to finance productions of his work he was not going to be the one to turn them away.

The Earl arrived, accompanied by a sizeable entourage. As a rehearsal was taking place in the theatre this created a chaotic scene in which the Earl's followers, who were somewhat drunk, rampaged throughout the auditorium and even on to the stage, seizing prop swords and conducting mock fights. They had dined well on their journey from Castle Hedingham, quantities of ale obviously forming a large part of their repast. Even their horses deposited so much fertilizer at the theatre entrance that approach to it was seriously impeded. Henslowe was dismayed at the thought that his Lordship might be expecting him to find accommodation for his unruly throng until he was reassured to learn that the intention was to travel on to

Thomas Walsingham's house not far away in Scadbury.

The Earl lounged, as far as it was possible to do so, on a hard wooden chair with an upright back facing Henslowe across his managerial desk. With almost regal insolence his lordship tossed a manuscript across to the manager and invited him to put it into production forthwith. Henslowe pointed out that his lordship had already sent him other scripts and he was awaiting reports on them from his production advisors. Oxford treated this news with disdain, expressing astonishment that there should be any need for advice other than what he himself, as a renowned poet and playwright, could offer.

Determined to be tactful, Henslowe explained that this was a technical matter of staging and casting, of deciding on the resources required for a particular presentation. Oxford wanted to know what was meant by resources and Henslowe explained that some productions required a certain amount of financial support. At the mention of finance a chill entered the conversation. Sensing this, the manager attempted to ameliorate his indiscretion by expressing his appreciation that his lordship would not wish to be worried by such mundane matters, succeeding as he did to a long line of distinguished aristocracy, with wealthy estates not only in Essex, but elsewhere in the nation. He went on to hint tactfully that a struggling theatre company would welcome anything in the way of patronage, particularly if it facilitated the production of a particular playwright's creative efforts.

His Lordship was blunt: "If you are looking to me for funds I must disabuse you from the start. It may appear to you and others like you that a fine castle and acres of land mean there are pots of gold ready to be disbursed to the apparently needy of this world, but nothing could be further from the truth".

There was the sound of a crash from the direction of the stage, cries of alarm from the acting company and roars of laughter from the band of invaders. His lordship waved a hand in that direction.

"Keeping a roof over the heads of that rabble out there and providing them with food and clothes on their backs requires a king's ransom, to say nothing of providing myself with the same facilities. You cannot eat a castle. A field does not yield a winter's rations unless someone has ploughed it and sowed it with corn during the summer. There is something called a balance. You yourself must encounter it in your theatrical dealings. It is a fine line that must be trod with care. Stay above it and you may enjoy a happy, useful life. Fall below it and there is nothing to save you from penury and even starvation. What you see in me now, Master Henslowe, is someone attempting to walk on that balance as if on a rope stretched between two trees and from which he might fall at any moment."

This speech was followed by silence. His Lordship quaffed from the wine thoughtfully been provided for him. Henslowe considered how it was possible that someone who owned so much property, who had the ability to create so much wealth and was responsible for the welfare of so many retainers could be reduced to penury. This was the man, Henslowe thought, who was proposing to inflict his ill-written, amateurish creations on the highly regarded, professional company he had established with so much care and diligence. He'd be damned if he would encourage it. On the other hand the Earl's influence spread far beyond the walls of the theatre. He could not afford to upset him. What he needed was to gain his patronage, if not his financial support, without necessarily committing himself to staging his wretched plays.

"Your lordship must understand", he began in a

voice on to which the honey of subservience had been poured in abundance, "you must understand that producing a play in a professional theatre such as this is a cooperative enterprise".

"Cooperative? I do not understand. What do you mean by cooperative?"

"Few of our authors write their plays individually. Most of them are produced in collaboration with others. Of all the writers with whom I have dealings only perhaps one or two have the ability and the dedication to complete a script by their own efforts. There is Thomas Kydd, whose Spanish Tragedy was such a success, but you see he has not followed it with anything quite as good. There is Kit Marley, of course, but he is exceptional, I mean really exceptional. I think he must be regarded as the finest writer of drama and verse in the land."

"Marley – yes, I have heard of him. Indeed, I am hoping to meet him at Tom Walsingham's. You do not think my plays could match his then?"

Henslowe knew how important it was to be subservient. He cringed: "It is a question of opportunity. He spent many years at Cambridge and since then has worked exclusively in the theatre. It is a technical matter, your Lordship, something difficult to apply unless you are involved day by day in stage working."

"Sadly, I can give very little time to writing. There are so many other matters that take up the time of – "

"Of course. You have estates to run, affairs of state to manage."

"I have travelled far and wide. I have experience of life seldom equalled by those who lead more humdrum lives. I have much to offer. You may think of me sir simply as a knight with aristocratic, even royal antecedents, whose contributions to the state are restrained by matters of political or perhaps religious governance, but that is not the whole man, sir."

He paused again and Henslowe thought: no, from what I have heard that is certainly not the whole man, but what else is there? He waited and was told.

"I have a soul like anyone else and my soul manifests itself in poetry, in the desire to enlighten my fellow man with the results of my experience. I do that in a small way with my own company, but it is parochial. I have a message for the world."

Henslowe, who sometimes had more insight than he was given credit for, thought to himself: yes, and perhaps you have a need for confession; then he quickly put such Catholic thoughts out of his mind in case some spiritual informer should report such heretical thoughts to a higher authority.

He picked up the manuscript and waved it in the air.

"You need someone else to work on this with you. To put it into – what might be called dramatic form. It would relieve you of the burden of finalising a script, release you to concentrate your valuable time on other matters, such as – " he hesitated, then almost as a question added : "redeeming your finances ?"

Oxford considered these possibilities: "How might I encounter someone who could assist me in this way?"

"You are visiting Sir Thomas Walsingham. He is a keen supporter of the theatre and plays host to many writers, most of whom work for me."

His Lordship finished his drink and got to his feet.

"I will think on what you say, although I may not necessarily act on it. You are an honest man Henslowe and I respect you for it."

Henslowe, reflecting that he had not often been described as honest, also rose and summoned assistance. The Earl with some difficulty managed to call his recalcitrant followers to order and somehow

202

succeeded in getting them mounted. As he left the manager asked him to be so kind as to remember him to Thomas and his good wife, something the noble lord disregarded as soon as it had been uttered. Nevertheless, although he would have been loathe to admit it, the Earl of Oxford, for all his arrogance, left the Rose Theatre wiser than when he arrived.

Chapter 19

Audrey Walsingham liked to think of herself as a good housekeeper. She had helped to run her father's small estate in Norfolk and had experienced no difficulties in managing the modest domestic affairs of her husband Tom as the younger son of a distinguished land-owning father. But on the death of Tom's brother Edmund he had inherited an estate covering a vast area south of the river Thames, including the family home at Scadbury, land in Chiselhurst, St Paul's Cray, Footscray, St Mary Cray, North Cray, Mottingham, Lee, Orpington, Bromley and Bexley. As if that were not enough, her husband was an active patron of what could be loosely called the "arts", but more specifically related to the activities that comprised the rapidly developing professional theatre and the characters who were involved in it.

Many of these seemed to occupy a world far divorced from the quiet secluded life she had known in her native Norfolk, where indeed even a visit from a travelling theatre group was a rarity to be experienced no more than once or twice in a lifetime. Now here she was not a metaphoric stone's throw from the latest permanent building to house regular theatrical performances and finding her new home invaded by as eccentric a string of personalities as might be found on the boards of those theatres.

There was an attractive young man named Christopher, or Kit, Marley, or Marlowe, to whom Tom Walsingham seemed to have become particularly attached. Then there was his wild friend Thomas Kydd, with whom he insisted on sharing a room for reasons that were not clear to her until her husband explained them, greatly to her astonishment. There was a surly character named Robert Greene, who seemed to carry with him a perpetual grudge against the rest of the world.

Then there were those not connected with the theatrical profession, but who seemed to make the house a staging post in their journeys about the country and the world. These added a more sinister aspect to the otherwise colourful atmosphere generated by the writers and actors. Chief among these was the enigmatic Poley, who seemed to act as a messenger between her husband and his uncle, Sir Francis Walsingham, who lived in London and was reputed to play a leading part in the network of agents protecting the Queen, anticipating Popish plots and actions against her person or her government. This aspect of her husband's activities was of particular concern to his wife, aware as she was of the shadow cast upon all civil life at that time by the storm clouds of religious controversy.

Despite this she enjoyed her role in her husband's new-found status, ruling her regiment of servants with a firm hand and ensuring that her guests received the kind of hospitality that was expected from the mistress of a large household. She even found time to listen to their complaints about the unfairness of the world, the state of the theatre, the iniquity of their fellow men. Some of them flirted with her, for she was a handsome woman and still young enough to turn heads. Sadly the ones from whom she might have welcomed attention seemed more interested in attracting the notice of their fellows.

Then one day she received word that her husband was to receive a visit from a guest of a rather higher social standing than any of those who had come before. Her household was already well populated and she was now to be hostess to no less a person than a peer of the realm, a noble earl, whose reputation as a man of taste and fashion had preceded him. The Earl of Oxford had been visiting Tom's uncle for reasons that were not disclosed. He had called on the Rose Theatre in London and was looking to the Walsinghams to receive him and his entourage.

Audrey's organisational skills and the resources of the surrounding countryside were stretched to their limits. They would arrive in the evening and would hopefully expect only a light meal before retiring, but the next day it would be necessary to mount a major banquet as the midday meal. A vast quantity of provisions was brought in and stored. Additional servants were hired. A whole suite of rooms was prepared for his lordship and special arrangements made for out-houses to act as sleeping quarters for his servants. New expensive linen was purchased to line his lordship's bed. Their horses would have to be refreshed or even replaced for their journey back home.

Thomas Walsingham viewed the portending visit of the Earl with a certain amount of trepidation. He had heard stories of his licentious life style and did not relish the prospect of admitting him into his household. He confided his concerns to Kit Marley and the playwright agreed. He told his host that the young Edward de Vere had spent but a year at Cambridge, even though he had matriculated there at the age of eight and a half. Since then he had led a life punctuated by incidents serving only to accentuate his reputation as a rabble-rouser. This was scarcely mitigated by the fact that his father's life had been even more reprehensible. At least the young Edward waited for one wife to die before marrying again. His father drove one wife away by his atrocious behaviour, married another without divorcing the former and kept a mistress at the same time. (She was later accused of being a whore by his brothers-in-law, who with their servants, dragged her from her house and cut off her nose as a punishment.)

These considerations were very much in the minds of Tom and his wife as they awaited the Earl. Their anxieties were not allayed as the time of his expected arrival passed and evening light dwindled into night. Host and hostess made repeated visits to the front door of their house and servants remained at their stations, fidgeting and yawning, scratching themselves, poking one another in the ribs, and sometimes lapsing into unseemly laughter. At last, out of the darkness, some torches could be seen and the sound of horses' hooves grew louder. Those waiting could hear much laughter and loud voices, sometimes carrying words that the mistress of the house did not like to have voiced before servants. As the entourage approached it was apparent that many of them were drunk. They rolled from side to side, on occasion in danger of falling from their mounts. Only their leader sat upright in his saddle, caparisoned in scarlet and gold, which shone even in the fading light. He waved a sword above his head and sang a song the words of which could not be deciphered by the listeners.

They drew up in disorderly array, with much cheering and carousing, and their leader leapt from his horse and swept his hat from his head almost to the floor in obeisance to the lady of the house. She curtseyed and Tom Walsingham bowed low. Then to the astonishment of all, the Earl stood erect, walked up to Audrey, flung his arms around her and kissed her roundly on the mouth.

Trying to hide his anger and dismay, Tom could do no more than introduce himself and his wife:

"Tom Walsingham, your lordship; my good wife Audrey. You are very welcome to our humble house."

The Earl released Audrey – much to her relief – and

turned to Tom.

"And very glad we are to be here, Master Tom. We have had a devilish journey, with only the foul refreshments from a pig-sty of an inn to sustain us on the way."

With that he marched into the house, ignored the rows of bowing servants, found his way to a settle by a fire in the large reception hall, threw himself down upon it and went fast asleep.

That night in bed Audrey Walsingham berated her husband, demanding to know how he could allow such things to happen. He asked what things she was referring to specifically. Her unhelpful reply was: "Everything".

Then on reflection she added : "Well, for a start. He comes right up to me and kisses me, not on the cheek as the French are reputed to do, but on my mouth, on lips I had reserved solely for you, my husband".

"I could hardly have stopped him. Even if I knew he was about to do it, what would you have me do? Get in between you."

"Then he throws himself on to my best settle. He muddied everything, the floor, my carpeting, cushions I had embroidered with my own hands. Following which those ruffians he brought with him rampaged through the house, fouling the bedrooms, chasing the maids. I caught one of them with Mary probably just in time to prevent her being ravaged."

"Oh! I hardly think it would have come to that."

"No? Then what was his head doing up her skirt? I pulled him out by his shirt tails, which might indicate that his nether garments were about his ankles. I have instructed the maids to remain in their rooms, lock and if necessary barricade their doors. The men have been garrisoned in the barn, where I hope they will remain."

"Where is his Lordship now?"

"He and Kit Marley and Robert Greene have sat up talking and drinking. No doubt they will all finish up insensible on the floor."

They did not finish up insensible, but they certainly drank a great deal. The ever hospitable Tom Walsingham had set up a cask of ale before a fire in what was known as the Great Room. The fire was stacked high with logs and the three authors settled themselves down for a literary discussion. Tom's own apology for not joining them was accepted almost too readily for his liking, but he escaped thankfully to the comparative sanctuary of his bedroom.

The Earl was particularly attracted to Kit Marley, in whom he saw a man of his own heart, fearless in his expression of views, careless for the outcome of his actions and a writer who had quickly established himself as among the greatest and most innovatory of the age. The Earl had seen Tamberlaine, but had yet to experience Dr Faustus, although its reputation had reached him as it had, indeed, all those who took an interest in the cultural developments of the age. He complimented the younger man on his "mighty line" and, as someone who would have dearly loved to produce such an effect himself, asked how he achieved it.

Kit looked at him in some surprise. The Earl was reputed to be a poet and playwright of experience and note and he wondered why he should find it necessary to enquire from someone lesser known how his work was produced. He confessed himself unable to explain the derivation of his verses. They came, he said, from somewhere at the back of his head. While at Cambridge he had read much and had accumulated a good store of literary nourishment.

"It seems to me", he said, "that one gets words from books. Actions come from people".

The Earl asked him if he wrote all his plays himself or if he worked in collaboration with other writers. At this point Robert Greene, who had sat silently during the conversation between the other two, broke in: "Most of us collaborate", he said. "It is a form of protection. The playwright's work has to overcome three obstacles: the mechanics of the theatre, the audience and, more difficult than all, the actors who speak your lines. You may take full account of the restraints imposed by the stage. You may ignore the reaction or lack of it from the ignorant mob that comprises your audience, but you cannot in the end control what the actors will make of your script. So you work with someone else, possibly someone who is an actor as well as a writer. In that way you can anticipate what liberties are going to be taken with your carefully created dialogue and business."

Oxford had not taken to Greene, who seemed taciturn and disagreeable, but he was very interested in this view, which coincided so closely with what Henslowe had told him.

"Would you be prepared to – what do you call it - collaborate?" he asked Greene.

Privately Greene felt quite affronted by the suggestion. He regarded himself as an initiator, not playing the secondary role of collaborator. He did not let this show, however. He was aware of the Earl's importance, not only in the theatre world, but in the wider field of political influence. Working with someone like Oxford could involve a degree of patronage and perhaps even financial gain. It was an opportunity not to be missed. So he tentatively agreed that he might consider it and flattered the Earl.

"I am surprised you are interested in the possibility of working with another playwright. You have a reputation as an accomplished writer of works that have been produced by your own company."

"Yes the Oxford Men are excellent performers, but I must admit they are only amateurs. Most of them have, or have had, other work: farmers, soldiers, lawyers' clerks. When I visit such establishments as the Rose or the Theatre in Shoreditch I can see that there is a world of difference. The man Henslowe has drawn my attention to the need for what seems to be an extra dimension, one that I would gain from someone with extensive knowledge and experience of the professional theatre."

Greene was about to respond, when Kit interposed: "If you are looking for someone to collaborate with I think I have the very man for you", said Marlowe. Greene looked at him in fury. Why was he interfering? This could spoil his chance of what might be a lucrative enterprise. Who, he wondered, did he have in mind?

"Who is that?" Oxford asked.

"His name is Shakespeare, William Shakespeare. The advantage to you would be that he is not only a writer, he also acts, and quite skilfully too."

"What is his background?"

A curious one. He has little education, but appears to have much learning, apparently derived from books"

"Books? Where would he find such books? In the University of Cambridge perhaps?"

"Strangely enough no, in Oxford."

"Oxford? But there is no library there. Not that I have heard anyway."

There is a proposal to establish one. William has told me about it. It has been instigated by a Sir Thomas Bodley."

"Bodley. Yes. I know of him. He is close to the Queen, I believe."

"The project is in its earliest stages, but many books have already been assembled, some of them from an earlier library that became defunct."

Greene interrupted: "In my view he is a very poor writer. He dabbles in verse, but most of his dialogue is in a turgid prose. He has produced a strange play about fairies and dreams."

"And a quite extraordinary piece of history", Kit said, determined to further the cause of his friend. "A whole series of plays on the Tudor dynasty. They have been produced with great success."

"Would he then be prepared to collaborate?"

"I think he might. It appears he has run into what we call a writer's block."

"A writer's block? What is that?"

"It is when inspiration ceases and ideas for new work no longer flow."

"I doubt if he will", said Greene, "I get the impression that he likes to work by himself".

Marlowe was becoming increasingly irritated at Greene's persistence. He was a man he did not like.

"I don't know why you say that Greene. He is a young man, trying to make his way in the world. He has an unusual talent, but lacks the kind of educational background and itinerant experience enjoyed by your lordship. I know for a fact he is searching for new fields to explore."

"Where will I find him?" the Earl asked.

"He is at Oxford, I believe. If not at the university then at the Bodley house."

The news that Oxford might become the site for a library rivalling Cambridge was of particular interest to the Earl. He felt he had not been well treated by the authorities at Cambridge, where they had failed to appreciate his special talents. He would welcome the opportunity to encourage anything that would increase Oxford's competitiveness.

The men drank in silence for a while, each with his

own thoughts. Greene was burning with resentment that a possible association with such a distinguished personage had been denied him. He blamed the renegade Marlowe for his disappointment and, knowing the playwright's reputation, wondered if he had supported the "talentless" Shakespeare for lubricious reasons of his own.

The Earl looked at Kit, a handsome man, flushed now with intake of alcohol. He had a fearsome reputation as someone who did not hesitate to make his views known either personally or through the medium of his plays. He admired this and wondered if it would make for a comfortable collaboration. He also thought he might become an agreeable companion to while away the cold winter nights.

Across the wide expanse of the massive fireplace Kit could feel the magnetism of Oxford's personality. He surmised the Earl's concept of collaboration was not confined to the production of a play manuscript. He looked up and saw the Earl's gaze upon him. A log fell from the fire into the open hearth with an eruption of flame. It brought to his mind the fires of hell he had summoned to consume the hero of his latest play. Were there really such things, he wondered. When he wrote "Oh! I'll leap up to my god." were they merely words for an actor to speak?. Sitting there in the glare of the fire, with the eyes of that strange man upon him, he had a premonition of doom. The flames and the words seemed prescient and he stood up, raising a hand to support himself against the mantle. The others looked in surprise at the swaying figure, the glow from the fire giving his face a red unnatural look.

"I must ask your Lordship to forgive me", he said. "I think I have drunk too much."

He bowed low and made his way uncertainly up the stairs that led to his room

Chapter 20

When Will returned to Oxford he found the Bodley household a changed place. The master had left for Europe on business so secret that he could not even divulge its nature to his wife. Their marital relationship, disturbed over the matter of young Anne, had been restored, but the restrictions imposed by Bodley on the young couple were being firmly enforced. The two must never be together again, nor even meet. Thomas had to board at the University, and the girl must remain in purdah, as it were, under the surveillance of her mistress. The domestic bliss that had been such an inspiration for Will was no longer there. In particular to ensure his commands were obeyed, Bodley had appointed a steward to "manage the estate" in his absence.

To all except his master this was an odious person. His name was quite aptly Malaver and Bodley had given him carte blanche over the personnel of the estate, with a particular admonition concerning the behaviour of Thomas and Anne. He had chosen his caretaker well as Malaver was one of those men who relish the prospect of imposing a form of despotism on any who come under their jurisdiction. When he was introduced to Bodley's wife he noted the hostile looks she gave him and almost salivated at the prospect of having a degree of authority over her. For her part, she was outraged at the development, but diplomatically kept her anger to herself, reasoning that tacit acceptance was better than outright protest. It was an unmerited intrusion into what she regarded as her realm, but she would deal with it in her own way and in her own time. Privately she raged to her maid and confidante: "Manage the estate!

What does he mean manage the estate? We have no more of an estate than the backyard of the local farrier.

So despite her outward compliance she sought ways to circumvent the authority of the steward by making his duties as difficult as possible for him and the rivalry between the two came to colour the atmosphere in the once-happy household. Will's reappearance was greeted with delight and he was glad to be back with his friend, but found that any intercourse with them was afflicted by the presence, actual or threatened, of the all-pervasive Malaver.

He was a large, portly man, much addicted to the gratification of his gastronomic needs. He was always first at table, ensuring he sat as near as possible to the choicest dishes. He disposed of the oysters before anyone could reach them. He slurped his potage and consumed vast quantities of capon without regard for the physical affects it was reputed to have on the person who overindulged. He took it upon himself to carve, claiming to know the various skills for dividing the game, the fowl, the fish, or the pheasant, thus ensuring for himself the tastiest morsels.

He seemed to wash but little and certainly not immediately before a meal, so that others tended to distance themselves from both him and therefore the best gastronomic delights. He disdained the napkin, preferring to wipe debris from his lips on his sleeve and the fat from his hands on his doublet. As he declined invitations from the lady of the house to have his clothing washed, it carried on it a record of the meals he had consumed days and even weeks before.

His ability to hold large quantities of food in his mouth while the rest of his body was trying to accommodate the results of earlier consumption did not deter him from attempting to dominate the conver-sation. He had travelled widely with his master and regarded himself as an authority on all matters incidental to the role of tourist in foreign lands. He had been lost in wonder at the strange sights he saw abroad and failed to appreciate that those to whom he tried to relate them were less than transfixed. How could he explain that there was a city in Italy where there were rivers instead of roads and residents travelled everywhere by boat; and another with a similar situation in Denmark, where women of loose morals (if he could spare his auditors' blushes) lined the banks of the canals to promote their wares? Water was also a major factor in the land that comprised what were known as the Low Countries, most of which lay under the sea to the great inconvenience of its inhabitants. Nevertheless they seemed to live excellent lives and had wonderful ways of preparing and cooking fish.

The saddest impact of his presence in the household and Bodley's concern over the good management of his "estate" was on the young Anne, and her erstwhile lover Thomas. The joyful lives they had been able to spend together were terminated without hope of redemption. The young girl deteriorated physically as well as mentally, her once robust young form shrinking as if under the weight of an indefinable disease. She spoke little and seemed to cling to the skirts of her mistress for comfort.

Young Thomas reacted by immersing himself even more deeply in his work, seeming to take on the colour and texture of those crumbling books and manuscripts, his face becoming grey under his scraggy young beard, his clothes resembling the leathery covers of the volumes he poured over for hours on end. Will did his best to lighten his mood, trying with little conviction to persuade him that things would improve, that Sir Thomas would relent and allow a match that was – as Will suggested in mitigation – so obviously made in heaven. Thomas, however, would have none of it. He was doomed to a life of celibacy, he said, without the consolation that a priest would derive from the spiritual aspects of his work. He wished he could have become a monk and even suggested (with a quick glance over his shoulder) that the lack of such an asylum was one baleful effect the dissolution of the monasteries had on young men of his persuasion – not to mention its impact it on the lives of the poor and sick..

Will found lodgings at the University and spent his daylight hours in Thomas's rooms, where he worked on Henry V. After the excitement and characterisation he had been able to inject into the two parts of Henry IV, he found this a tedious task and in an attempt to introduce comic relief tried to draw on memories of his childhood encounters with peasants from the west of England and in particular Wales. He seriously began to wonder whether his inspiration was waning and spoke about this to Thomas who suggested he should study the Greek plays, which managed to integrate personal and domestic problems into affairs of state. Will admired the concept of inevitability and was intrigued with the device of the chorus, but decided that, although this was a useful way to introduce a commentary, it seemed to interrupt the action.

One day Will was surprised to receive a message from Castle Edingham, in Essex, which puzzled him greatly. It was a summons from the Earl of Oxford for Will to attend him there. In the first place, he could not understand why an earl in Essex should be called Oxford and why he would then send to Oxford for Will to visit him in Essex. Thomas, the fountainhead of all knowledge enlightened him:

"When William of France invaded our country he divided the land up among his followers. The de Veres were granted vast estates in Essex, Middlesex, Suffolk,

Cambridgeshire and elsewhere. Years later when Audrey de Vere – also known as Audrey the Grimm – was made an Earl for acquitting himself so well in a crusade he had the opportunity to choose his title from several counties, and decided on Oxford. But that did not mean he had to live here."

Will's first inclination was to ignore the invitation. Problems with his work were absorbing him and he was not anxious to desert his friends at their difficult time. Thomas took a different view. He was impressed by the invitation from such a distinguished nobleman and insisted Will should accept.

"He is one of the proudest and grandest lords in the land", he said. "You cannot refuse".

"Is he very rich then, this Earl?"

"You would think so, but for years the family has been in decline, morally as well as financially. The Earl's father began it. He was a man totally lacking in moral character and it is perhaps hardly surprising that his son has ended up among the most dissolute in the country. Sir Thomas took me to visit him once because he claimed to have a quantity of books and manuscripts he said might be of value. We were greatly disappointed and not only in the quality of the material. Far from wishing to donate them to us he wanted to sell them. Fancy such a rich and noble lord stooping to such a level. But it all seems part of the man's nature. When his father died he became a ward of Sir William Cecil, who must have found him a grievous responsibility. He practised sword-play and there is a story that during a fencing match he accidentally stabbed a bystander who died from his wound. A jury found that the unfortunate man had committed suicide by throwing himself on the sword. As a result he was denied a Christian burial, his widow and son were stripped of their assets and the earl walked free."

"It sounds as if he would make an excellent character in a play."

"Oh! there is worse to come. He married Cecil's daughter. She was 15 at the time. That didn't stop him from spreading his sexual activity far and wide. He took himself – and a five year old choir boy - to Europe and, to the relief of all and sundry, spent some time in Italy. Then he returned to this country, where he and his lawless band of followers involved themselves in murder, pederasty and sedition. It all ended in a drunken brawl when four men were killed and a number, including Oxford himself, injured, since when he has been lame".

"And this is a man you want me to visit."

"I don't see how you can refuse. He is still a man of influence and power. It is reported that the Queen has intervened in the Earl's behaviour, since when it has been modified."

"But why on earth would he want to meet me?"

"Once again I'm surprised you don't know. He has pretensions as a playwright, writing plays produced by a company of amateur actors. He also writes verse, some of which I have read, but it is poor stuff. Perhaps he wants to collaborate with you."

"I hardly think I am likely to do that."

"Well it won't harm you to go. You should if only to view the castle, which is a marvel. It is one of the grandest in the land. Look out for the chevron pattern in the archways, particularly the one in the banqueting hall, which must be the highest in Europe."

Once again Will marvelled at the encyclopaedic knowledge of his friend, but thought he did not propose to travel all the way to Essex just to look at chevron patterned archways. Then he received a letter from his friend Kit, who wrote that he had recommended Will as a potential collaborator to the

Earl. If he received an invitation he urged him to take advantage of it. Will felt he owed it to his friend to accept and so one day set out on another journey, along strange roads and to an unknown destination, unsure of its purpose or where it would lead him. It was a journey that would influence the course of his work and life forever.

Chapter 21

As William Shakespeare rode up towards Castle Hedingham he was astonished at its size and grandeur. At least one hundred feet high and standing as it did on a rise it dominated totally the countryside around, which no doubt was the intention of its builders. The Castle's influence, however, spread far beyond the limits of its walls and even the immediate outer defences and moat. There were out-houses, sturdily built in stone, presumably providing comfortable and commodious accommodation for staff and visitors. There were a few cottages, obviously the homes of farm labourers, scattered around the outer walls or clustered near the tiny chapel. From these one or two inhabitants came out to stare curiously at William as he rode by.

It had been quite a long journey from Oxford, what roads there were being narrow and in poor condition. He had spent one night at an inn and was glad to be arriving refreshed at his destination. The morning was fine and sunny. His horse stepped out well and he sat upright in the saddle. Approaching the great building he began to experience a feeling of excited anticipation. He would be meeting a scion of a noble family reaching back to the very beginnings of the country's emergence from what were thought of as its dark days. Ever since childhood he had dreamt about the chivalric wonders that had been brought from across the sea by the conquering Normans. In recent years he had immersed himself in the dramatic struggles endured by the noble families to establish themselves on the throne and ensure that their country, and his, was secure and prosperous.

Finally, it had reached an apotheosis, with a golden Queen, sitting on a golden throne, and leading the country to a golden future. He was proud to be living in such an age, proud to be among such great men and, now, about to meet one, a noble Earl who had actually summoned him, William Shakespeare, to appear before him. The picture of him painted by Thomas had not been exactly complimentary, but to William this was all part of the world he had studied and committed to the stage. It was not for him to judge, only to observe and take whatever advantage might arise from the encounter.

If he thought he was moving into an environment of nobility and grandeur, however, he received the first hint of disillusion as he approached what appeared to be a guard-house, with a round top, a single unglazed window and a door open to the elements. A man emerged from it and approached him. He was a rough, uncouth sort of fellow, large, his fat belly extending over his doublet, his face red and distorted, his breath, as he drew near, stinking of alcohol. Will thought it best to be polite, doffed his hat and said: "Well met, good fellow".

Instead of responding the man tried to seize the horse's bridle with one hand and grabbed at Will's leg with the other. Will, not a man to take such behaviour lightly, kicked out at him and managed to hit him in the face. The man staggered back, clutching his nose from which blood began to ooze.

"What did you do that for?" he demanded.

"I do not permit you to touch my horse", Will said. "It is a spirited animal. You could have caused him to bolt."

"I'll cause him to bolt!" exclaimed the man and rushed at Will, who did not stand on ceremony, but urged his horse on. The animal gave a little leap and kicked his hind hooves out, catching the gateman in the chest and knocking him down. Will turned to make sure he was not severely hurt and saw him start to get to his feet with many a curse and threatening gesture. He then spurred the horse on towards what turned out to be a further obstacle.

He was required to stop and give an account of himself by two ruffians, somewhat less unprepossessing than his earlier encounter, but determined not to let him pass. He thrust the Earl's missive under their noses. They were obviously unable to read, glancing at it upside down, but were impressed by the sight of a signature and crest and agreed that one of them would go ahead to announce his arrival. While Will waited he looked with interest at work in progress on the drawbridge, involving scaffolding and a team of workers who belied that description by lounging on the nearby grass and drinking beer. Will asked what was happening and the remaining gate-keeper explained that the drawbridge had ceased to function effectively, because the machinery operating it had not been maintained. It was being replaced by a fixed bridge.

The drawbridge certainly was in a bad state of repair and when at last he was allowed to cross it he did so with care. There were holes in the wooden flooring and gaps in the rails on either side. Ending up in the moat might not have resulted in drowning as it was not deep enough, but the smell emanating from it suggested that it had been the receptacle for centuries of ordure from the castle and its attendant out-buildings. Will held his hand to his nose until he dismounted at the entrance to the keep. He was led past a stone building that appeared to be some kind of prison, with a heavy metal door and bars on the window. Then he was taken down a narrow dark passage and wondered that so grand a castle should be approached by something so mean and unprepossessing. His view changed, however, when the passage, with dramatic effect, opened up into the most splendid room he had ever beheld.

He had encountered halls as wide, but never seen one so high, nor one dominated by such a magnificent arch. His heart actually leapt at the sight of it to think that man was capable of something so noble and inspiring. In his ignorance of architecture and knowing nothing of such matters as keystones, he wondered how it was possible for a structure so large not only to remain standing, but to maintain the weight of the whole building. As he walked under it his gaze was drawn upwards so that he was at first unaware of the man who lounged in a large chair by the blazing fire and watched him with a slight smile. A young woman sprawled on the ground by his chair, her head and one hand resting on his thigh. Two dogs lying at his feet growled and trotted up to Will in order to test his credentials with their tongues.

"You like my little house?" the Earl asked.

Will hastily recovered himself, drew off his hat and bowed low.

"William Shakespeare at your service, my lord. It is a magnificent hall."

"Yes, but it costs a king's ransom to maintain. Come and sit by the fire. May I offer you some refreshment?."

"Thank you. I am thirsty after my journey. A little ale would be welcome."

He sat across the fireplace from the Earl. The woman gave him a languid look and he noticed with embarrassment that her dress was in some disarray. To Will's astonishment the Earl clipped her across the head and sent her away with a wave of his hand. Then he gestured to one of the servants who stood nearby and sent him for Will's drink. Others sat at a distance, drinking, playing dice, or simply watching the

224

newcomer with various degrees of interest. William felt that, despite the grandeur of the surroundings, there was about the whole scene an air of decadence, almost decay. Attendants the Earl certainly had in plenty, but they seemed to treat him with scant deference and Will suspected that it would be difficult to maintain discipline over them if they chose to pursue their own aims.

Will tried to appear impassive as he looked around him and the Earl watched him with a smile: "We lead a relaxed life here", he said. "I expect dinner will be served in an hour or two. In the meantime, if you are hungry – "

"Thank you. I stayed at an inn overnight and had a good repast before I left .this morning. I did not want to feel obliged to your lordship."

"But you may, my dear boy, you may. You have come a great distance to visit me. I owe it to you."

"You honour me, but I am sure you are not in my debt", suggested Will trying to be polite without seeming deferential.

"Then you are the only one", said the Earl with a laugh. There was a sudden shout from a group of servants by one of the great arched windows. A scuffle followed and the Earl looked at them in irritation. He stood up and Will saw he was tall, a grand figure of a man, although with a stomach that overlapped his tightening doublet.

"We can't talk here. I have a little den."

He shouted to one of the servants to bring Will's drink. Two of them stood up and hurried to stand by the door, bowing and touching their foreheads as he passed them. Will followed him up flights of stone stairs until he found himself in what appeared to be a long gallery.

"You are now", the Earl said, "inside the castle wall,

which is 18 feet thick here because on this side we were more vulnerable to attack. I say we, but I really meant the builders. We are certainly still vulnerable, but from enemies within not from across the sea."

He led the way to a door by which a servant sat sleeping on the floor. The Earl kicked him awake and he sprang to his feet with a cry of alarm, then hastily bowed and opened the door. Will entered the room and looked around him in astonishment. It was if he had stepped back into the world of the university at Oxford. Books and papers were everywhere, on a long table under the window, in piles on the floor, on a ledge in the window alcove, even on the hard wooden chairs that constituted the room's only seats.

"This is where I work", said the Earl, with what sounded like a note of pride. "As you may have heard I have been responsible for inflicting my literary efforts on a long-suffering world."

He swept books and papers off two chairs and gestured to Will that he should sit, which he did, uncomfortably and with an air of uncertainty about what was expected of him.

"Yes", he said, "I had heard of your Lordship's prowess in such matters".

"Have you indeed. And what do people say about them – no never mind. It is of no account."

"I am surprised that your Lordship has time for such activity when you are responsible for an estate of such dimensions."

"You have hit upon it exactly. It is not easy – my father – he was not a careful man and I took over when – well – let us say I have had to work hard to keep body and soul together."

Will thought that there had to be worse ways to keep body and soul together than in such surroundings, with so many attendants, and such apparent wealth. His lordship seemed almost to read his thoughts.

"There is no money here, you know. The whole place is going to rack and ruin. The drawbridge is about to collapse. We dare not raise it. If we did we might not be able to lower it, then how could we cross the moat - by swimming?"

No, thought Will, that did not bear contemplation.

"I have begun a programme of trading activities, of investment – oh! I can't tell you: imports and exports, tin mining in Cornwall, anything to earn an honest shilling. I have even tried to sell my plays. I took some to – what is his name? Henslowe. He didn't seem to like them. Didn't like them! And me a master poet, acclaimed throughout the land."

Will thought, yes, but who acclaims you and why?

"I don't want to run a castle. I don't need a castle. All I need is a little room, pen and paper. Oh! and, of course, a place to rest my head when my day's labour is done."

A day's labour, thought Will. An hour or so spent wielding a feathered plume. And there were those who scarcely have time to put their heads on a sack of hay at the end of one day before the next one takes them out to the field or the barn again.

"I have so many ideas", the Earl was saying. "I have travelled, you know. I have travelled widely. Not so much to the new lands in the east. Such was never my inclination, but in Europe and particularly in Italy. Italy – ah! there is a land."

"They tell me it is a beautiful country", said Will.

"No. You are wrong. It is not a country. It is a land, yes, but a land of cities, of states. There is Rome you see, and Verona, and Venice – Ah! Venice – you cannot imagine the beauty of that city. It is built on the sea. Can you imagine that? Where there are streets in our cities, Venice has lanes of water. You can wander for hours in little boats they call gondolas. You can row up to a doorway and enter a palace of great magnificence – not a gaunt castle like this, but a place with rooms and balconies that look out at the maritime traffic plying the great lagoons. And Rome – a city that has been there forever. Rome, from which we in this country have derived our civilisation."

"I thought Greece had something to do with that."

"Greece! A decadent civilisation. Greece has little to offer us today."

He fell silent and sat looking out of the window, perhaps Will thought, living again the times he spent travelling.

"You must have encountered many strange experiences", Will ventured.

The Earl turned and looked at him, a long enquiring look.

"I have stories, many stories. Italy is a land of stories. In every city state there are tales that are too recent to be legends, that are talked over – even still fought over. I have long wanted to place some of them in plays. They would create wonders in those who attend the Theatre, the Rose and the inn-yards of this land."

"Such as?"

The Earl looked at him again, as if assessing the degree of his interest.

"So you will go away and write plays about them and I will have lost them."

"I assure you my lord – "

But in his heart Will could not speak with assurance. He would long to have access to such material. The historical well he had been drawing on in Oxford seemed to be drying up. There were other books there, which he had yet to explore, but he was uncertain what path to take. He became aware of a long silence between them. He looked up and saw that the Earl was again looking at him enquiringly.

"I have read some of your work", the Earl said suddenly. "I also saw one of your plays at the Rose".

"I am honoured my lord", said Will and looked down, feeling his cheeks flushing with embarrassment.

"I was astonished."

"Astonished, my lord?"

"Yes, astonished. I am still trying to work out how you do it. I have written a number of plays, most of them well received and up to now I have been satisfied with them. But they have all told a single story. There is a small set of characters, who speak their lines, further the plot, fall in love, marry, die, do battle. Then I saw your – what is it – your play about a dream – a dream no less. One would have expected it to be of no account, but the audience was engrossed, I was engrossed."

"Your lordship is too kind."

"No. I am not kind enough. I do not have words to describe it. One minute there is a fairy telling how he circled the earth, next there are fairy kings and queens – fairies mind you – and they are quarrelling. Then lovers appear and they quarrel. Then a whole gang of yokels gather and plan a play. One of them is transformed into an ass. The Fairy Queen falls in love with him, with an ass! You would think that by now all would be confusion, but no, it all comes together at the end. The audience go wild with joy. How did you do it?"

Will realised that there was no way he could answer. He waited for the Earl to continue, still wondering what his purpose was, why he had summoned him there.

"Then I read one or two of your history plays. I do not know how you acquired the knowledge they contain. It certainly does not come from the books I have read on the subject. But it is not the content, it is the way it is put together. You have written about one of the Henries, the fourth I think, and you introduce this character – he is a hard-drinking, blustering fool, I have seen many of them, but I would never in a million years have thought of putting him into a play."

"If you mean Falstaff – "

"Yes. I believe that is his name."

At this point the door opened and, without ceremony, a servant entered with a tankard of ale, which he placed among the papers on the table. The Earl rose in a fury and clouted the man around the head: "Where are your manners, serf!" he cried. "You should bring it on a tray and not set it among my papers."

The man cringed and turned to go, receiving a kick in the rear for his pains.

"I am so desperately served here", he said. "So many matters occupy my time. Money matters. Money matters. There! That's what would you call it? An aphorism. Money matters matter." He laughed broadly at his joke. Will smiled politely.

The Earl went on: "Do you know what it is like to have your mind full of ideas, of plots for plays, of characters, even dialogue and not have the time or energy to put them on paper?"

Will thought he did, but for very different reasons. There was another long silence. Will sipped his drink, which quenched his thirst, but tasted foul. He knew that etiquette did not allow him to lead the conversation so he waited and eventually his lordship continued.

"A few years ago I acquired the Earl of Warwick's players. That caused, incidentally, a certain amount of unrest. For some reason law students from the Inns of Court protested and my men had to protect my interests. They tend to do so rather violently, I am afraid. One or two of them finished up in jail, but then

230

that's their problem. We produce – when we do – at the Theatre. You will know of it, of course. Very good man Burbage, far superior in experience and intellect to that moron Henslowe. I have a couple of playwrights working for me. There is John Lyly, for example, and Anthony Munday. We put on some good shows. What is your arrangement with Henslowe?"

The question took Will with surprise. He was still uncertain where the conversation was leading. Did his lordship have some idea of involving him in his enterprises? It was not a prospect to be relished.

"My arrangement? Well, he pays me as an actor when I am there, which has not been often of late. And I get a fee for each play I write for him."

"Not for each production?"

"Well, no. He buys the play, as it were."

"If you worked for me you would receive payment every time the play was performed."

"Work for you?"

"Well, for Burbage, I suppose. I don't bother myself with management details. But Burbage is a true man of the theatre. Henslowe is a property dealer – property that is sometimes of a dubious nature – not that there is anything wrong with that – but not for a theatre manager. I want to see plays of real quality produced at the Theatre – and, incidentally, at the new places Burbage is proposing to develop. You know he is going to build south of the river."

"No. I did not know that."

"Then there are the indoor theatres in Blackfriars. Where you don't have to worry about the weather, or the light. That's where the real future is. Once this dread plague has left us.

Will's mind was in turmoil. He thought Henslowe had been good to him, had helped him place his feet on the ladder. It was true, however, that he had earned very little money from it and would be hard pressed to survive were it not for the generosity of his hostess in Oxford. The Earl looked at him shrewdly.

"You could go far, you know. You could make a lot of money. More to the point you could make money for me."

"For you?"

The Earl got to his feet and went to the door. He opened it and hauled a waiting servant in by the scruff of his neck.

"Go and fetch ale for myself and my guest", he said. "And viands. And make sure you bring them on a tray. Come back with others. Let us have service here".

With that he flung the poor suffering creature on to the floor. He scuttled out and the Earl returned to sit on a corner of the table and lean over Will.

"I have plays that need working on. I need someone who can help to lift them above the ordinary. Some of those who work for me now – they are run-of-the-mill, commonplace. They can turn a line and give a few words to an actor to say – then it is up to the actors to make something of them – and they do, but it is not good enough. I have read your plays. I have seen them. They have something special."

"Surely, your lordship, that is something you could provide."

The Earl seemed reluctant to reply. He strode to the door and shouted through it.

"Bring me some ale, for God's sake. Do you want me to die of thirst?"

He came back and sat, his head in his hand. Then, at last, he looked up at Will.

"Yes, I could, I could, but I do not have the time. Henslowe, for all his faults, put his finger on it. There are those who can write, perhaps brilliantly, as indeed I believe I do, but we are not – what would you call us?

232

Professional. Full time. At the best we can only produce an occasional work of art. At worst we are capable of nothing but dross. As I said I have a mind bursting with ideas, information, background knowledge, colourful characters. They buzz around in my head like so many bees in their hive. But I cannot release them. I cannot produce the honey that my brilliance justifies. And that is where you come in."

All the fears Will had kept back while the Earl was speaking began to surface. He was to be a writer held in the background, while his lordship took the glory he produced. He was to be the Earl's shadow, his ghost almost. He stood up, determined to defend what he knew to be his creative genius to the last.

The Earl looked up at him and Will was surprised at the sadness in his face. The mouth was drawn down, the eyes were half closed. In a lesser man Will might have expected to see tears on his cheek. This was a great lord, scion of a noble family. Will had approached him in fear, but now he found himself confronting a normal human being. This was a man who had feelings and emotions like anyone else. Despite his family and power he was a man like any other. Will was no longer afraid of him. He could even be his master.

"Your lordship does me great honour in proposing that a humble playwright like me could share in the work you are so triumphantly presenting to the public, but even a humble playwright has his own aspirations. I have successfully, by your own estimation, presented a number of plays to the public, some of them based on the work of others it is true, but many produced entirely by my own hands. You have been gracious enough to speak well of my work. I do not think I could exercise my skills so adequately if I did so under another's name."

"Another's name? I think you misunderstand me. I

was not proposing that I should present your work as if it were mine. There are those who speak ill of me and say I have many faults. It may be true that I have not lived my life in as Christian a manner as society requires, but I would never try to pass on someone else's writing as my own. That seems to me to be the ultimate in knavery. No. What I am suggesting is that you accept from me a lifetime's store of knowledge from travel, from experience, and with my support turn it into work that will grace our stages and perhaps increase our country's fame for centuries to come."

Will was stunned. For a moment he was quite unable to respond. A small diversion came to his rescue when the door burst open and several servants entered carrying tankards of ale and foodstuffs on trays. The Earl hastily gathered up papers on the great table and placed them in piles at one end so that they could set the trays down. He then clouted one of the servants round the head and cried: "Napkins, you dogs. Napkins. Would you have us clean our hands on our raiment. And fetch a bowl of water or I'll have you all drowned in the moat."

They scuttled from the room. The Earl took a chicken leg from a plate and began to devour it. He gestured to Will, who was glad of the chance not only to assuage his appetite, but to avoid the need to respond to his lordship's proposal."

"You see how evilly I am served. I need a housekeeper. I need a wife. Oh! I have had those, but they never seem to stay long enough to take control of my domestic affairs."

"The young lady downstairs?" Will ventured. The Earl roared with laughter.

"A whore! Well, I must have something to satisfy my natural appetites. Mind you, women do not always satisfy one's wants."

He stood close as he said this and Will judiciously leant away so that he could help himself to food.

"You are married, no doubt?"

"Yes, your Lordship. I am happy to say. With a dutiful wife, who looks after my home and my children during my absence. Sadly they are in Stratford on Avon."

"I have estates there", said the Earl. "In Arden, a place of ill repute I believe from a notorious play of that name. There is some good forestry, however, and reasonable game."

He took a generous slurp of his drink, stood up and wandered about the room. Will waited again for him to continue.

"When I was in Venice I came across a story, about a Jew. You know young Kit Marley's play – The Jew of Malta – it had a great success, I believe. People love plays about Jews. It activates their capacity for hatred. Well, I have drafted a play about a Jew. I call it The Jew of Venice, or perhaps to avoid comparisons with Marley, The Venetian Jew. Then there was a curious tale about a rich widow who had many suitors and forced them to undergo a kind of lottery to decide whom she should marry, a pretty concept that I have also turned into a play. I would like you to look at them. See what you can make of them. You have no commitment? You are not needed anywhere? You could stay here. As you gather I have many rooms. You may not be well served, but many of my guests seem able to fend for themselves. And we feed quite well. It will shortly be dinner-time. You will see."

One of the things Will had learnt early in his writing career was that in order to produce a satisfactory play it was important to have background material, or "sources" as some of his acquaintances called it. The imagination was all very well, but you could not build a wall without stones and mortar. Working on the histories had shown him that. Here was an opportunity, he thought, to draw on the knowledge of an experienced writer, one who had travelled and garnered in his journeys the raw materials for many a dramatic production. Perhaps he could fill the gap left when he no longer had the books to rely on.

.Seeing Will's continuing hesitation, the Earl thought the story about the Jew did not appeal. He bent closely over the young man.

"Well, perhaps the idea of the Jew does not appeal. There are plenty of others. In Italy they have these factions. There are wars and contentions between cities. Even within cities. In Italy they are always fighting one another. When they have finished fighting their enemies, they turn on their friends, even their families. In Verona there were two warring parties whose young men could never meet but they would drew swords if one would do no more than bite his thumb at another. One of them fell in love with the daughter of the opposing side. Can you imagine that? It would be like a Lancastrian involved with a Yorkist, only worse, because they are living side by side in the same city. It all ends in disaster, of course. The young people die. It is very fetching."

"Have you written these plays ?"

"The two Venetians, yes. I can show them to you. Yes?"

"I have certain provisos."

The Earl turned on him angrily: "Provisos You sound like a notary. What provisos?"

"They are not onerous and I hope your lordship will think them fair. I would be honoured to work with you and develop your ideas, but the finished result will be mine and in my name. Your Lordship will not begrudge the small amount of recognition that I will gain from such an arrangement. You have your estates and reputation, both for your standing and for your literary achievements. If I produce something original that derives from my creative abilities, such as they are, I think I am entitled for that to be acknowledged."

The Earl looked at him and smiled: "You are a shrewd negotiator. I will recommend you to Burbage. I think you will go far."

"I have one small favour to ask. I have with me a play promised to Henslowe. I need to deliver it."

"Then you shall. I will expect your early return. Take my plays with you and when you come back our partnership can begin."

He held out his hand. Will took it. Then, in a sudden gesture of affection the Earl put his arms around him and embraced him warmly. Despite some aversion he had for the man's character Will was unable to resist a certain attraction towards him. He was released and felt himself slightly pushed away.

"Then let us to dinner and we will carouse a little to celebrate our arrangement."

Chapter 22

Christopher Marley – or, as he was sometimes called, Kit Marlowe – was holding forth. It was something he greatly enjoyed. Not being an actor he welcomed any opportunity to disport himself before a captive audience, expressing views he knew were often greeted with concern, amazement and even alarm. He would also read passages from work in progress, declaiming in a stentorian voice and acting out his lines in ways that often made professional actors squirm in embarrassment.

His present arena was the house of his benefactor, Thomas Walsingham, who was in the audience together with Marlowe's sometime room- and bed-mate Thomas Kydd, Richard Baines, Richard Cholmley, and Robert Greene, a sallow fellow, who seemed to delight in joining company with which he had little sympathy simply for the opportunities it gave him for disputation and argument. Kit was reading excerpts from the draft of his play based on the life and death of Edward the Second when he was interrupted by Greene.

"When I knew you were going to regale us with a play on this monarch", he said, "I took the trouble to see what our good friend Hollingshed had to say on the subject. I cannot recollect that he mentioned this fellow Gaveston at all, even though you seem to have made him one of your principal characters."

"Unlike you Greene, I do not confine myself to a single source. There are many commentators to draw on and I can assure you Gaveston played a principal part in the life and eventual downfall of the king."

"Even if he did, to provide him with the opportunity to open the play is surely dramatically unacceptable."

"Who says so, Greene? Who is it who lays down these rules? You are as bad as Gabriel Harvey, who would have us all writing in strict hexameters."

"But you suggest he has an active homosexual relationship with the king and your writing actually seems to favour it."

"On that basis you could say I favour the Jew of Malta and become a usurer, or follow Faustus and descend to hell. You should know better as an aspiring playwright that the writer does not necessarily relate personally to his characters."

"What do you mean aspiring? I have written many plays that have been well received, even though they might not contain your bombast and braggadocio."

Thomas Kydd, who knew his friend's tendency to become involved in worthless controversy especially when confronted by someone like Greene, tried to intervene.

"I am told, Walsingham, that our good friend Shakespeare will be visiting you today. What time is he expected?"

"Any time now", replied Walsingham. "I understand it is something of a farewell visit. He is due, I believe, at Hedingham Castle."

"So our fine-feathered friend has taken up with the Earl then", said Greene. "I cannot imagine his Lordship will benefit greatly from the relationship."

Kydd's attempt to keep the two combatants apart was doomed: "Why do you speak ill of Will Shakespeare?" asked Kit. "He is a fine writer, an excellent actor and a good fellow to boot."

"Good fellow he may be and an indifferent actor, but as a writer he is a time-server, a quill-pusher."

"Well, I think he will turn out to be worthier than any of us."

"And how would you know that?" Greene had

found a tasty bone to satisfy his appetite for contention and was not going to give it up easily. "Do you claim a special relationship with god so that you can foresee the future?"

"I don't claim any relationship with god. I do not even claim there is a god."

Now Kydd was seriously concerned. He went up to his friend and took his arm: "Will you continue reading from your play Kit?"

Once again he failed.

"If there is a god", said Kit, "and if he is supposed to have created the world, then he has made a damn bad job of it."

"That is blasphemy, sir."

"If it is blasphemy to speak the truth as I see it, then I confess I am guilty of it."

"Come Greene", said Kydd, "we are not going to spoil this company with an argument about religion".

But Greene had found a tasty bone to satisfy his appetite for contention and was not going to give it up easily: "If you do not think there is a god, perhaps you also deny the existence of our lord Jesus Christ."

"Not at all. He certainly existed, but he was not a god, nor the son of one. His mother was dishonest in our sense of the word, which makes him a bastard. The Jews knew that. They also knew his father was a carpenter. When it came to a choice between him and Barabas, they made the right choice, even though Barabas was a thief and a murderer."

At this there were cries of outrage from some of the others in the company. Baines in particular cried "shame". Thomas Kydd got up quietly and left the room. Several of those remaining sought to silence Kit, but he was not to be deterred. Once he had the oratorical steed between his legs he tended to ride it to exhaustion. He got up and strode about the room

240

declaiming.

"What good does religion do? It only serves to impress the populace. In which case the Roman Catholics do a better job. At least from them we get ceremonies, the elevation of the mass, organs, singers, shaven heads. Protestants are all hypocritical asses."

Unnoticed Audrey Walsingham quietly entered the room and stood by the door listening. Kydd was close by her in the passageway. He had brought her to the scene in the hope that she could help to mollify an atmosphere that threatened seriously to get out of control. Baines went to a table and picked up a Bible. He waved it at Kit.

"It would serve you Kit to read the good book again, to learn what it has taught men throughout the centuries."

"Tosh, sir! It is filthily written. I could do better myself. It fails to say what people were really like. The Woman of Samaria and her sister were whores, John Baptist was Christ's bedfellow."

Baines went up to Kit and rested a hand on his shoulder: "It worries me to hear you say such things. It worries all of us. You are held in so much respect it makes us begin to doubt our own faith."

"You see how god-fearing folk are affected by what you say", said Greene.

"God-fearing folk? You mean the ignorant masses. I care nothing for them. All those that love not tobacco and boys are fools."

At this Baines turned away, put the Bible down and sat with his head in his hands. Kit went up to him: "Baines, Baines, don't you realise - the apostles were fishermen and base fellows of neither wit nor worth. St Paul was only concerned to make men subject to the church. As for the Angel Gabriel, I think his relationship to the holy ghost was very suspect because

241

he brought the salutation to Mary."

Richard Cholmley was one of those who had been admiring Marlowe's outburst and even applauding it. He leapt up and cried: "Kit you are right. All religion is a mockery, a foil to keep men in thrall. From this day forth I shall be an atheist" and with that he embraced Kit and danced round the room with him.

The others started arguing among themselves, until the noise reached a climax. At this point Audrey Walsingham made her presence known by coming to the centre of the room. The dancing stopped and the noise subsided. Greene went up to the lady and spoke seriously: "You see what he is doing my lady. He is corrupting us. In your house. He will lead us all to the gallows and hell fire."

"My first request to you gentlemen is to behave with more decorum. The servants may become aware of you. My second is that I wish to have a few words in private with my husband."

She moved towards the door and beckoned him to follow her, which he did reluctantly, but obediently. She led the way into her private room where she berated him soundly.

"What do you mean by allowing such goings on in her house?"

"It is a little high spirits, nothing more", he protested.

"I'm not referring to the uproar, offensive although that is. I am talking about the views that were being expressed, particularly by this man Marley".

"It is a private activity", he said.

"Private? With people like Greene there. And did I see Poley and Skeres lurking in the background."

"It is just a dispute. It causes no harm".

"Harm! Supposing Sir Francis gets to hear of it."

"But he is family."

"He may be, but also the head of secret diplomacy, appointed by the Queen no less. One word in his ear and the whole household could be in danger. The fact that he is our kinsman would not help."

"Marlowe speaks only in jest. He is a playwright. Such words are customary to him."

"Well, they are not customary to me. And men have been tortured in the Tower for less. Well, I tolerate most of the rabble you entertain here, but I cannot rest while that man is in the house. Marlowe, or Marley, or whatever his name is must go."

"You cannot mean it. He is a great poet, perhaps the greatest in the land. He speaks his mind that's all."

"Well, he can speak it elsewhere. I must insist."

Intimidated as he usually was by his wife, she had touched on something that was close to his heart. The freedom of men like Kit to come and go as they pleased in his house was a sources of great satisfaction to him: "And I also must insist. He is my guest. This is my house – "

And who knows where such an argument might have led were it not that there was another uproar, in which shouts and cheers were interspersed with laughter.

"Now what!" cried Audrey in despair. Followed by her husband, she left the room to find that the outburst had been caused by the arrival of a newcomer. It was William Shakespeare, who was standing in the hall, surrounded by his acquaintances, some of whom were delighted to see him, others less so. Kit marched him into the living room, relieved him of his hat and cloak and sat him down. Then he pulled off his boots and tossed them over his shoulder, to the annoyance of Audrey, who sent a maid to retrieve them. She found this latest visitor less objectionable than some of the others and offered him refreshment, which was gladly accepted. She left to superintend it and the rest of the company gathered around him or sat at a distance according to inclination.

Kit sat at his feet and complimented him on his latest offering, the second part of Henry the Fourth. He had special commendation for the character of Falstaff.

"I gather from the epilogue that you are planning a play on Henry the Fifth, when no doubt he will feature prominently", he suggested.

"Sadly no", said Will. "I wrote him for a fine actor, whose physical form and natural proclivities suited the character, but I am afraid he acted out the licentious life of Falstaff too closely in his own life and has died as a result. I kill off Falstaff in Henry the Fifth without actually showing him on the stage."

"And after that, what plans do you have? There are rumours that you are going to work with the Earl of Oxford."

"Yes it is true and this visit sadly is to bid farewell to you all for a while. I am going to Castle Hedingham. His lordship has been kind enough to suggest we might work together"

"You are going to be a hack for that amateur", cried Greene.

"I believe it was a proposal you would have been glad to accept", said Kit. Then he turned to his friend and said seriously: "I hope you have made an appropriate arrangement with him".

"I believe so. I have tried to make it plain what my reservations are I think he and I understand one another on that point."

This produced a burst of merriment from the company, some of whom bowed extravagantly to Will and there were cries of "yes your Lordship, no your Lordship". Will laughed with them.

"What about his own company – will you be writing

for them?" asked Marlowe.

"I have no idea. That presumably would mean working for Burbage at the Theatre. I have no plans to leave Henslowe."

"Burbage is a good man and a fine producer. I sometimes wish I had been associated with him", said Marlowe.

"Perhaps you will Kit. Perhaps you will. When I become established in Essex you must come and visit us. Hedingham is a magnificent castle. You will be amazed."

"I may", said Kit. "I may. But then who knows what the future will bring."

"Who indeed", said Will and took his friend's hand in a moment of close friendship.

Chapter 23

"You've combined them into one."

The Earl sprawled his languid length across the hearth. The grate bore no fire as it was approaching summer and the weather was already warm. In his hands was a clutch of papers. Some lay in his lap; others had fallen to the floor. From the other side of the cold hearth Shakespeare looked anxiously as the results of his labours were being dispersed and criticised.

"You've taken two perfectly good stories and combined them into one play – and for good measure you've added another one. How do you think audiences are going to make sense of them?"

"The more complicated plays become, the greater is the appreciation of audiences. I believe they will accept changes of plot being developed before their eyes and will wait eagerly for that development. I have seen them become restless when one scene is drawn out too tediously."

The Earl was silent for a while, gazing at the pages before him. Then he remarked quite angrily: "And I cannot identify one single line of my own writing."

Shakespeare was silent at this. As he set himself the task of rewriting what the Earl had given him he found his own words formed themselves on the page. He knew of no way in which to stem the flow of both verse and prose as he allowed the plots to develop. This led to a kind of apotheosis in his mind, culminating in speeches that he could hear himself as an actor declaiming.

To mollify his Lordship, however, he lied: "Oh! much of your writing is still there. Maybe it is such a long time since you wrote perhaps you have forgotten it".

"I have to admit some of it is very fine, very fine indeed", said the Earl almost grudgingly. "The quality of mercy is not strained. It droppeth as the gentle rain from heaven upon the place beneath'. How do you write such stuff? It even scans You make it scan: 'it is twice blessed' – all in good old iambic pentameter."

Will felt a flush of pleasure at the praise and accepted it in silence. His lordship read on, occasionally nodding his head in appreciation.

"I am going to show this to Burbage. He knows more about audiences than I do. If he likes it we will put it on at the Theatre."

"Not the Rose?"

"by that old reprobate Henslowe. No. You can do better than that. I hate to say it young Shakespeare, but you do seem to have an extraordinary talent."

"Your lordship is very generous."

"We make good collaborators. I have other ideas I want to share with you. You will remember I told you of my journeys in Italy."

"Yes I do and I am anxious to begin work on them. But I have a favour to ask of your Lordship. I have had a letter, from my friend in Oxford. Ostensibly it is about a book he has received and would like me to see."

"A book? You can't go halfway across the country to see a book. We have books here. Lots of them".

"This one is rather special. I heard of it when I was at school, but the translation is only just beginning to circulate freely. It is by an ancient Greek writer, Plutarch, and contains the lives of many famous heroes and statesmen".

"The Greeks – pooh – an ignorant superstitious race. You'll find all you need in Rome."

"This book contains stories from both Greek and

Latin. I am hoping to derive some material from it."

"I have material enough for you. You don't need books."

"Oh! but I do. You were kind enough to praise my history plays. They would not have been possible without my sources."

"Your sources! I am your sources, whatever that means."

Will walked about the room anxiously: "Besides. I have another reason to visit Oxford. As I think I told you I became very attached to a household there and it seems they are very troubled. They ask my advice and even my help, although sadly I do not know what aid I can give them. Nevertheless I feel I need to go to them in their time of need."

"Remind me. Who are these people?"

"It is the family of Sir Thomas Bodley. You may have heard of him."

"Indeed I have. He is someone of great repute. It is a connection you cannot neglect. Well you are not a prisoner here."

He gathered his papers together in some sort of cohesive bundle and waved it at Will: "But before you go I must insist you come with me on a shorter journey close to London. Now we have completed out first play together I want to show it to someone without delay. I propose to visit James Burbage at the Theatre and I need you to come with me."

"Close to London, you say? In that case I will come with you, but ask your indulgence to travel on from there to Oxford."

Reluctantly the Earl agreed and so Will found himself joining his unruly entourage on the short journey from Essex to the outskirts of London. Their destination was in Shoreditch, close to the City walls. The building itself was not unlike the one familiar to

Will south of the Thames, but it was surrounded by gardens, outhouses and even a little lake. It was still morning so no performance was in progress. They were met at the entrance by James Burbage himself.

His first impression on Will was of a Henslowe clone, the same portly stature, similarly formal, but unassuming dress, hair greying and thinning. Talking to him later he found other similar characteristics. He spoke in practical terms of theatre production, concerning himself with sizes of casts, ease of staging and – apparently most important – the possibility of making a profit – or otherwise.

"Surely", Will said to him at one point, "the essential quality of a play is its artistic merit, the quality of the writing, the ability of the actors to portray the characters."

"Artistic merit – fiddle-dee-dee! Artistic merit is not of much account if you don't have an audience to appreciate it. The only thing that counts is the number that comes through the door. That means money and money pays the rent, the salaries of the actors –"

"And the profit in your pocket", suggested Will.

Burbage looked at him sharply: "What other motive do I have? I do not have the satisfaction of creating mighty lines like Marlowe; I do not receive the plaudits of the house when I orate a fine speech. My emotions are not stirred by the delivery of a love song. No. I could make more money running a whore house, or bear baiting. I could brew foul beer and import even worse wine and sell them at a huge profit to drunken farm labourers, but I don't. I provide an opportunity for people like you and our worthy Earl here to share the results of your creative genius with the general public. In doing that I am performing a public service, but I expect to be paid for it – and rather more importantly I do not expect to suffer a loss as a result."

Will laughed: "You sound exactly like Master Henslowe".

Burbage became quite angry: "Don't talk to me about that charlatan. Now he really is a whore master".

"Well, he employs your son."

"And don't even mention that prodigal. Your Lordship, why have you brought this mountebank along to pester me".

He led the way into the theatre and had a table and chairs arranged on the stage. The Earl's followers remained on the field outside. Will looked around him and noted that the arrangements of the building were much like the Rose. He noted that the auditorium was not raked and mentioned that to Burbage.

"You have to remember this was the first, which is why it is called the Theatre. As new ones are built improvements are obviously added. But it is all makeshift. We really need to be indoors, but we can't afford the lighting. We need daylight so we leave the roof off. There will come a time when all drama will be indoors."

"I believe there are already plans for something of the sort in London", said Will.

"In Blackfriars. Yes. I have acquired property there. We just need to be free from the rules and regulations of the government in London."

He turned to the Earl: "Well, what have you brought for me?"

"A very interesting concept – the product you might say of both our minds".

"What is it called?"

"'The Jew of Venice'. It's all about – "

"But Marlowe has a similar play. People will think you are just copying it".

"It is very different I assure you."

"Yes, but they won't know that. Anyway titles

containing the word Jew do not attract audiences these days."

"What about the Merchant of Venice", suggested Will.

"Well, he's hardly the main character", said the Earl.

"It's better than the jew", said Burbage. " Do you have any other stuff for me."

"We are thinking of doing a series", said the Earl.

Will looked at him in surprise: "Are we?"

"I told you about the Moorish general who murdered his wife out of jealousy."

Will shuddered. He thought of the coldness with which he was received on his last visit to Stratford.

"I don't like that idea."

"But it really happened."

"Because something's true, that doesn't make it dramatic. How are we going to make it plausible on stage."

The Earl laughed: "I'll leave that to you."

"Thank you very much", said Will with asperity.

The Earl turned to Burbage with a sigh: "you see the difficulties we playwrights have".

"I feel for you", said Burbage with heavy sarcasm. "Well, leave this one with me. I just hope it has more depth than some of the recent work you have shown me."

"It is not my work", said the Earl. "I only produced the idea. What you have here is the first work of a new literary star in the dramatic firmament".

"Hardly new", suggested Burbage. "I understand a number of his works have been produced at the Rose".

"It was my first port of call when I arrived in London", explained Will. "Kit Marlowe introduced me and it does seem that Master Henslowe's company of actors is a fine one."

"If that is the case I wonder why you have brought

your present work to me here."

"It was at his Lordship's suggestion."

"I see. Well, his Lordship will no doubt explain that I expect my writers to show me loyalty. If I am going to risk my money and reputation producing their plays and finding them an audience, it is only right and just that they should offer me the first refusal of future work."

Will chose his words carefully: "Speaking for myself it is important to know you value what we have written. Our relationship will surely depend on whether his Lordship and I can produce something to our mutual satisfaction."

Burbage looked at the Earl in some surprise, expecting some reaction to what he might be expected to regard as the impertinence of his protégé, but the noble lord merely shrugged his shoulders and grinned as if to say: what else do you expect?

Receiving no other response, Burbage said: "Well are you returning to Essex today or do you want me people to find accommodation for you and your people?"

"No, I shall take my people as you call them into London to see what sport we can find."

"And you Master Shakespeare? Are you to go looking for sport in London?"

"No. I have an errand of mercy that takes me to Oxford."

And with that they separated. Will set out with a feeling of triumph. He had challenged a member of a family with a lineage going back to Norman times and who could if he chose reduce Will to dust beneath his aristocratic feet. That man also had a reputation as a playwright and poet, who had agreed not only to supply the plots and schemes for future plays, but was apparently willing to allow Will to mould them to his own design and with his own materials, taking credit for his efforts.

Only one thought cast a shadow over his otherwise sunny prospect. The news from Oxford was not good. He dreaded what he might find there.

Chapter 24

His anxiety was justified. What he found was a deeply unhappy household. He was greeted by Ann Bodley and embraced warmly. Neither her maid nor Thomas James was anywhere to be seen. The large figure of Malaver, the steward, hovered in the background. Will bowed politely to him, a courtesy that was not returned. Will was anxious to speak to Ann privately, but they seemed never able to rid themselves of his presence. Will asked after the young Anne. Her mistress answered hesitatingly.

"She – she is confined to her room."

"I hope she is not indisposed."

"No. No. It was thought better for her to withdraw for a while."

"And Thomas James. Have you seen anything of him?"

"Not lately. He is very busy at the University."

During dinner she had an opportunity to slip a note to him, with warning glances directed towards the steward. He secreted it until he had an opportunity to read it. Ann suggested he should come to her room after dinner. It was her custom to retire there at that time when Malaver was usually sleeping off the effects of the meal. The prospect of meeting her *a deux* excited him, but he tried to put such thoughts behind him. He was, after all, dealing with a woman who might be in need of brotherly counsel not amorous dalliance.

Eventually the meal was over and the large man dozed noisily in a chair. Ann supervised the clearing of the table and, with a knowing look at Will, went up to her room. After a suitable delay, Will followed. He knocked lightly on her door, which was immediately opened to admit him. Once again she embraced him warmly, then kissed him gently on the cheek and drew him to a small armchair by her bed. He sat there, while she stretched herself out with a sigh.

"Oh! Will", she began, "this is a very unhappy household. That dreadful man is ubiquitous. He has locked up poor Anne and keeps the key."

"Locked her up!"

"Yes. The silly girl betrayed herself. She and the boy - they were – well – they were found together. I think it was quite innocent, but you won't get that blockhead to believe that. They had arranged to meet, don't ask me how, and were walking, hand in hand – as innocent as that - in the garden of all places. And he surprised them. I think they were betrayed, perhaps by one of the maids he has suborned to spy for him. Young Thomas should not even have been here and as for her – well – the two are obviously so much in love. It is very sad. Who knows what my husband will do when he comes home - they may never be able to see one another again."

"Can anything be done?"

"I hope so. I hope so. I thought perhaps you could help."

"How?"

"I do not know yet. Have you spoken to Thomas ?"

"No. I came straight here."

"You must speak to him. He seems to have given up. From what Ann told me he seems to have resigned himself to a life of celibacy."

"What a waste!"

She looked at him and smiled: "Yes. I think so, but then I am a woman. I think any young man who denies himself the benefits of male potency is wasting his natural gifts."

Will looked at her sharply. She smiled at him. Was

she flirting with him? As she lay on the bed, her clothes displayed negligently about her robust form, her dark hair loose and spread about her on the pillow he became even more acutely aware of the magnetism he felt whenever he was near her. Her eyes had a look he had not seen in a woman since he first wooed his wife in the fields and forests around Stratford. He was profoundly disturbed, anxious to assist his hostess, but concerned not to betray a man he respected and in whose house he had been welcomed.

Almost as if she read his thoughts, Ann sat up and seemed to adjust not only her dress, but her person. She became businesslike, leaned towards him and placed a hand on his. She looked him earnestly in the eye

"I am so concerned for her Will. She is my protégé and I love her dearly. I cannot bear to see her wasting away in forlorn virginity. She deserves to have the love of a good man. Go and see him. Tell him there is a young woman with a broken heart and only he can mend it."

Will thought this a vile phrase, but agreed to do as she asked: "I propose to go to the university tomorrow. There are books I wish to consult and he has one he particularly wants to show me. Of course I will speak to him on your behalf."

"Not on mine. On Anne's."

"I will do what I can."

"Thank you. You are so good. I have always felt I could rely on you."

She leaned closer and kissed him, this time on the mouth. She did not immediately remove her lips and he was overwhelmed with desire for her. Very slowly and carefully, so as not to disturb the moment, he put his arms around her and drew her close. Then he returned her kiss. She placed her hands gently on his chest and disengaged herself.

256

"Oh! Will. If only things were different."

"I love you, you know."

"Do you? I was hoping you might. But it cannot come to anything, you know that."

"It already has. I have feelings for you that I know cannot be consummated, but they are there nevertheless. And I can express them in my thoughts, in my poetry. If only I could dare to hope that you might love me in return."

"Oh! Will. I do. I do", she cried out with tears in her eyes and clasped him to her. "I feel so much pleasure in your company and when you are not here – well – then the world is a poorer place. So let us be friends, lovers if you will, but you must understand -."

Will did understand, but only partly. He thought it strange that he should love this woman with whom he should have an unconsummated relationship, yet he had enjoyed the intimacy of someone he knew he did not love.

There was a loud knock on the door. She pushed him into his chair and leaned back on the bed. Then she called: "Who's there?"

It was Malaver: "I need to know if you have any requirements for the rest of the day, my lady".

"I will be there shortly. Kindly wait for me in the hall."

As his footsteps faded away along the passage she said to Will: "I must go. It would not do to give him any cause for mischief making."

"I will talk to Thomas. We will think of something."

"Give me time to go down to him. Then follow shortly after. I am sorry we have come to this."

"So am I, my lady. So am I."

That afternoon he went to the University, where he found Thomas very much as he feared – morose, resigned to a loveless life, totally absorbed in the work of listing and calculating the multitudinous volumes and manuscripts his master intended one day to incorporate into his library. The book he wanted to show Will was a translation of Plutarch's Lives by one Thomas North.

"I know of this", said Will. "It was mentioned at school. But Plutarch was a Greek. I am little interested in the history of that nation. They seem to me poor people in comparison with the Romans. The Latins are the bed-rock of our civilisation."

"You mistake it", said Thomas. "He wrote about the heroes and statesmen of both nations, comparing them side by side. It is an amazing work of scholarship. You would derive much useful information and even inspiration from it. Sir Thomas brought a number of copies with him last time he visited. I could let you borrow one if you wished."

"Will he not notice it is missing?"

"I doubt it and if he does I can make some excuse. Take it Will."

They spent some time studying it and Will was astonished at the wealth of stories it contained and also in some cases the quality of the writing.

"This Thomas North was a great scholar. His knowledge of the Greek language must have been profound."

"Far from it. He translated from the French. Plutarch was Grecian living in Rome and writing about Greeks and Romans in his own language. His work is transcribed into French and now, hundreds of years later appears in English."

Thomas returned to his books and Will became engrossed in the Plutarch stories. There was silence for a while; then Will looked at his friend anxiously. He had promised to speak to him, but did not know how to raise the subject.

"I spoke to the Lady Ann", he said at length.

"How is that great lady?" Thomas asked.

"She is well. Not in good spirits, but well. I do not think the same came be said for young Anne Underhill."

At the sound of her name Thomas looked up, biting his lower lip, his eyes wide.

"What is it with her? I hope she is not ill."

"Not so far as I can ascertain. She is confined to her room. Locked in there, I gather."

"It's all my fault", cried Thomas. "I felt I had to see her. We thought we were being discreet. We did nothing improper, I assure you. We talked and held hands. But that dreadful man – what right has he to terrorise a household so?"

"What do you propose to do about it?"

"I? What can I do? I am destined to live a life of celibacy."

"So you will never marry, never know the love of a woman, never have children."

"It cannot be such a loss. You are married yet you never see your wife, nor your children."

"But they are there. I have experienced it. And one day, God willing, I will return to them. It is a man's destiny. How else can the human race be perpetuated?"

"I know nothing about the human race. I have enough on my mind with this mountain of books."

"Books! Books! Books are for the scholar."

"And for you too, apparently."

"I am a playwright who needs to mine their treasures for my own purpose, but they cannot be a substitute for life. And think of young Anne. Can she find consolation in books? She needs a man to love her, to help her bear children."

"I cannot answer for her. I cannot."

"So you do not love her. You have been merely dallying with her affections."

Thomas threw the book he was studying on to the table and stood: "I will not allow you to say that. I do love her. I love her more than anything in the world".

"So then what are your intentions towards her?"

"My intentions? My intentions? What intentions can I have? My intentions are driven by my patron and controlled by that odious man he has installed to watch over his household. I would do anything to woo her – yes and marry her, but what can I do? I am reliant on my work here for my livelihood."

He picked up several volumes and put them down again. Then he turned on Will almost fiercely: "And incidentally she is even locked in her room. Would you have me break the door down and run off with her."

Will confronted him: "Yes, if necessary. Think positively. The lady Ann wants to help you both. I want to help you."

"But how? What are we to do?"

"Take your paramour and flee that house."

"I cannot betray Sir Thomas. I owe him a great debt and must repay it."

"By remaining in his subjugation. Are you prepared to spend the rest of your life in slavery. "

The word seemed to stimulate Thomas. He got to his feet and went to the window. Will could sense the conflict that was tormenting him. Eventually he turned. His eyes were brighter:

"Do you think it's possible? We are watched day and night."

"Everything is possible if the determination is there. The first thing is for you to agree."

Thomas did not reply immediately. He looked around at the shelves of books, the manuscripts on the tables. It was as if he was assessing their value against the prospect of a life with the young woman of his dreams.

"So what do you want from me?"

"At this moment one word only – yes."

Again there was a long pause. Then Thomas said, quietly at first: "Yes, yes, yes, yes".

It was worked out like a military campaign. Ann was the prime instigator and Will was tremendously proud of her, said she was like a latter-day Jeanne d'Arc. She laughed at this and expressed the hope that she would not suffer the same fate. Her original plan had been to say that she would visit her family in Bristol and take Anne with her, but the steward refused to surrender the key of the room where the girl was still incarcerated.

It was decided that Italy should be the couple's ultimate destination. In any nearer country, such as Denmark, the Netherlands, or even France, they might be discovered by Thomas Bodley or his agents and brought back to England. However they had no knowledge of that country and were at a loss even what city even they should aim for. Then Will had an idea. He thought of his patron in Essex and the years he had spent in Italy. Would he be prepared to advise, even perhaps help? In the short time he had been working with the Earl he had received the impression that he would be inclined to encourage such an adventure.

He hastened to Hedingham with fast post horses. Typically the Earl was in his cups and laughed uproariously at the plan. He was delighted to assist in what he saw as a little knavery, providing letters of introduction to places where the couple could stay en route and even offering his house in Venice as a place of refuge.

Back in Oxford Ann told him that she had managed to visit the girl and explain what they were hoping to do. The principal difficulty lay in persuading the steward to part with the key to the room and for this Ann devised a plot that seemed to Will devious in the extreme and even fraught with danger. It involved his ingratiating himself into the steward's confidence. The man was fond of his tipple and enjoyed a convivial drink with anyone who was prepared to tolerate his offensive manners. Subduing his natural revulsion, Will allowed himself to carouse with him and encourage him to partake even more liberally than his wont.

He raised the subject of the imprisoned girl and exchanged much prurient banter with him. It appeared that the steward lusted after the maiden and would have dearly loved to take advantage of her purity, but. advances had been repulsed with contempt. Will suggested a way in which he could enjoy the young woman by proxy. He professed himself enamoured of the girl and urged the steward to allow him access. He offered by way of bribe an account of what transpired as a form of surrogate satisfaction and even subtly suggested that once the girl had been introduced to the delights of intercourse, she might be more amenable to approaches from other males. He also waved a gold coin at him as a further inducement.

In his inebriated state the odious man was delighted with the idea. He would achieve a kind of revenge on the upstart young tart who had rejected his advances so peremptorily and also opened up the possibility of potential satisfaction for his own carnal aspirations. On an agreed night he rendered up the key and wished Will good fortune in his endeavours. Then he went to his own bed and dreamed who knows what perverted imaginings might take place in the young girl's room.

The next morning Malaver awoke late, being aroused by a maid who told him she needed the key to the girl's room so that she could fulfil her duties there. He asked her if Will Shakespeare was about and she said she had not seen him. Cursing the volcanic eruptions of his stomach from the previous evening's over-indulgence and the even greater disturbance in his head, he staggered from his bed and went in search of Will. He was nowhere to be found. The mistress of the house was still confined to her room and was not to be disturbed. He was in a quandary. Could it be that the young man was still in there? If so, it would not look well for him to have granted him admission.

He sent the maid away and, when he was fairly sure he was not observed, hammered on the door and called Anne's name then Will's. There was no response to either. The disturbance in his stomach was beginning to make itself felt in his bowels and he found it necessary to retire to an appropriate privy. When he emerged some time later, feeling as if his insides had been drawn out slowly and painfully through his nether regions, he checked the door again and found it still locked. He knocked again and, mindful of people who were in the vicinity, called softly to Anne. At this point her mistress appeared and asked him what the difficulty was.

He said he had lost the key to the room and was unable to gain admittance. Ann first of all expressed her astonishment at its loss and then asked how he thought her maid could assist when she had no means of opening the door. He then asked her if she knew the whereabouts of Will Shakespeare and when she wanted to know why he was forced to admit grudgingly that he had lent the key to Will.

"Lent it! Lent it! To another man! When you would not even permit me to use it! How dare you. I hope the young lady has come to no harm. You will be answerable to it if she has."

"Oh! no. No harm at all. He is a highly respectable young man. But he is an actor and well versed in matters of deportment and the like. He was going to give her lessons."

"Lessons! Well I hope that is all he was going to give

263

her. We must obviously find him."

"He may still be in the room."

"Still in the room! Why should he? You do not mean he has spent the night there?"

"Well no. I mean that was not the intention."

"Oh! and what was the intention pray?"

"I've told you. It was just to be a brief visit."

"A brief visit and he may still be there!"

She made a great show of banging on the door and he joined in. As with all the other doors in the house, however, it was very solidly built of good old English oak and, like her majesty's ships, designed to repel all boarders. She then had the household searched, inside and out, but to no avail. Eventually, it was agreed that the door should be broken down, regardless of the damage. That took quite a while and it was nearly dinner time before they were able to force their way in. When they did they were confronted by an astonishing sight.

Sitting on the bed was Will. His hands were tied behind his back and his feet were tethered to the bedposts. A gag across his mouth had prevented him from answering the knocks. They released him and he fell sobbing on the floor. He was picked up and stretched on the bed, where he lay gasping for breath.

Ann held his shoulders and begged him: "Where is she? Where is my darling maid?"

Will could only gasp: "Gone. Gone. They have taken her."

"Who? Who have taken her?"

"Kidnappers. Brigands. They may demand ransom, thinking she is the daughter of the house."

She turned on the steward: "This is your doing, you stupid man. The master shall hear of this. You'll pay for it, see if you don't. Get out of here."

He protested, but she shook her fists at him and

chased him from the room. Later Will was able to explain to him and the rest of the household how he had called on the girl as agreed to give her tuition. Masked men had entered the room, tied him up and seized her. Malaver, who despite appearances to the contrary was no fool, suggested this was obviously a plot devised by her lover. A piece of paper found in the room afterwards addressed from Thomas to Anne suggested that they were bound for Portsmouth, where they would obtain passage to Le Havre or Rouen.

Ann instructed Malaver to recruit the help of local men to go in pursuit towards the coast, knowing the two lovers would in fact be on a boat sailing down the Thames, en route for Calais. She had been happy to award the girl for her loyal service by providing her with a substantial sum of money to ensure that the couple were able to endure their elopement in reasonable comfort. She also sent a messenger to her husband's last known destination and awaited with a certain amount of equanimity the wrath of his return.

For Will the happy outcome of the event left him with a sense of anti-climax. The play had come to an end. After all the days of preparation the audience had left and the players had gone their various ways. Without Thomas he could no longer justify his remaining in Oxford. Once again he was turning his back on a home and family, as he had done his wife and children in Stratford. Although he bid farewell to Ann with deep regret he realised that his feelings were transient. He had come to love these people, but was in reality little more than a spectator in their lives. The characters he wrote about were more real to him.

The people he was meeting in Essex or London would also be strangers to him, collaborators, business partners. He was alone in a world whose inhabitants would pass him by, with nothing but their stories to write about and perhaps console him. As he spurred his tiring horse through a landscape of fields and woods that left him largely uninspired only one bright star lightened the shadow clouding his mind, one friend who still lit the future like a beacon at the end of a distant journey. That one exception to his gloomy prognosis was Christopher Marlowe. Despite the differences in their personalities and their views on life, he felt he could love him as a brother, an elder brother perhaps, certainly a mad brother, but a brother nevertheless. He would try to find the earliest opportunity of getting to London to be with him again. But before he could do that once again his work would intervene and he must direct his steps once again towards Hedingham.

PART 5

Chapter 25

In the August of 1592 the plague returned to devastate the population of London and its environs. Theatres and all other places where people congregated were closed or bereft of audiences. As the great monster death stalked the streets of the stricken township, some of its brightest literary lights were extinguished, among them Thomas Watson, a man honoured among the literati; and Robert Greene, less well loved, who died slowly and presumably painfully, comparing himself in his writing to a swan singing melodiously at his demise. While he repented for a life spent too licentiously among the temptations put in his way he still poured out vituperation for his fellow scribes, including a man who had neither wished, nor caused, him any harm, but who had achieved what he had failed to do and had stood in his way when he might have gained preference with a noble lord. Writing as a dying man in what he described as a "groat's worth of wit", he dismissed Shakespeare as: "an upstart crow, beautified with the feathers of others and with a tiger's heart wrapped in a player's hide", thus echoing a comment made about Shakespeare many years before in very different circumstances.

For his part Shakespeare was safe from the dread disease in Castle Hedingham, where he was lodged in a cottage on the estate. His lordship had much to occupy his mind and left the playwright very much to himself. The experience was more congenial than Will had expected and the words began to flow from his quill. He still felt himself, however, very much a jobbing playwright dependent upon his patron not only for his board and lodging, but for the very stuff on which he built his literary creations.

He began to be depressed at his lot and wondered if he would ever find himself acknowledged as the master poet he felt sure he was. Unlike others who were writing at the time he did not have the advantage of a classical education and had arrived perhaps too late at the cultural scene in London. Financially he was in a perilous situation, presently dependent entirely on the generosity of the Earl. With the theatres closed because of the plague, he had no income as an actor. Even when they reopened the return from the production of his plays would scarcely make him a rich man, although he hoped that the arrangement he would make with Burbage would be more advantageous than that with Henslowe.

As is so often the case, however, when the skies are darkest and the future bleakest, the sun will burst through the clouds and suddenly it is summer again. Will arrived late for dinner in the great hall one day to find that the Earl had a visitor, or rather a whole army of visitors. The Earl of Southampton had called with his entourage.

The Earl of Oxford, not usually noted for his formality, on this occasion chose to introduce the newcomers with a flourish. Will found himself facing a young man, several years his junior, of a grace and beauty that lit up the dark, lofty interior of the great hall like a morning star. Quite dazzled, Will bowed low and hardly dared to lift his head until the graceful creature, rose from the table and, to the playwright's astonishment, walked towards him and offered his hand. Will took it and made a formal gesture towards it with his lips.

"Master Shakespeare, I have heard great things of you."

"Your grace is too kind."

"And seen something of your plays, particularly those about our earlier monarchs. Fine, I must say, very fine."

"Once again your grace is pleased to flatter me."

"Nothing of the sort, I assure you."

The young man resumed his seat and Will took a place near the bottom of the table. From there he had an opportunity to study the noble visitor. He was particularly struck with the contrast between him and his host, the one so delicate in his manner, so courtly in his gestures and conversation, the other gross and abusive to all around him except his guest. It was, Will thought, a living example of the great contrast existing between individual members of the human race. Here were men of similar background, wealth and position, but with souls reflecting the opposite poles of good and evil. He knew little about Southampton's background, but found it difficult to believe he could be guilty of anything that was base or degenerate, unlike Oxford, who from his reputation was capable of anything that was ignoble and depraved.

After dinner Will found himself in conversation with Southampton. Lacking the pomp and aggressive superiority displayed by Oxford, he talked to Will almost as if they were equals and if anything appeared to make a conscious effort not to appear condescending. He asked Will if he had written poetry as well as his plays and Will confessed, almost for the first time to anyone, that he had, in particular sonnets written to particular friends of his.

"I am a great lover of poetry", the Earl said. "Oh! I enjoy a good play, but once seen it is over, although not always forgotten. A poem is something one can cherish for ever. I have many, some of them kindly written for me by poets of the age. There is poetry in your plays. I can tell. The words are very beautiful. Would you

271

consider writing a poem for me?"

For a moment Will did not know how to reply. He felt himself blushing.

"My sonnets were written out of affection for particular people – " he began.

"No, no. I am not talking about sugared sonnets made to a mistress's eyebrow."

Will laughed with him at the conceit and made a mental note for future use.

"I mean a real poem, about real events, or a tale from history or legend. Think on it."

And with that he left to carry on a private conversation with Oxford in his "den".

The young Earl stayed only a few days and when he left reminded Will of his promise. Oxford asked him afterwards what the promise was about and demanded to know if he was seeking patronage elsewhere. Will reassured him that it was only the question of a poem, not of a play. Oxford reacted more favourably to this and suggested to Will that he could do himself much good if he accepted the other's invitation.

"He has made the reputation of many a less worthy poet than you", he told him.

Later he explained the reason for the Earl's visit. Financial constraints had made it necessary to sell Hedingham. It was the only part of his estate that would realise sufficient return to satisfy his debts and responsibilities. Southampton had at one time been ward of Lord Burghley, and had agreed to act as an arbitrator between him and one of the few members of the nobility with sufficient funds to capitalise the purchase. Will suggested that it would be a wrench for Oxford to lose such a wonderful heritage, but the other merely shrugged.

"What is it but stones and mortar", he said. "I shall be glad to be shot of the place. Perhaps I can begin to enjoy life again. I have many other estates where I can stay. Perhaps return to my beloved Italy."

Will thought about Southampton's offer of patronage. It was an exciting prospect. There was no doubt that the publication of a major poetic work was a better way of establishing oneself on the literary scene than writing a play, which as the Earl suggested, existed only for its life on the stage and rarely found its way into print. A poem, however, needed a sponsor to ensure its distribution among the great ones of the land as well as the general public.

What should he write about? It would have to be about love, perhaps unrequited love. His mind returned to his encounter in Oxford with the dark beauty who had desired him so warmly, but whose fire he was unable to return. Somewhere in classical literature there would be a story that paralleled his. On the wall of the Earl's den there was a picture, one of a number obviously enjoyed by their owner rather for their prurient nature than their artistic nature. Most of the figures portrayed were nude or dressed in various forms of disarray. The one that caught Will's eye showed a young Adonis, one hand covering his eyes, the other decorously concealing his manhood. He was standing repelled at the spectacle of a rather fleshy Venus who was behaving in a less bashful manner, making no attempt to conceal the delights she was offering him.

"Yes", he thought, "man can reject even the most desirable prize when it is offered. It is the choice that makes him a man and divides him from the animal. I can write that."

And there, while the theatres were closed to his plays, while his host caroused and drank away the terrors of the plague, in the relative quiet and security of his nearby cottage, he told the story of Venus and Adonis.

Chapter 26

Christopher Marlowe also escaped the terrors of the plague by taking refuge once again at the house of the Walsinghams, near Deptford, a few miles out of London. He had another reason for departing precipitately from the city. He had a run-in with one Allen Nicholls, constable of Shoreditch. It was a typical confrontation for Kit with what passed for the law and his reaction to it was in character. The man had attempted to prevent him from going along a particular London street for some trifling reason (a crime, possibly a murder, had taken place there) and Kit resented being told where he could or could not go. The pair came to blows and on this occasion his opponent got the better of him. He was brought before a magistrate, who fortunately took a lenient view of his misdemeanour. He was released on agreeing to pay a fine of 20 guineas in three months' time and obviously hoped by leaving London he would avoid having to do so.

He asked his bedfellow, Thomas Kydd, to join him there, but Kydd said he wished to remain behind, so that he could to take advantage of the theatre closure to work on a new play, possibly a sequel to The Spanish Tragedy. He did not tell Kit he had a more covert reason for wanting to spend time there on his own. He had become increasingly concerned at his friend's heretical outbursts, particularly his latest one at the Walsinghams, and feared he may have committed some of his views to paper. He proposed to go through them and destroy any that might be used in evidence in the event of any witch hunt by the authorities, something that was always a possibility. When Kit expressed concern for his health he undertook to shut himself in his room to escape the ravages of the plague unaware that in doing so, he would not be able to evade a fate awaiting him from a more totalitarian source.

That plague in human form was Gabriel Harvey, who in his plague-free Cambridge *sanctum sanctorum* looked down upon the stricken city and identified the hand of god in the punishment inflicted on its wayward inhabitants. His spy Poley had kept him informed of the heretical activity spreading its corrupting influence insidiously among those who frequented places of entertainment, not to mention the ale houses, brothels and stews that proliferated around the new theatres north and south of the river. They might be closed as a result of god's intervention, but those responsible for purveying the gospel of evil in their walls remained largely untouched.

He also had a personal, academic reason for disliking the freedom of expression playwrights adopted not only in their stage presentations, but also in their occasional verse. To Harvey language reflected the morals of the population. Lack of discipline in writing demonstrated moral decay. The application of correct scansion in the writing of verse went hand in hand with a proper regard for social proprieties. In this way he regarded himself as the only savant in history attempting to improve the morals of a nation by the application of the hexameter.

Braving the ravages of the plague he came down to London and approached Sir Francis Walsingham, who had been appointed head of a department set up by the Queen to control dissent and ensure that proper intelligence was gained about any rebellious spirits abroad in the realm. Harvey was welcomed with the respect due to a man of such influence in the intellectual affairs of the nation. Wrongs were being perpetrated, Harvey told him, even as the shadow of the Black Death hovered over the population. He regretted having to mention the name of Walsingham's kinsman, Thomas, but it was a matter of scandal that his house had become a hotbed of dissident talk and unrest. Many gathered there, including the most invidious of them all – Christopher Marlowe. Among the others was Marlowe's pederastic companion, who at this very moment was living in his former lodgings in London.

Walsingham was no fool. He knew Harvey by repute and recognised a repressed academic when he saw one. The man's obvious anathema for the rapidly developing theatrical scene had to be regarded with caution. Her majesty was known to favour such activities and, indeed, had expressed a wish to be entertained by the players in her own court. Nevertheless the stability of the realm depended upon a strict adherence to the established church. Dissention of any kind represented a threat. Patriotism served to keep Roman Catholicism in check. It was associated in the popular mind with threats from countries like Spain and France. Heresy was a different matter. It seemed to arise from the actions and pronouncements of individuals, people disillusioned by what the established church could offer in a modern world. It had to be suppressed and the best way to do so was to identify one or two perpetrators who would serve as examples. The closure of theatres because of the plague represented an opportunity to do so without threatening the structure of something with support at all levels of society.

It was an easy matter for him to set the wheels in motion. He called on an agent by the name of Maunder and, having briefed him, left it to him to carry out the necessary work. So it was the unfortunate Thomas Kydd who was the first to feel the impact of Walsingham's operation. He was awoken quite early one morning to hear the sound of heavy footsteps on his stairs and find his door burst open by sword-bearing agents of the queen. Despite his initial alarm he thought he had nothing to fear. Then they started examining in minute details the papers scattered about his room. One in particular seemed to capture their interest. They showed it to him and demanded an explanation. He told them that it was not his. It belonged, he said, to a former room-mate. They asked his name and, reluctant to lead them to such a beloved friend, he declined to give it.

As a result he found himself in the dread precincts of Bridewell, where the interrogation continued. After a night spent uncomfortably on a stone bench he was taken to a different room where a hard pallet was the least of his concerns. The persuasive instruments of a previous Christian authority still furnished the room and he could hear the screams and appeals of other sufferers through the walls. As the rack took its toll on his joints and sinews, he continued to protest his innocence, but could only gain relief from his suffering by giving them the name they sought. He told them the paper denying the divinity of Jesus Christ belonged to one Christopher Marlowe. It was all they wanted to know. They released their bruised and bloodied victim. The results of their questioning were communicated to the Privy Council. Agent Maunder was despatched to hunt down their new quarry and arrest him. He was advised, in view of the playwright's violent reputation, to take with him whatever aid was necessary.

However, with the theatres closed and writers and actors dispersed the difficulty was how to find him. Maunder referred back to Walsingham, who, irritated at being bothered with such details, passed him on to Harvey, who was anxious to shake the stews of London off his clerical garb. So he called on his confidante

Poley and asked him if he knew Marlowe's whereabouts. Poley was reluctant to tell him the writer would be at the Walsingham's because of the possible danger to a family whose hospitality he had enjoyed and the members of which he regarded as his friends. Harvey could be very persistent and persuaded him that they would not be in jeopardy. The only suspect in this matter was Marlowe.

Harvey left London as soon as he could, but he made his way not to Cambridge but towards Castle Hedingham. He had become increasingly concerned at rumours regarding the possible establishment of a library at Oxford and although he did not imagine that the eponymous Earl had any connection with it, he understood that someone was staying there who did. If the noble lord was going to bestow his patronage anywhere it should obviously be Cambridge rather than Oxford. He knew his reputation as a poet and playwright and there were those who had dedicated poems to him, such as his friend Edmund Spenser, Greene and Lyly.

He was welcomed with courtesy by the Earl, which flattered Harvey, unaware that his lordship was prepared to receive anyone who might be in a position to assist him at a time of severe financial pressure. As he had anticipated Harvey found Will Shakespeare there, but surprised at the warmth the Earl seemed to pay him when, as playwright he appeared to have no academic qualifications whatever. He had read a little of his work and thought it of small account, the writer apparently unable to apply even the most basic tenets of prosy.

He expected to have a private audience with the Earl and said as much, but Oxford waved a casual hand at those gathered around him, including Shakespeare, and insisted that all were friends. Despite himself Harvey found himself caught up in the casual even unruly atmosphere of the household, allowing himself to partake rather more than was his wont with an excellent wine that seemed to flow endlessly. The Earl asked him what had taken him to London during the perils of the plague and although he had not intended doing so, the pedant's vanity, combined with the lubrication of the alcohol got the better of him and he spoke of his visit to no less a person than Sir Francis Walsingham. This immediately aroused the mistrust of the Earl. He was not one to take kindly to political machinations. They could so easily have an adverse affects that spread much wider than those who might be directly concerned. The spectre of a conspiracy raised its head. He knew Harvey's reputation as an instigator and questioned him closely.

He began by complimenting him on his reputation as one who opposed heresy and searched it out assiduously, offering him assistance in his endeavours. Flattered, Harvey related the arrest and torture of Kydd and told him that steps were being taken to deal with similar malefactors, particularly the iniquitous Marlowe. By doing so the forces of rebellion would be crushed and, incidentally, the quality of English verse preserved.

"Amen to that", said the Earl. "But how can this be achieved. You say this man Kydd has been apprehended, but it will not be so easy to prise Marley from the bosom of his friends".

Harvey became boastful: "Oh! there are ways. He is currently with the Walsingham's – not my acquaintance, Sir Francis of course, but his nephew Sir Thomas in Deptford in Kent. He is known to express himself forcibly there, expanding on his heretical views and generally corrupting those around him. Action has already been put into motion with a view to apprehending him, or failing that, taking whatever is necessary to silence him".

Will could hold back no longer: "Silence him! He is the finest poet in the land".

Harvey looked at him in surprise: "That may be your opinion young man, but I think you should accept the views of wiser men than you. His work is full of bombast. Worse than that it contains passages that are heretical. Combined with the comments he is reported to have made it seems there is good evidence at least to have him questioned by the appropriate authority."

"You mean tortured. Stretched on the rack."

"Oh! come now. Such things might have been customary under a former religious regime, but I do not think you can accuse our humane Christian church of such practices."

At this his lordship got to his feet: "My dear Harvey. I did not realise it was so late. You will be wanting to get to Cambridge before dark". Harvey also rose, concerned to find he was not being offered hospitality.

"But your lordship – my horse – "

"We'll have a horse for you. Hey you!"

He stirred some of his servants with kicks to the rear and buffets to the head.

"Get some horses ready. Our guests are leaving."

Will was surprised to learn that he might be included, but the Earl motioned him to stay. He ushered Harvey unceremoniously out and then returned.

"It seems your friend Marlowe is in mortal danger."

"My lord it does appear so – and not only him. He will be at the house of the Walsingham's – Sir Thomas that is. The axe might fall on all of them."

"The axe being an apt word. You must go to them Will. Warn them."

"If your Lordship will allow me."

"Of course. Of course. It could be a matter of life or

death. Take a horse. But don't hang about in London. We don't want you going down with the plague."

Chapter 27

The household of Sir Thomas Walsingham was not a happy place. Since the birth of his son, his attitude towards his wife had cooled and he had begun to absent himself habitually from the conjugal bed. Audrey associated this with his preference for the company of the men who visited the house. Most of these were the usual rowdy, troublesome males, whose manners and language made meal times an increasing burden and there was one for whom he seemed to have a special affection; that man was Kit Marley. She was well aware that pederasty was punishable by death and was not anxious to bring about a situation that might lead to her premature widowhood, but she nevertheless found the relationship increasingly irksome. She found herself consumed by a jealousy made the more emotionally disturbing because it was directed towards a man rather than a woman.

One day someone she knew as Poley arrived without invitation and on a horse lathered by hard riding. He had come, he said, to warn them of the threat to their guest Marlowe. Although Walsingham was aware of the risks his friend took in the expression of his views, he did not think there was any immediate danger. The wheels of authority turned slow and were hardly likely to be directed towards such a respectable household.

His wife took a different view and agreed with Poley that they should persuade Marlowe to return to London, or at least leave their house. Thomas refused. His relationship with Marlowe might not have had the physical connotations feared by his wife, but he was certainly in thrall to the younger man. Totally lacking himself in creative ability, or even imagination, he was almost mesmerised by the power of the other's rhetoric, both as represented on the stage and in the relative privacy of his household. He welcomed the company of many writers to his home, but for none of them could he feel the same esteem and affection. Only one came close in the quality of his work on the stage and that one was William Shakespeare, but Walsingham found him a curiously cold person, who held himself apart from the rest of the company and treated Thomas with nothing more than deference.

Poley was invited to stay to dinner, where the company was sparse, most of the usual visitors having returned to their homes during the plague. In addition to Sir Thomas, his wife Audrey, Christopher and Poley, there were two who were little more than servants, but were tolerated at the table. They were Fritzer and Skeres, who sat either side of Poley and made up a baleful trio sharing one another's intimacies with sniggers and guffaws. Occasionally they would break off to pay attention to Christopher, who was holding forth in his customary manner.

His flow of invective against the received wisdom of Biblical references was interrupted by a question from his host. Sir Thomas reminded Marlowe of his play Edward the Second and asked him why he had opened it with a lengthy monologue by an apparently secondary character, Gaveston.

It was a question the playwright had been asked before: "But he is not secondary. He is central to the whole tale. Consider if you will –" and he began quoting, declaiming in an extravagant imitation of an actor:" 'What greater bliss can hap to Gaveston Than live and be the favourite of a king? Sweet prince, I come; these, these thy amorous lines Might have enforced me to have swum from France, and, like Leander, gasped upon the sand, so thou would'st smile, and take me in thine arms'. There, you see Thomas. You have only to place yourself in the person of the king and one of your guests – say me - as Gaveston to appreciate the wealth of devotion there is in those lines".

"Why Kit, you make me blush", said Walsingham and hastily turned towards his wife engaging her in conversation. She listened to him coldly, while eyeing Marlowe as he stood uncertainly for a moment, then, with a wave of his hand, sat. The others around the table turned to one another and continued their conversation. Marlowe seemed to feel he had lost his audience, a rare occurrence for him. He got to his feet again, pushed his chair back and, proclaiming: "I need the privy", left. Walsingham called after him: "I would have a word with you Kit" and followed, leaving Audrey the only woman present except her maids. She turned towards Poley, Fritzer and Skeers and found them looking at her with something she interpreted as derision, even contempt.

She was overwhelmed with anger to think that these lowly members of her household could be so condescending towards her. She challenged their looks and rose. They hastily stood in turn and bowed towards her. She gathered her maids to her and as the men replaced their hats upon their heads she said pointedly to them: "I would there was someone who could rid me of this pestilent poet". They returned her look without reply and she left the room.

The three men took their drinks to sit outside in the warm sun. A storm was threatening and already thunder could be heard in the distance. There they were joined by Christopher and as the case is when men get together after a few drinks they began to gossip. One opinion shared was that all was not well in the Walsingham household. Kit agreed and said that

Thomas had gone to attempt a reconciliation with his wife.

"I think", said Poley, "that we should give our worthy host and hostess a little time to themselves. I know of an excellent inn nearby where we can drink and eat some more, spend the night and, if that is our inclination, enjoy the company of a fair maid or two."

"If that is our inclination", repeated Christopher.

So they left messages of apology with the servants and set out. The inn was only a short ride away in Deptford and they were welcomed there by a landlord who saw them as potentially good-paying customers. They were provided with a private room and served with viands and excellent ale. Their carousing went on into the night, with many a song and much laughter. A considerable amount of liquor was consumed until eventually silence fell.

Will set out from Hedingham, desperately anxious for his friend's safety. He hoped to make a quick journey as from Colchester the road was a straight one laid out by the Romans, but he found the horse he had so generously been given by the Earl was little more than a pack animal, insisting on travelling at a quick walk or foot-pace He thought with bitter irony of the horse he had described in the poem he carried in his saddle bag and decided his current steed did not excel a common one in shape, in courage, colour, space and bone. He had brought the manuscript of Venus and Adonis with him in the hope of finding a printer for it in London. If that proved impossible because of the plague he proposed to see out his patron in the hope that he would be able to assist or at least advise.

To add to his problems he had hardly reached St Albans, when the weather took a turn for the worse. At times the rain was torrential, which not only stung his face, but made conditions underfoot difficult. The wretched animal he rode balked at every flash of lightning and seemed to regard each step it took as a possible hazard. Will had hoped to reach London by nightfall, but his progress was so slow he eventually had to rest himself and his exhausted horse in a hostelry at Chipping Barnet, still some 20 miles from his destination on the other side of the city.

After a sleepless night spent in the greatest anxiety, worrying about the possible fate of his friend, he set out at daybreak. The storm had subsided and it was a fine bright morning, but he now faced a further difficulty. When he reached the outskirts of London he realised he did not know his way across town. In the narrow streets the buildings almost met overhead and he could not identify any landmarks. He looked for someone to ask directions, but there were so few people about it was almost like a city of the dead. Those who had stayed behind to brave the dangers of the city were obviously the poorest of the poor, scuttling along with hoods over their heads as if hoping that the plague would not notice them, or consider them unworthy sport for its death-dealing darts. More gruesome were the occasional forms lying at the roadside or in doorways, waiting for the cart of death to come and carry them off to a common grave. Some of them were almost naked, bearing the signs of the post-mortem injuries inflicted by the rats that scuttled away as Will's horse approached them.

At last he saw the tower of St Paul's and urged his reluctant horse on. The road widened and ahead of him he saw a figure of a man stumbling along as if finding it difficult to put one foot before another. Occasionally he would hold his head in his hands, then fling his arms into the air as if sustaining great pain. As Will approached he fell, or threw himself, on the ground, causing the horse to stall. There the man writhed in obvious agony, foaming at the mouth, his eyes staring. When he saw Will he lifted a weak arm and cried out: "Water, for the love of god. A little drink to save my life".

Will was uncertain what to do. He could see the man was sorely smitten, with running sores on his naked arms and legs. He was desperately anxious to hurry on, but his charitable instincts went deep and he felt he could not refuse succour to a dying man. A flask of brandy water had been refilled at the inn. He could offer the man a sip. He dismounted and tethered his horse to a post. Then he carefully poured a little liquid into the stopper and offered it. The man seemed too weak to lift himself and Will had to bend down towards him, finding the stench of his wounds almost overpowering.

The man took the drink and knocked it back. As Will reached down to recover the stopper he found himself seized round the neck and thrown to the ground. Then with surprising vigour for such a sick individual the man leapt up and bestrode Will, holding a knife to his throat.

"Thanks for that young master", he said with a thick guttural accent. "Now I'll have the rest of your belongings."

"I have little of value", said Will. "I am a poor man like yourself".

"Poor you might be, but like me you're not."

"What I have you may take, only spare me. I am on an important mission to save someone's life."

"Is that so? Well, that might mean two of you will have to die."

"You have no reason to kill me."

"If I let you live you will inform on me and that'll be

my end, and a nasty slow one on the gallows. At least yours will be quick."

Will was not a coward. He was not afraid of death, but he hated having to face it in the filth of the gutter and at the hands of such a ruffian. He supposed there was nothing left for him but prayer. He closed his eyes and tried to remember one that was appropriate to the occasion. The man's grip on him was strong, the knife felt sharp against his throat. Then the grip relaxed. The knife was no longer there. He could hear other voices. He opened his eyes. His assailant was in the hands of two men, large capable men, dressed partly in leather, with swords in their belts. He sat up.

"It was lucky we came along", one of them said. "We have been looking out for this one. He's a galliard, or what you may know as a counterfeit crank."

"He was very convincing. Those sores look as if he had been eaten by rats."

"Ratsbane more like. We get them all. Abraham Men, Tom O'Bedlam."

"I met one of those", said Will. "He said he was cold: 'poor Tom's a cold' he said."

"That's him."

At this the miscreant clutched at his captor's hand and cried: "Don't turn me in. They'll hang me for sure".

"And the rest. You'll be flayed, quartered, opened up before you're dead."

"I meant no harm. I don't want to die."

"You would have shown no mercy to him if we hadn't come along."

They bid farewell to Will and dragged their protesting prisoner off. Will mounted his horse slowly, chastened by his experience, aware of the little group of beggars who had gathered round to watch the proceedings. The morning was half over. He continued his way through the near deserted town. Even the traders on London Bridge had given up and deserted it. He made better time on another of the Roman roads, but it was still dinner time before he reached the Walsinghams. When he did he was met at the door by an anxious looking Sir Thomas's wife who greeted him by asking: "Have you come from the inn?"

"What inn?"

"At Deptford. A group left here last night and haven't returned. My husband has gone to find out if something has happened."

"Why should he think that?"

"Marlowe was among them and we had a warning. Poley came down from London and told us the word has gone out against Marlowe. He is in some form of danger."

"Yes. I heard that too. In fact I have come to warn him."

"It appears they have taken Kydd, who was living in Marlowe's place. I'm just worried that my husband will get involved."

"I will go and find out. The Deptford Inn you say."

He turned his horse to ride off. She put out a hand and let it rest on his leg.

"You are a good young man Master William", she said. "Not like the others".

Blushing at the unexpected compliment he doffed his hat and rode off. When he arrived at the inn he found a crowd gathered outside. Someone told him there had been a death and he was full of foreboding. Inside people thronged the hall and stairs and he had difficulty in making his way up to the bedrooms. As he approached one of them, Sir Thomas emerged, his eyes wild and full of tears. He saw Will and gripped him by the shoulders:

"His eyes!" he cried. "They took out his eyes".

Pushing onlookers aside he went to the stairs and

289

would have stumbled down them were it not for the press of humanity. Will fought his own way into the room, where he saw his friend lying on the floor, bloody stab wounds in his neck and body, dark hollows where his eyes had been. Someone, presumably a medico, knelt by him, fussing unnecessarily with an examination. It was Will's first encounter with death and he was horrified by its violent form. He stood as if paralysed, unable either to move or turn his mind to any coherent thoughts. Poley came up to him and took him by the arm.

"Come away Will", he said. "you can do no good here".

He allowed himself to be drawn through the crowds, down to a quieter room downstairs. There he found Fritzer and Skeres being questionned by someone who was obviously an official of sorts, perhaps a local sheriff. He finished his interrogation and told them there would have to be a crowner's court. Then he left them to make arrangements for moving the body. Slowly Will pieced together what had happened.

Poley explained: "It was stupid. Nothing. A quarrel over the settling of the inn's charge. Kit had a quick temper, you know that. We had a good evening, drank, caroused a little, one or two of us had – well there were a couple of pretty young women there, although Kit would have none of them. Well, you know what he's like."

He shook his head and sat silently.

"He attacked me," said Fritzer."

"Kit did?"

"Yes. I was unarmed and to defend myself took a knife from Skere's belt – just to try and deter him, you understand, but he came back at me." He stood up and demonstrated the fight with dramatic gestures. "So I stabbed him in the chest, like that, just to disarm him, but still he came on, so I aimed at his face. That brought him low."

Will turned to the others: "So you were all there? You can confirm this?"

They grunted and nodded their assent, then sat silent looking, Will thought, shifty. Did it all happen like that? A drunken brawl?

"Why were you at the inn?"

"I came down to warn Kit", Poley said. "They had taken Kydd, you know, and Maunder was asking for Kit's whereabouts. I was afraid the Walsinghams might be in danger too."

"So you brought him here?"

"That's right."

"To be killed."

"Yes. No. That was something we could not have foretold."

Will remembered something he had read about the death of the Roman emperor, Julius Caesar, when several had been responsible for his death. These men were Kit's friends. Had they each contributed to his fatal stab wounds? He got up and went towards the door: "I must find Thomas Walsingham. He appears very distraught".

Fritzer bared his teeth in a grimace: "His wife will not be so sorry", he said.

Will looked at them, sitting there like three guilty men: "And his eyes? Why was it necessary to take out his eyes?"

Nobody answered for a moment, then Skeres explained: "Well you know in death if they have no eyes they cannot come back to haunt you".

The others nodded as if in agreement with this absurd notion. Will looked at them almost pityingly, then without another word left them. He found Sir Thomas was sitting on a bench outside the inn, his head in his hands. He lifted up a perplexed, tear-riven face and said: "He was my friend, Will. He was a good loyal friend".

Will sat beside him and put an arm along his shoulder: "Yes, Thomas. He was my friend too."

He was silent for a while, unable to offer any comfort. Then he suggested: "Shall we return to your home?"

"No. I want to stay here, but you go on. You will be tired after your journey."

"I have an errand to perform", said Will. "Perhaps you can advise me. I need to deliver something to the Earl of Southampton. Have you any idea where I might find him and what road I should take".

Sir Thomas seemed to welcome something that took his mind off his immediate distress.

"Yes I can help you there. He is also Baron of Titchfield and his family has long had an association with the village. He built its market hall and is often to be found there. If he is not I am sure the local people will be delighted to direct you to him."

"Titchfield you say?"

"Yes. Go out on the Roman road towards Southampton. You will find it signposted."

"Then I bid you farewell. I will not trouble you further at your time of affliction."

Sir Thomas stood and embraced him warmly.

"Goodbye Will", he said. "You are always welcome at my house, a sentiment I am sure my wife will echo".

Will thanked him and mounted his horse, directing its nose south again. Once again he was turning his back on a family and friends. He was setting out into an unknown future, with only his writing to keep him company. It worried him that he had been unable to save his friend's life. If only he had set out earlier, his horse had been speedier, he had not been delayed by the assailant in London. The tears of Sir Thomas had affected him and he was particularly troubled to find that he seemed to have no deep feelings for the death of his friend. It was as if the emotions he should have held were being directed into his work. Instead of mourning he involved himself in academic considerations. Had he witnessed a tragedy in the classical tradition? According to the Greeks a tragic event was brought about by the fates. But could that be seen in a tavern brawl over a reckoning? Or was there perhaps a conspiracy, arising from the environment of the day and the character of the protagonist? Was his friend's death the inevitable result of a preordained destiny? He himself had been involved in a similarly fortuitous event. A knife had been held to his throat and he had prepared himself for death, but it had been forestalled. By destiny? Or by the happy accident that brought two rescuers to his aid?

The road was a good one and he even found a signpost directing him towards Southampton. Perhaps that in itself was an omen. The work in his saddle bag was good, he was sure of that, and no doubt his lordship would approve. Maybe there would be payment for it. Maybe he would ask for another, although Will did not relish the prospect. Writing that kind of poetry was something of a domestic chore. His satisfaction lay in the creation of dramatic plots. The plague would subside. The theatres would open again. Now that he had been introduced to Burbage it was no longer necessary to rely on the rogue Henslowe. He hoped the new manager would allow him to act, to strut his stuff about a public stage. And what was really exciting, what made this absurd, comic, tragic, unpredictable life worth while was that the stuff he would be strutting, the words he and other actors would declaim, the lines echoed in many a homestead, tavern, or bawdy stew, would be his stuff.

Epilogue

The explanation of Marlowe's death was accepted by the authorities. Although mourned by many there were also those who were relieved at his passing. Thomas Walsingham might have wept at the loss of a friend, but his wife saw it as the removal of a burden, a threat to her domestic stability. Sir Francis Walsingham decided the death of Marlowe represented a satisfactory closure to a campaign with little more than the vindictiveness of Harvey to support it and called off the hounds of justice in the persons of Maunder and his men.

The crushing debts of Edward de Vere finally brought down the noble line of Oxford and the 17th Earl was forced to sell Castle Hedingham, which was snapped up at a bargain price by Lord Burghley. The Earl told Will he would take up residence in Stratford, and invited the playwright to visit him there. Will was delighted at the thought that there would be opportunities to visit his family at the same time. He was not sure where the Earl's place was, but knew he had an estate in Warwickshire and assumed it was that to which he was being invited.

He took the earliest opportunity to visit his home, where he was greeted coolly by his wife, uncertainly by his children and by his father with his customary air of bewilderment. As soon as he had settled in he set out to find the Earl, but could not locate him and all his enquiries were in vain. It was true Oxford had estates in the region, but had never been known to visit them. The only sizeable house in the neighbourhood was Bilton Hall, where they denied any knowledge of him. Will began to be concerned at losing contact with so valuable a patron.

After spending an appropriate time at home he returned to London, where enquiries regarding his lordship's whereabouts were greeted with derision. Many Londoners had never heard of Stratford-upon-Avon. To them Stratford was a village to the east of the city where the Earl had a property by name of King's Place. Feeling stupid and embarrassed at the mistake, he made his way there and renewed his productive partnership with the noble lord.

Will delivered Venus and Adonis to the Earl of Southampton. Writing the 200 stanzas had been a tedious labour, not at all like pouring out one's feelings in a sonnet, but he had brought all his technical expertise to the task. He offered it diffidently to the Earl, fully expecting him to reject it, but to his astonishment and relief the Earl expressed himself delighted with it and presented him with a prize of £1,000. To raise that, Will thought, would have required the sale of many thousand gloves. His future was secured for years to come and was further indemnified when the Earl commissioned another poem from him. The result was the Rape of Lucrece, which represented more hard graft from a literary point of view but much satisfaction financially.

He invested the money in Burbage's company and was taken on as his business partner. With the income from his appearances as an actor and for the production of his plays he became comparatively rich. Even his father had to admit that perhaps his son's extravagant ambitions had not, after all, been empty dreams. Burbage began work on his new theatre on the south bank of the Thames, which came into direct competition with Henslowe and eventually drove that manager out of business. The new building would embody all the latest devices of modern stage technique. It was to be called the Globe, which was,

Shakespeare thought, an apt name. He and his fellow actors and writers would bestride it, masters of the theatre, masters of a Globe, masters of a round world spinning endlessly in space.

For himself he was content. Only one matter, concerning someone close to his heart, remained unresolved and one day passing through Oxford on the way to visit his home in Stratford he called on the Bodleys. Thomas Bodley had been relieved of his duties on the Continent by a grateful Queen and allowed to return home permanently. He was tired of the constant pressures and competitiveness of political life, and relished the opportunity to concentrate on the development of his beloved library.

When he was confronted with the colossal task involved in assembling the vast array of books and manuscripts, however, he found himself totally at a loss without the assistance of the diligent Thomas James. He needed someone to act as a librarian and there seemed to be nobody fit for the task and certainly none having a historic knowledge of his embryonic collection. His discerning wife had been waiting for an appropriate moment and, when she thought the conditions were favourable, raised the possibility that he might reconsider his constraint on the errant couple. She explained they had been married in a Catholic church in Italy and very much wanted to return home to a formal protestant wedding. Moreover a child had been born, a little earlier than expected, but healthy and, Ann thought, probably beautiful.

At first Bodley would hear none of it, but under persuasion like many good men he allowed expediency to overcome his principles. He agreed at first merely to interview the young man in the expectation that he would find a diplomatic solution to the impasse. He thought perhaps they could be lodged at a respectable distance from the house with the young man travelling to his work at the University. When Thomas arrived, however, he was accompanied not only by a mature and very beautiful wife, but also by an amazing creature not much more than a couple of feet long and hiding its dimpled complexion behind a blanket. Curiosity got the better of the stern and forbidding Sir Thomas and he moved this impediment gently aside with a gnarled finger. A tiny hand reached up and grasped it. A pair of startlingly blue eyes gazed at him and a gap resembling a mouth opened in what could be taken for a smile. As must have happened to millions of elderly men since the world began, the defences of a hitherto unassailable heart were breached and the fortress was lost.

Lightning Source UK Ltd.
Milton Keynes UK
UKOW04f0616150915

258655UK00002B/15/P